Aᴿ

HAD I NOT CHOSEN

JOSHUA LOYD FOX

Published by Watertower Hill Publishing, LLC

Copyright © 2020 JLFoxBooks, LLC
www.jlfoxbooks.com

Cover and internal artwork by In the Blackwoods Design,
Rogue Blackwood, Artist.
Copyright © 2021 JLFoxBooks, LLC

Author's Note;
All character and names in this book are fictional and are not
designed, patterned after, nor descriptive of any person, living
or deceased.
Any similarities to people, living or deceased is purely by
coincidence. Author and Publisher are not liable for any
likeness described herein.

Library of Congress Control Number: 2021918455

ISBN: 978-1-7362983-9-8

This story is dedicated to
Cheryl Z.
She showed me twenty-five years ago to run the long course, even when I could have taken the short cut like everyone else.
Thank you, Sunshine.

"I call the heavens and the earth as witnesses against you, that I have set before you life and death, blessings and curses: therefore choose life that both thou and thy seed may live."
Deuteronomy 30:19 NIV

Energy Drives,
Fear Decides,
Time Derides,
Fate Divides.
Book of the Tower and the Traitor—Strophe One

Prologue

There is a place, which in a way, resides in the same place as the reality of a material world, but which cannot be seen by that world. Or any world, for that matter.

The Material would never be able to see the Spiritual.

Well, not yet.

A pink robed being stood on a heightened level of the Spiritual plane, with a specific world in the Material spread out below him and pondered his most recent Mission, given by the Father of All. It had come the normal way, down to one of the older Ilk of the Host. And unfortunately, at least to the tall being searching the world below, that would be he.

He sighed heavily and twisted energy in one hand, not unlike a human would do with a strand of hair when agonizing over a choice. Because even in the Heavens, the Host could make choices.

To an extent.

What the Material did not know about the Host, was that they were, all fifteen of them, extremely lazy, if given the choice. With the fighting, the Missions, and the praises, they were rarely given that choice.

The figure breathed in using lungs that did not exist in this Realm, with air that was not present around him. It was a matter of habit, he knew.

The Host frequently, and without thought, mimicked those below, of which they could never join. Both the older Ilk, and the younger often mimicked human behavior.

The Host could guide the Free-Willed. They could interfere when given the Missions, but never could the Host join the Free-Willed beings in the material.

It was just as well, most of the Host had been known to say amongst themselves, when they were allowed to talk freely, away from the confines of the Heavens.

At one point in existence, on a world very far away in both space and time, they had tried to assimilate with the Free-Willed. For a brief few generations.

That experiment had ended in disaster. Of biblical proportions, the being snickered to himself. The bible had yet to be written, in this time and space. That would come, much, much later.

Time was relative in the Material Realm. In the Spiritual, it did not exist at all.

The being took one last non-breath and began to make plans for the two free-willed children he watched below.

The two who were born into the Material, leagues apart, but whom the ArchAngel who watched over them would guide together, eventually.

It was a matter of pushing the right motivations, the right manipulations of that free-will they took for granted.

Humans were so gullible and easily swayed. The Host had known that since the Garden. Which, the being thought to himself again, did not exist yet.

He snickered to himself again, finally amused, and in a better Spirit. The aura around him brightened and became a lighter hue of pink.

The ArchAngel then looked down on a world on the brink of extraordinary change.

And smiled.

Oh, this was going to be fun, he thought to himself, as he winked out of existence in the Spiritual, and took a different form in the Material.

Chapter 1

The room was painted stark white. Cinderblock walls were counterbalanced by plain cream-colored tiled floors. The furniture in the room looked old, well used, but sturdy. Three beds were lined up, facing the same way, like soldiers standing at attention. The covers were tightly tucked in, and it was all done with uniformness and picture-perfect precision.

"I want the room to look like this every time you leave it for the chow hall, or school, or wherever."

The man standing behind ten-year-old Benjamin Reeves had a grating, yet nasally voice. He was also standing too close to the young boy for comfort. Ben could smell the man's cheap aftershave, but when he glanced up, it didn't appear as if the man had actually shaved in a week or more.

"One bathroom for every two rooms, three boys in each room, six boys to a bathroom. And you ALL WILL keep it absolutely spotless, or you'll be scrubbing the walls with a toothbrush until it shines!" the man said gruffly.

Ben, who held the only thing he had from his father in both sweaty hands, placed the dented suitcase on the floor near the bed closest to the door. He then didn't know what to do with his hands, so he held them together in front of his dirty, holey jeans. The man sniffed, like he smelled something distasteful, turned, and stalked back down the long hallway crisscrossing the middle of the dormitory.

Ben assumed he was meant to follow after and hurried his short legs to catch up.

It had been a whirlwind few weeks for young Benjamin Reeves. Named after his father, who had left his mother shortly after his birth, young Ben was trying to find his breath after his life was upended, and he felt like he had done three cycles in a dryer.

Two weeks ago, his mother, Lorraine Reeves had had a massive heart attack while sitting at her desk in the Chrysler Building in New York City. She had been a certified public accountant at a large firm. Putting herself through night school while young Ben was a toddler gave her the first feelings of accomplishment in her own young life.

She had had to do something after her older husband had surprisingly left in the middle of the night soon after their only son was born. She had known he had moved back down to Texas where he had family, but she had had no contact with him since.

When she had died, Ben was at school on Long Island, where they had rented a small two-bedroom home.

Lorraine couldn't afford much more than what they had, but she saved everything she could from her CPA job, as well as doing odd jobs for neighbors. She hardly ate, had been very thin, but Ben remembered how strong she had been. She worked very hard and had to learn to make it on her own, as she herself had been an orphan who grew up in the City.

Ben only passingly knew about his father's family down in Texas, but for all of his short life, it had just been him and his mother. He was as independent as she was, and very protective of her. She had not had any men in and out of Ben's life, of which he was grateful.

A couple of his friends' mothers who were divorced spent all their evenings down in corner bars and talking to strangers on 1-900 numbers to try to find a replacement for the men who had broken their hearts. Ben's mother Lorraine hadn't stooped to that. He knew, even at a very young age that most people just wanted someone else there.

But his mom was perfectly fine just being his mom. At night, when he thought about that, he was sad. But in the morning, his mom singing in the kitchen while she made breakfast, he thought that the way it was, was just fine with him.

Because, for all of Ben's life, it had just been the two of them, taking care of each other, and finding happiness in the times spent together, mostly on the beaches of Long Island, but once in a while in a car trip to upstate New York, and one time a wonderful trip down the coast to the Chesapeake Bay for a long weekend.

When the principal of the school came to get Ben out of class the day she died, Ben almost threw up in his mouth. He was never in trouble, got good grades, and tried not to be noticed. The principal knowing his name and announcing it as he stepped into the classroom made goosebumps rise on the back of his neck, and a pit open up in his stomach, which, two weeks later, still had not left him.

The rest of that day had been a whirl. They took him to the police station and a fat elderly police officer had given him a cold can of Coke and some crackers. He was promised dinner later on, but that had never happened. Ben sat on a hard-wooden bench in the waiting room of the police station, watching the police bring in men and women in handcuffs, and escort them into the back, where they disappeared, but did not reappear.

The same thought went through Ben's mind for the countless hours he sat on that bench. His mother, his whole world, was gone. He wondered when she fell over at her desk if her head had hit the keyboard sitting in front of her, and if it had, did the letters of the keys leave imprints in her forehead?

He couldn't get that image out of his mind. Was there now, and forever, the imprint of the "F" through "K" letters etched into her forehead? She would go to heaven with those letters on her forehead and that made no sense.

He wanted to cry. He wanted to laugh. He remembered being more scared than he had ever been in life.

"We will go down to the chow hall, and after, we have to take you over to the schoolhouse and get you signed in. What grade are you in again?" The nasally man's voice brought Ben out of his memories.

Ben replied in a shaken voice, "Fifth grade sir. That's what grade I was in in New York."

"Well, you aren't in New York anymore sonny, that's for sure."

As they walked outside the oversized dormitory, Ben looked around at his new surroundings. No, he

4

thought, we definitely aren't in New York anymore. He couldn't smell the ocean like he could from the little house he had shared with his mother.

Instead, he smelled cow shit. He didn't know it was cow shit at that moment, but he knew it was some kind of shit. When his mom took him into the City to see a museum, or to walk in the park, he had smelled shit coming from the alleys they had hurriedly crossed in front of.

This shit was a different shit, but in his young mind, he still knew it was shit.

On the plane from New York to Texas, he wondered what his life would be like now that his father was going to be back in it. He had never met the man. But a social worker from the state had informed him the day after his mother died that he would be going down to Texas to meet his father, who the state had located and told that young Benjamin Reeves was homeless and abandoned.

According to the state worker, his father had reluctantly agreed to maintain custody of the boy, with the understanding that Ben would be placed into a boys' home nearby, down in Texas. He assumed his father was just busy and couldn't care for him, but the truth was much more hurtful.

B. Joseph Reeves, Sr. had a whole 'nother family down in Texas, and his "mistake" from New York wasn't to get in the way of that new family. Ben had not even met his new brother and sister when he landed in the hot, arid Texas countryside.

Instead, he was met by the tall, nasally man, who had then taken him to the boys' home.

Ben hadn't seen his father that day, or any day after that. All Ben saw that day was the miles of scrub brush and dark brown dirt out the window of the white passenger van

5

he rode in, as the miles of flat and ugly land disappeared behind him.

A tear had fallen from each of his eyes as he tried to remember what his mother's face looked like the last morning he had seen her. He couldn't remember. And he hated himself for not being able to remember. His life had abruptly changed, and he had no control over what happened to him from here on out.

All he could do was remember one of the things his mother had always told him in her singsong voice:

"Don't ever let this life get you down baby. You have to be strong, and always think about what comes next every time you do something. Always look farther down the road instead of down at your two feet. If you're looking at your feet, you won't see what will make you stumble, until it's too late."

Chapter 2

"I can't believe Freddie died! Like, what is Queen going to do now, without him?"

Kristin swept her long dark, perfect hair back over her shoulder and smacked her Bubblicious gum loudly. Gwendolyn Murphy glanced at her best friend jealously and thought for the thousandth time how ugly she was next to her tall, skinny bestie.

"Now Queen's music is totally going to suck. But I'm still totally going to watch the Tribute Concert. I hear it'll be on MTV," Kristin said with a typical teenage sigh.

Gwen looked at herself in the floor-to-ceiling length mirror taking up one whole wall of her spacious room. Bright rust-colored red hair that fell in waves to the middle of her back framed a heart-shaped face, covered in freckles. Her bright green eyes looked over her twelve-year-old body, and she knew how skinny and gangly she was starting to look.

7

Being the tallest girl in her class was not what she thought it was going to be like. The boys all sneered at her behind her back, and she could feel the glares of the other girls in the seventh grade.

She loved the freckles on her face, thought they made her look European, but hated the ones on her shoulders and chest. She always felt like she had lizard skin, perpetually dry, and repugnant to the two boys she had allowed to kiss her so far. One in the sixth grade, and the most recent boy, Billy England, behind the gym one perfect fall day.

He hadn't spoken to her since, and every time she walked by Mrs. Summer's English class between fourth and fifth period, Billy and his two best friends would be standing at his locker, and they always tended to be laughing right at her. She looked at her rust-colored hair and didn't even want to think about it. Today, her hair felt like her father's beard. Same dryness, same texture. She sighed heavily.

"So, did you hear that Brittany Doty let Tommy Smith kiss her behind the cafeteria yesterday?" Kristin said with a giggle. She lived for this drama, Gwen thought again to herself. She laughed along, as she was expected to do, but she wondered at the same time if Tommy was going to stop talking to Brittany now that she let him kiss her.

Gwen knew that she was what her father would call "boy crazy." But every girl she knew in the seventh grade was trying to not think about how all the boys were starting to lose their baby fat, and were playing sports, and looked so yummy.

She knew that many of the girls her age were doing exactly what she was doing on a Saturday afternoon in Napa Valley, California. They were gathered together in twos and threes, discussing who had kissed who, and who

8

had been developing boobs sooner than the other girls, and why was Billy so tall for the seventh grade?

There wasn't much else to excite them at this age, other than waiting to start their periods and hoping they didn't do it in the middle of class. Gwen had sworn off wearing white pants just for that very reason and started noticing that a lot of the girls her age were wearing black leggings a lot more often than they had in the sixth grade.

Gwen knew that if she thought about it, she was much more interested in learning all she could in school. She loved to learn. She was starting to figure out that she was really good at it too. She was often conflicted in allowing how smart she was to show, as well as how easily things came to her. She also didn't want to look like the know-it-all in front of the boys.

But she was starting to realize that most of the other kids in her school just didn't understand the things that she did. So she hid her intelligence. She didn't want to be known as the "smart girl" that the boys didn't like, and were intimidated by.

"Girls, come down for a snack, and I want to talk!" Gwen's mother, Joy Murphy, yelled from the kitchen downstairs.

Gwen and Kristin looked at each other, sighed, and marched resolutely down the carpeted stairs in the large country-decorated house. They knew that Gwen's mother, who all the kids in Santa Rosa Elementary called Mrs. Murphy, but who Gwen had heard some of the boys call "Mrs. Big-Tits," probably had another one of her crazy food drive ideas, or some other volunteer activity for them all to do this afternoon.

The girls just wanted to play with some makeup that Gwen had snuck from her mother's over-stuffed makeup bag and listen to the last Queen album ever to be made with their real musical muse, Freddie Mercury.

Walking into the bright kitchen, Gwen saw her petite, yet overly top-heavy mother practically bouncing around in her workout clothes. Ever since Gwen's little brother, Daniel McCarthy Murphy II, was born, her mother had been obsessed with losing the "baby fat."

Gwen knew her mother had been perpetually skinny, and looking down at her own growing body, knew that she, too, would be cursed with no curves or hips, and just hoped for half of what her mother had up top. She could practically hear her knees knocking together as they all gathered in the kitchen, little Daniel McCarthy Murphy II, playing happily in the playpen in the living room, but close by so that her mom could hear him if he got out.

"Your father has a company dinner tonight in Sonoma, and I want to ask you girls a very important question." Mrs. Murphy looked seriously at the two girls shuffling their feet, as both glancing over at the stack of brownies, steam rising from them, sitting on the oven top. Both girls smiled. They had smelled the brownies as they were coming down the stairs.

In an even more serious tone, Mrs. Murphy continued: "Your father and I think that you have grown up a lot this year Gwenny, and I think you are ready to start earning a little money by babysitting."

Gwen could feel a little excitement catch in her chest. Finally! A way to make some money, so she didn't have to keep asking her father for money to go to the mall, or the movies, or to buy the flare-legged jeans she had been eyeballing at Aeropostale in the mall. But maybe, she secretly thought to herself, she could buy Neil deGrasse's new book on the expanding universe. She had been eyeing it, as well as the jeans, at the mall.

"We want you two to watch Danny tonight while we are at the dinner. We won't be gone more than two or three hours, but if you do this well, we can start doing this more

10

often, and every time you watch him, I will pay you twenty bucks," Mrs. Murphy said.

"Thirty dollars," Gwen replied back before she could stop herself. There went her big mouth, she thought.

"Okay, thirty bucks. For each of you. But you have to feed him dinner and get him down. You know he likes to be read to, and then rocked if he starts to cry."

Gwen silently congratulated herself. A negotiated win against her mother was rare. Suddenly, they all heard the garage door open from the other side of the kitchen.

"Daddy's home!" Gwen shouted to her little brother. He gave a squeak and yelled "Da Da!"

Gwen's father was a giant of a man. Six-foot-three inches and had worn a full beard since Gwen could remember. She also got her bright red hair from her Irish father. He came in, wearing his normal wrinkled suit, tie askew, and picked up her mother in a great big bear hug, kissing her noisily in front of the two teenagers.

Gwen embarrassingly looked away, but saw Kristin watching intently. Gwen's mother giggled like a schoolgirl and yelled to "put me down, the kids are watching!"

Gwen was so often embarrassed being aware of her parents' love for each other.

The pair had grown up on the same street, had been together since they were both old enough to notice the opposite sex, and Gwen knew that their bond was growing stronger every year. Gwen often daydreamed and night dreamed about a boy loving her as much as her father loved her mother.

She just didn't know how a boy could love her skinny legs and freckled shoulders. She sighed and glanced back over at her parents in time to see her father and mother share an intimate gaze at each other before moving off to do their separate duties with the children.

Her father swept by Gwen and kissed her on the top of her head before heading into the living room to pick up Daniel McCarthy Murphy II in his own little bear hug. Gwen's mother grabbed the plate of now-cool brownies, offering the teenagers one each.

"Just one! Don't spoil your dinner. We will let you two order a pizza, but you have to make the macaroni for Danny. You know he won't eat anything else if we aren't here." Her mother chided the teens and they both sighed heavily, rolling their eyes.

Joy Murphy yelled at Gwen's father that she was going upstairs to get ready for the dinner, and Gwen heard her father mumble a reply from the living room where he was throwing her little brother almost up to the ceiling and catching him, the little toddler laughing hysterically.

Gwen and Kristin took their brownies back up to Gwen's room, and the girls started discussing what they would buy with their newfound wealth when they went to the mall tomorrow afternoon. While they talked, they ate their warm brownies, getting dark crumbs on the white carpet of her room.

Gwen again saw her thoughts going to her kiss with Billy behind the gym, and superimposed that on how her father looked at her mother, and knew that Billy England was not the boy for her.

She sighed, finished her brownie, wiped her hands on her jean shorts, and started crying with her best friend over the loss of the greatest male singer in human history and what their favorite band would sound and look like now without the fashion icon singing the lead part for any new albums.

Chapter 3

"Motherfucker, I'll kill you!" Ben yelled as he again punched Turtle in the face. Or at least tried to punch the much heavier boy. Ben bled from his busted upper lip, but Turtle was breathing so hard he was going to pass out soon.

At fifteen, Turtle, whose real name was Nicholas Beans but who everyone had called Turtle since the first grade, was a year older than the smaller Ben. That didn't stop Ben from trying to fistfight the bigger boy after school.

Turtle had talked back during the shift at the dining hall that morning, and Ben wasn't going to let it slide, even if Turtle was bigger. Ben knew he was dumber, and slower, and would tire out faster.

"Bitch, you can't even hit me!" Turtle flew back at Ben with one last attempt to finish the fight.

Ben swung out of the way of Turtle's waylay arms wind-milling at his head, and stepping back, aiming one last haymaker at Turtle's eyebrow. A solid fleshy smack made Turtle's eyes roll back in his head, and he went down like a fat bag of goo, his legs folding under him.

"Alright, he's asleep, he's asleep!" Junior stepped in and kept Ben from aiming a few last kicks at Turtle's prone body.

The other ten or so boys, who had surrounded the two fighters once the last bell of the day sounded, started to break up. Ben could hear their laughing to each other, ass-grabbing, and general hullabaloo, and soon, Ben found himself alone with Junior, as the much older boy tried to wake Turtle up.

"Give him a minute. I don't think you killed him. Not with those skinny arms." Junior looked over at Ben, and saw that Ben had a tear in his eye.

"It's okay, kid. Why don't you head back to the dorm, and I'll tell anyone that asks that you ran into a wall, with that busted lip."

Ben felt grateful for the older boy. Junior, who everyone at the boys' home respected, gave him one last wink and a wave, and picked up the stirring Turtle. Ben made his way back to his dorm, not noticing the fading light, nor the fact that he was supposed to head to the chow hall for dinner.

He was alone with his thoughts and could feel his heartbeat start to slow during the long walk back to his dorm. He started to shiver from the cold, late fall wind, and the adrenaline leaving his system. He pulled his jacket closer to himself, noticing that he had gotten a tear in the front of it.

He didn't even know at which part of the quick fight it had been torn. He sighed to himself, bent into the wind, and walked the rest of the way to his dorm.

He didn't like to fight, but for some reason, he kept finding himself in them almost weekly. When you had over 300 teenage boys in one place, fights were going to happen.

14

Ben was just so damn angry all the time. Anything provoked him. He was constantly in trouble for talking back to his dorm parents, but he couldn't help it. He just saw red and couldn't control what he did.

Turtle hadn't done anything to him, really, had just made fun of his new haircut, and the verbal sparring had gone back and forth until Turtle had broken the rule and said something about Ben's mother.

All during school, the insult had ricocheted in Ben's mind, until he felt that if he didn't fight Turtle, he would fight the first person who said or did or looked at him wrong.

They had met in the back of the school building, where two hallways stretched from the main long hallway, forming a pocket area between each hallway. There was grass in this area, but it was usually shaded, and in the winter, the snows would build up between all the hallways, and wouldn't disappear from the dark corners until mid-June.

Ben didn't even say anything when Turtle showed up with a bunch of other boys. He just went in swinging. Turtle had him by about thirty-five pounds, but Ben was pure rage. Turtle had gotten in the one jab that had split Ben's lip, and after Ben felt the blood trickle down his chin, he didn't see anything but white-hot rage.

Now, almost back to his dorm, Ben started to feel bad. He felt bad he had knocked Turtle out, but he also felt bad that he couldn't control himself. He never used to be like this. Four years in the boys' home, with no visitors, and no letters, and no phone calls, he felt so alone in the world, and that just pissed him off.

That's what started the vibrating in his chest when he woke in the mornings, and that's what created the vibrating headache that he got most evenings. He had to mentally unclench his jaw a couple times a day, and he

15

didn't even know what had made him clench up in the first place.

At fourteen years old, he was old enough to know that he needed to channel his anger or find an outlet before it ate him up. At least, that was what his counselor told him; every week he had to go and talk to her. She knew that he was a very angry young man.

He had that counselor, and several teachers who tried to talk to him after classes, asking him how he was, and what he was doing with his life, but he wasn't able to talk to any of them. Not about what mattered. The fact was, he missed his mother terribly, and he had no idea what he wanted to do with his life.

He was in the ninth grade, and people were already asking what he was going to do when he graduated and left the boys' home. He was as confused about the world outside the home as he was about girls and sports and everything else all the other boys seemed to completely understand.

"What are you doing here? You're supposed to be at dinner," his dorm parent, Mr. King, asked him when he walked through the screen door into the living room of his dorm.

"Stomach hurt. Thought I was going to puke," Ben answered him as he walked back to his room.

"Let me know if you need anything. Just get some rest," Mr. King called out to him as he rounded the corner into his room and threw himself on his bed. At least he didn't see my lip, Ben thought to himself.

Ben reached over to his prized possession, his new Sony stereo, which played CDs and tapes, and turned on the CD he had been listening to when he fell asleep last night. He grabbed his oversized headphones, plugged in the wire to the outlet hole on the front of the stereo, and put them over his ears, drowning out the world.

Nirvana's *Unplugged* sounded in his headphones, and he closed his eyes as Kurt Cobain sang about teen spirit while playing an acoustic guitar. Dave Grohl on drums was why Ben listened to the album. He just let the beat of the song bang back against the throbbing in his head.

His thoughts drifted to his mother, standing in the sun, on the beach on Long Island, and he saw her wave at ten-year-old him as he collected shells. He couldn't quite remember what she looked like, but when he let the music play, and drifted into semi-sleep, he could see her well enough for the tears to come.

The tears came because of his fight, the pain in his head and mouth, but the biggest pain was from his heart. He couldn't let the other guys in the dorm see him cry, but when he had a couple of minutes like this to himself, it didn't take much for the tears to fall.

He wished for the millionth time that his mom was still around and would marvel at how tall he had gotten, but still chide him for being too skinny, while she herself was a toothpick.

He smiled through the tears, and felt himself drifting, the beat of Dave Grohl's drums in his ears, and a trickle of blood slowly moving down his chin, falling on his neck, his chest rising and falling as he fell asleep. His last thought was of his mom and knowing tomorrow he would be just as alone as he was today.

Chapter 4

"Steer right, steer right!" Gwen's father practically yanked the emergency brake off as Gwen maneuvered her new car down the country road but had mistakenly hit the gas instead of the brakes as she went around a sharp turn.

"It's okay. Just breathe and get back on the road. There's no one around," her father said shakenly.

Gwen had somehow steered the little two-door red Ford Aspire hatchback onto the right shoulder of the road and sat in a slowly dissipating cloud of dust. She took a shaky breath, squared her shoulders, and bravely put the car into first gear and pulled back onto the road, just as a large Chevy pickup screamed by, horn blaring and an angry man shaking his fist in the air.

She slammed on the brakes of the car again, and because she had not pushed in the clutch, she felt the car shake and the engine die.

"It's okay honey, it's okay."

Her father was sweating in the full blast of the air conditioner coming from the vents of the little car. He looked so big sitting in the passenger seat.

Gwen this time looked in her mirrors, checked over her left shoulder, and turned the ignition back on, with the clutch firmly pushed to the floor. She put the stick into first gear, again looked over her shoulder, and pulled slowly back onto the two-lane country road.

She could hear her father's breath start to even out, and she smiled, feeling the rush of adrenaline slowly fritter away from her tall, lanky body. It was very exciting, she thought, to be in control of her own car, knowing that when she got her license in two weeks, she would be totally free.

She glanced over at her father, smiled at his look of discomfort, and gunned the engine to catch up with the rude guy in the truck. It was way in the distance, but she was driven. She laughed to herself. Driven. While driving. She was amused at her own quip.

Her father had taken her and her brother to so many classic car shows and had taught them both more about cars than either wanted or needed, but as she got closer and closer to having her own car, her appreciation for all her father had shared with her, his own love of cars and machinery, grew and grew. It was just one more thing in the world that excited her mind.

She would be turning sixteen in just two weeks, and two months after that she would be the youngest person to graduate from her high school. Taking accelerated classes all through high school and maxing out the scores on all the pre-placement tests she had to take to graduate assured her a spot at almost any college she wanted. She had won three science fairs in a row, another school record, and felt sure that her place in the STEM world would be assured with her theories on quantum mechanics mixed with terrestrial ecology theories.

She wanted to study multiple scientific avenues because she believed that a mixture of several types of science is what would be needed to change the world. She abhorred the idea of a single course of study.

A paper she had written as a fourteen-year-old sophomore assured that she would be recognized by the academic world, and she had been. MIT had offered first, followed by Harvard, and a host of lesser-known colleges.

She didn't want to call herself a prodigy, but others did. She was just happy to be loading up her car at the end of the summer and heading off to who knew where. Of course she knew where, but it was nice to say it like that. Off to who knew where?

She savored the possibilities like a starving person at a buffet, pondering which delicacy to try first, but the rumbles of hunger in their belly telling them to start somewhere, and fast!

She was so excited to take her first solo trip across the country, she could burst. She felt fearless. She finally felt freedom. Breathing in deep, relishing the mixture of numbness and exciting fireworks bursting in her chest, she turned the car towards home, and looked forward to the longer roads of her trip across the country, and the beckoning future, bright with possibilities.

"Let's get home quick, kid. I'm going to shit me pants." Her father brought her crushingly out of her stupendously beautiful dream world, and reminded her that here, back on Earth, people had to poop.

She gunned the little four-barrel engine, and shifted into fourth gear, heading faster towards the house, as she saw her father squirming in his seat next to her, a small fart escaping from under him.

He laughed, rolled down the window, and seeing the look of horror on her pretty face, laughed harder.

Chapter 5

Ben was shaking with nerves. He usually never felt this way, but this was a big day. Today, he would find out if he really did have a gift. If what he thought about himself could be replicated in the minds and opinions of others.

He sat in the waiting room of the poshly decorated office of the highest acclaimed literary agent in Texas. He had submitted his book of short stories exactly one month and two days earlier, and about three weeks later, was called by a nasally voiced secretary, setting this appointment, concerning his essays.

Never before in his seventeen years of life was he so scared of being judged and to be found wanting.

He was bouncing one leg up and down, up and down, as he chewed nervously on a fingernail. His mind rebounding with ideas on how he was going to sell himself, and maybe his book. He knew his writing was solid. Many people had read the stories he had started writing when he was fifteen, as an exercise given him by his counselor.

He hadn't thought much of what he produced at first, but when his roommate at the boys' home, a rather good friend, got ahold of the loose sheaf of papers in his closet, and started to read his ramblings, all the praise he had received from everyone who read what he wrote after gave him a sense of pride.

It also made him think for the first time in his short life that he may very well have a gift.

The secretary looked over at him bouncing his leg noisily, sniffed, and went back to clacking her long fingernails on her keyboard. Ben wondered if she had been the same one who had called him a week and a half ago with this take-it or leave-it interview.

Another pretty blonde woman came out of a back hallway, called his name, and when he embarrassingly raised his hand and said "here" like a first grader, she asked him if he wanted anything to drink, and that "Mr. Peabody will be with you shortly. He's just taking a phone call," said all in one breathe.

He asked for a water, and she nodded in agreement, like she knew the kid needed some water. Turning, he couldn't help but look at her tight bum in her skirt. That settled his nerves a little. Not for the first time did he resent his own young age and inexperience with the opposite sex.

He looked down at the folder in his lap. It was packed full of loose copies of everything he had ever written. *The Tower and the Traitor*, the title of his book of short stories and poetry, prominently displayed on the first 120, double-spaced pages.

The rest of the folder was full of cleaned up copies of other shorts, as well as the start of a longer novella. He

23

still didn't think he had the ability to write a full-blown, 160,000-word novel, so he stayed with the 30k-and-below stories. Good stories, taken in small doses, which was his way of writing.

Maybe one day he would write something longer, but for now, he was happy with what he had written. Not perfectly happy though. No writer, he had read, was completely satisfied with everything he or she had written. That's what kept the edge sharp, he had read in the same how-to book. The author's name eluded him, but he could probably look it up.

He didn't know why he was fixated on thinking of all these things, when he should be focusing on presenting his ideas to Mr. Rudyard Peabody, Esq. The literary agent to the stars. Or at least those from Texas.

Being a local (or so they had called him during the single call for this meeting) made him more marketable. Or so he thought. He really had no idea why someone with Mr. Peabody's reputation would want to talk to a seventeen-year-old kid from a boys' home in West Texas, but here he was, and as his knee started to rhythmically tap again, he could feel the cold sweat beading down his spine, beneath the only dress shirt that he both owned and that had fit him.

He gulped loudly, and started pawing through his writing, in the manila folder on his lap. He tried to read his writing as his knee bounced the stack of papers almost off his lap. He couldn't focus. He was startled by a sound, but it was just the pretty woman bringing him a cold bottle of water.

He mumbled his thanks, and barely heard her tell him it would "only be a couple more minutes."

Ben took a deep breath. Then another. He tried to loosen the tight muscles of his back. He closed his eyes and started listening to his breath. In and out, in and out. Just

24

like his counselor, Jane Rommer, taught him whenever he started feeling overwhelmed. He wished she was there with him now, but she had given him a big hug this morning before he left for Dallas, commenting on how tall he was getting, but also how skinny he was.

She had said he looked "dapper" in his Sunday clothes. He liked the way she talked.

She was young for a counselor, but she knew her stuff, and she really cared. He had been seeing her for two years, ever since she got her first job as a therapist at the boys' home.

He still didn't have any idea what her life was like outside the home, only that she talked about her dog, an aging beagle she had since she was a teenager, and she had lost her mom when she was young as well. She shared these things with him to make him comfortable talking about his own losses, but she didn't talk about anything else.

He had a bit of a crush on her but knew that she just saw him as another damaged kid. That was okay to him. He needed the help she gave him every week. Since he started seeing her, he felt a little bit of peace. He still needed the exercises though. Those made him calm more than once a day.

He was shaken out of his mental reprieve by the secretary's nasally voice telling him to go to the back, second office on the right.

He got out of the comfortable waiting room chair, swallowed his growing panic, squared his shoulders, and walked down the bright hallway to the second door on the right. He knocked, heard a loud voice inside telling him to come on in, and taking a deep but shaky breath, he opened the door to his future.

The man sitting behind the desk was fat, but he was the type of fat that people would comment "carried it well."

He was dressed in an old-fashioned suit jacket with denim patches on the elbows, and tight jeans that were held up with a big shiny gold belt buckle almost lost under his voluptuous gut overhanging it. Pure Texas, Ben mused to himself.

He rose up, balding head shiny in the fluorescent lights overhead, and held out his hand.

"Rudyard Peabody, but people jus' call me Rudy," he said loudly. Everything about this man seemed to be done loudly.

Ben shook the man's hand, feeling his own hand crushed in the big meaty palm of the older man.

"Sit, sit. Let's talk about this here book," the man said, sitting back down with a grunt.

Ben took one of the leather chairs in front of the oversized cherry desk. The heavy wood desk was covered in papers and empty Styrofoam coffee cups. He had no idea where in the overflowing masses of papers was his manuscript, but the man shuffled through it, and brought out a copy of his short stories, bound together, and held with a large black clip.

"Here we go, here we go," the big man said in a deep Southern drawl.

Ben sat uncomfortably as the big man quick read his work, mumbling to himself the whole time. His hands starting to wrangle in his lap again, Ben watched the man intensely, with the feeling that the older man held his future in his big, meaty hands.

Sweat started forming on Ben's lower back, where it pressed against the now hot leather chair.

"I'm gonna shoot straight wit'cha," the man said to the sweaty Ben. Ben gulped loudly and held his breath as the man continued.

26

"I ain't read something I've liked in a spell, in a long spell, but this here, I liked every bit of it!" Ben let out his breath in one loud explosion.

The older man chuckled in a knowing way, seeing how uncomfortable the boy was. The truth was, Rudy thought to himself, he was lucky he had found this kid. This kid was an exceptional writer, being so young. And so unrepresented.

"Here's what I wanna do wit'cha," Rudy said with a smile.

"I want ta represent cha and get you a book deal. How much do ya write ever'day?" he said.

"I try to write around 500 words a day, depends on the story. Some of them, I can't stop until it's finished," Ben answered back.

"Keep it up. I'm gonna farm this 'un here around a bit, with yer permissin'."

"Do you think a publisher will want it? Do you think it has feet?" Ben asked, starting to get excited at the prospect of having a real published title under his belt.

"Don't get yer panties in a twist, but yeah, I think it'll sell."

Rudy stood up, indicating the meeting was over. Ben stood quickly and held his hand out. They shook rather gruffly, and the man sat back down, dismissing Ben, and went back to looking like he had a million things to do that day. On the way out, Ben turned, and said an excited "Thanks so much!"

Rudy glanced up at the departing teen, smiled, and put his head back in the stack of papers in front of him.

"Girls'll have some papers fer ya to sign up front," he said to the papers in front of him.

Ben smiled one last time, and hurriedly left the large office. He stopped in the hallway, his chest growing in size, and felt tears well up in his eyes. He quickly wiped

27

them away and finding the attractive blonde woman still at her desk holding out a sheaf of papers for him to sign, he felt true joy for the first time since he could remember.

He almost lost control of the pen in his shaking hand. Signing his name three times, he gave the pen back to the woman who smiled and told him to keep it. She winked at him and told him under her breath that she wouldn't tell anyone.

Ben smiled back, and floated out the office door, back to his life. But for the first time, he didn't cringe when he thought of the future.

His question was answered. He did have a gift.

Chapter 6

Gwen hugged her mother one last time. She pulled away, but stayed within arm's reach, looking into her mother's tear-filled eyes.

"It's going to be alright mamma. I have maps, and snacks, and money to get me there. There's nothing to worry about. I have Triple-A and a charger for the cell phone. I'll be okay!"

Gwen felt bad about being impatient to leave on her cross-country road trip. She knew her mother and father were very hesitant to let her go, and she wanted to get on the road before they changed their minds. She was only seventeen years old but was amazingly intelligent and mature for her age. Without that being true, they would have never agreed to let her take this trip to her college on her own.

She had spent the last year since graduating high school doing science fair expos and traveling to different parts of the world. She knew that taking a year off of college was a risk, but if she would have gone straight to MIT as a sixteen-year-old, she knew in her heart she would have missed out on a lot of the experiences she would have been too afraid to try.

Now, at seventeen, she felt surer of herself, and surer of her future. She was now caught up with the other people her age, and the year of school that she had tested out of was gone, but she didn't feel bad about that. She needed the rest in the year in-between. There were only positives to the year she took off.

Gwen looked at the faces of the other people standing next to her car in the driveway on a hot, sunny, Northern California morning. Her father was trying very hard to hold his tears in, and her little brother, now not so little, was shuffling his feet, ready to get back to his summer routine of videogames and snacks, alone in his room.

Gwen's long-time best friend, Kristin, was also holding in the tears. Her too-young pregnant belly showing under the tight white t-shirt she was wearing.

Gwen felt the worse about going off on adventures and seeing the world while her best friend stayed here in the same place she was born, being forced to marry the boy who had gotten her pregnant senior year of high school.

They had discussed how Gwen felt the night before, when Kristin had slept over like so many hundreds of nights before. Kristin did everything she could to dissuade Gwen from feeling guilt over her choices and told Gwen in no uncertain terms that she was laying in the bed she had made.

30

"It's getting late and I have to get through Nevada before tonight. I have to go everyone," Gwen said to her family.

They all gave her one last look, a hug each, and Gwen got into her little red car, bursting with excitement, and scared out of her mind. This was it, she thought to herself as she waved one last time and slowly backed out of the driveway. This is the moment she had waited on for all of her short seventeen years.

By the end of her street, she was so excited she could burst. By the time she got outside the town limits of her childhood home, she had to pull over and let the tears come. Great, she thought to herself, if they could all see her now. She felt alone for the first time in her short life, but it was a happy alone.

Letting the tears stream down her face, she put her Hootie and the Blowfish CD into the car player and turned up the volume. As Darius Rucker sang his soul out in the song "Hold My Hand," her tears coming slower and slower, Gwen once again squared her shoulders, as was her way, put the car into drive, looked over her shoulder as she conditioned herself to do, and pulled back onto the road heading east.

It was a bright, sunny, August day, and she wasn't going to let homesickness stop her from her dreams. Singing along to the song playing through the speakers in her car, she pressed the gas, felt the tires gripping the blacktop, and she didn't look back.

She was tired and sore once she stopped that night. The country unfolding under her tires had quickly impressed her with its size. She had been on plenty of road trips in her life, but she had never been the one driving. Her butt felt numb as she climbed out of the little red Ford, and grabbing her bag out of the hatchback, she entered the hotel lobby of the Motel 6 she was staying at her first night away from home.

She had driven ten hours that day. From Sonoma, CA, to Salt Lake City, Utah. She stopped on the western edge of the city, the lights twinkling in the mountain air in front of her, and was stayed the first night at the cheap motel.

In the morning, she would be heading south on I-15 to catch I-70 into Colorado. Her first real stop that she was dying to make was a place called "Bishop Castle" outside of Pueblo, CO.

She had watched through the years as a man, who was a mason by trade, had built his very own medieval castle in the mountains of Colorado. She had watched, fascinated, online, as the castle came together over the last couple of years.

She was very excited to see it.

Getting her room key, and tugging her oversized suitcase into the room, she was more tired than she had ever felt before. But she was still exhilarated from seeing all of the country she had driven through that day. Mountains, and deserts, and beautiful sight after beautiful sight.

She had gone through three disposable cameras, stopping at overlooks and roadside attractions, taking picture after picture of things that she was excited about. She only had five cameras with her but was so excited about the land she had never seen before that she used up three of them before she knew what she was doing. She made a mental note to get a couple more from a Walgreens before she made it to the castle.

As she got settled, she used the pre-paid phone card her father had pressed on her yesterday to call home and told everyone that she was okay and described to her mother and father what she had seen that day. She knew that they were not taking her leaving off on her own very well. But they, as always, put on brave faces, and told her how proud they were of her, and still worried.

They warned her not to open her door for anyone, and to keep the mace on her keychain close to her all night. She told them she was ready for a shower and wanted to just sleep.

"We love you so much," they both told her, talking on different phones at the house where she grew up. She could picture them both standing near the phones, looking at each other across the living room where her father would be, looking into the bright kitchen, where her mother would be gripping the phone in her hand.

She suddenly missed them with all her heart, once again letting tears slide down her tired face. She told them in a shaky voice how she felt, but that she had to get to school, and this was the best way for her to grow. They both knew she was right, and soon said their goodbyes once again.

She promised to call the next night, when she got into the western part of Colorado. They had her itinerary down pat. She hung up the phone and sat on the edge of the hard motel bed, head in her hands, and tried to pull herself together. She was just exhausted, she told herself. But all day, she had had so many misgivings about leaving home. She was sure all teenagers who left home for college felt the same way.

She looked at the emotions with her scientific mind, and filing away the sensations for later study, she got up, and got ready for a shower, and finally bed. She wasn't hungry, so told herself that she would eat a large breakfast before she got back on the road in the morning.

After a dismal shower, where the hot water quickly turned cold halfway through, she got into her favorite flannel pajamas, and was sound asleep as her head hit the pillow. The last thing she remembered was the sound of the big trucks driving past the motel on the highway, heading who knows where.

Arising early the next morning, as was her way, she started looking over the maps she had brought into the motel room.

She needed to get to Grand Junction, CO that day, and head south on Route 50, towards a tiny town called Cotopaxi, and then south again on Route 69 to Westcliffe, CO.

She was hoping to stop there for the night and press on the next morning the hour or so over the mountains and get to Bishop Castle first thing. She didn't want to have to deal with crowds. She wanted to spend as much time at the castle as she could.

She carefully folded her map of the western United States up and closed the Rand McNally Atlas book she was using as a double-check to the state maps her father had pressed on her.

She could have used the internet and printed out MapQuest directions, but her father insisted that she learn to use the Atlas, as well as other maps, so she could never get lost.

She was once again grateful for her father's teachings about seemingly unimportant, yet very practical things. It was him who had taught her to drive, cook Irish food, fish in the streams back home, and change a tire.

She was on the verge of choking up again thinking of home, but distracted herself with getting her things all together, and after another crappy shower experience, headed out to her car to find a gas station and the road south.

The road south was a long way, but she was excited to see more of the beautiful country as she went. She knew that she would be seeing the Western Face of the Rockies that day and was so excited to travel those mountain roads. She loved the mountains more than anything, and always had.

She got back into her little red hatchback, after stowing her suitcase carefully in the trunk, and drove to the Shell station between the motel and the highway heading east.

As she was walking into the Shell station to buy more snacks, and to see if they had any disposable cameras, there was a man holding a portable vacuum cleaner and some cleaning supplies.

He looked homeless, but Gwen did not like to presume that about anyone. As she approached him, she could see that he was middle aged, and had an air of misery around him. Her heart suddenly went out to the man. He was about to ask her if he could clean her car, but before he could utter his spill, she asked him,

"Have you eaten yet today? Can I buy you some food?"

The man looked her deep in the eyes. He just shook his head no, without uttering a word.

She reached into her clutch, hanging off her right shoulder, and grabbed a twenty-dollar bill.

"Here," she said. "Please buy yourself some breakfast. Don't worry about cleaning my car. I have a long way to go. But please buy something good to eat."

She pushed the folded bill into the man's dirty hand and went into the gas station. With snacks in hand, and having paid for gas with cash, as her father taught her to do, she walked back outside. She had assumed that she would see the man cleaning cars for money come into the station to buy something to eat, but he had not come in.

When she walked back towards her car, she did not see the man, but she saw that the twenty-dollar bill was laying on her driver's seat. Next to it was an old, wrinkled piece of paper.

She picked up the wadded, heavy paper and smoothed it out while looking around for the man. She couldn't understand why he had given back the money. Looking down at the heavy paper she had unwrinkled as best she could she saw that it was an old bi-folded Valentine's Day card.

On the front cover was a big red heart on a field of pink with the words "You're so Loved" in black across the large red heart. Opening it, the simple phrase "Won't you be mine?" was inscribed in bold. There was no other writing on it at all.

And then she flipped to the back and saw where a child could write in a "From" and a "To."

On those lines, what she saw stopped her in her tracks.

On the "From" line, she saw a single name. It was her own, written in a first- or second- grade scrawl. She knew she had written it, because it was her full first name, "Gwendolyn," as she always had written at that age, being so proud of being able to spell it, as well as her secret that she has two names.

A short one, and a long one, that no one usually used.

On the "To" line was the name "Ben."

She did not remember ever sending this particular Valentine's Day card. But she did recognize her own childish handwriting.

She looked around one last time, not seeing a trace of the older man, shrugged her shoulders and threw the old Valentine into the back seat, where she unconsciously thought it had come from, and drove around to the gas pumps.

Before she even got back out of the car to pump the gas she had forgotten all about the man.

She was unaware that the man, in his eternal form, had not forgotten about her. He watched her approvingly from where the material could not see the spiritual.

After pumping the gas, getting back into the car, and heading out along the highway, she reached into the plastic bag of road trip snacks, rolled down her window, cranked her new Boys II Men CD, and headed towards the mountains, and more of the country she was exhilarated to see.

Unbeknownst to Gwen at that moment, a very heated debate was going on between forces she could not comprehend, even in her advanced genius. It was a very quick discussion, and both sides were passionate.

For once, the Being who had been disguised as the homeless man on a hot morning in the state of Utah, and simultaneously the same man on a street corner in New York City, won the discussion, and started making preparations for what lay ahead in the two individual yet connected lives, moving swiftly towards each other.

Chapter 7

Ben once again looked out of an airplane window at his future. Instead of thinking he was going to land in a cotton field in the middle of West Texas, this time, he wondered if the plane would hit any of the tall, slate-gray, shining skyscrapers of New York City.

He was finally coming home, he thought to himself. He could feel the excitement in his chest. He wanted to grin from ear to ear, but then he was reminded of the last time he was in New York, and what he had lost that day.

Looking down at his lap, his momentary relapse into depression nearly forgotten, he fondly looked at what was bringing him home.

A glossy black covered book, the words of the title in equally shiny silver. *The Tower and the Traitor* by Benjamin Reeves. He turned the book over and saw the black-and-white photo of himself, looking very mature for his eighteen years of age.

They had taken the picture right after his graduation from high school, and as he turned eighteen, they were legally allowed to publish his book without his father's permission. Ben had made sure no word of the book got back to his absent father. He had fatally and finally shut THAT book in his life. He wished his other "family" well, but was finally content to just be on his own.

As one of the Big Five publishers had bought his book of short stories, they were flying him out to the home offices for a tour and a couple of book signings around the City.

Having been from the City, he was once again the "hometown" boy, but in reality, they had said the same thing over the summer during his many, small stops in towns all over Texas.

He really felt like a person out of time, with no real home. Or, he thought to himself, the whole world was his home. That thought made him smile.

He had really come a long way in the last year.

Leaving the boys' home, graduating, getting paid in advance enough to live off of and start his life, was all very exciting, and happened very fast.

All of his teachers, as well as the staff and boys who became friends were all very complimentary and happy for him, but he could hear their undertones.

He had needed to get out of the small area that he had called home since he was ten years old. He felt surer than anything that he had outgrown his upbringing.

The world was his now, his counselor had told him two days before he left. She was super proud of him, but he could see the worry in her eyes. He was being thrust into a world he didn't know, and she wondered if he was ready for it.

What she didn't realize, what none of them had realized, was that this was what he was made for. He got into the swing of the book tour very comfortably, and already had written half of his next book before this trip to New York.

He was excited to see the city in the early fall. It was still very warm, but they had had some cool nights, so he knew that the heat wouldn't be baking off the sidewalks and streets, and the air would smell a little cleaner than during the long, hot summer.

He left the terminal that he had flown into, and seeing a man wearing the traditional black tuxedo, holding a white card with his name on it, he motioned with one hand that he had seen the man, and with the other pointed down the long passenger hallway to the baggage claim.

The man fell in step with him, and as they retrieved his single suitcase, he led Ben out to the holding lanes on the upper level of the airport. They dodged taxis honking and buses polluting the environment. Ben gave the chauffeur his suitcase, got into the back of the jet-black Lincoln, and made himself comfortable.

As they made their way into the city, towards all of those tall, shining skyscrapers, Ben practiced what he would say about his next project. They were clamoring for details of his next book. He, with Rudy, his agent, had sold his book to the highest bidder. Rudy had never been a part of a bidding war for a book, especially one from a seventeen-year-old boy, but he was excited to have a part in the whole scheme. Ben felt bad that, when he signed his long-term contract, he had done it without the guidance of his agent.

But he had been given some very practical advice and knew that Rudy was a little too "small town" for his goals and where he had wanted his books to go.

So, using a loophole in the contract he had innocently signed with him, Ben had gotten out of a long-term representation from Rudy in Dallas. Rudy had received a very favorable amount as recompense, but Ben didn't like the feeling he had felt as he walked away from the downtrodden look on Rudy's face.

He knew he would have to make it up to the man somehow, but for now, he was enjoying the attention in the most important city in the world.

The car pulled up to a very beautiful, and very tall building in Midtown. Ben stepped out of the car, before the doorman could open his door, and started walking up to the front revolving doors.

As he approached the front of the building, a homeless-looking man sitting almost camouflaged against the stones of the limestone foundation caught his attention.

The man looked middle-aged, but very dirty. Ben guessed he had not eaten today. Maybe a couple of days. The homeless man did not have his hand out. Didn't even have a collection cup like Ben remembered most homeless beggars having out in front of them as they sat on a piece of cardboard usually. He was just sitting quietly, not moving, and staring right into Ben's eyes.

Ben walked over to the man, almost drawn to him. He didn't break eye contact. He could hear both the doorman and the chauffeur calling his name behind him, but nothing could stop him from approaching the dirty man sitting, staring at him so intently.

"Do you know me?" Ben asked the man as he got close enough to smell him. It wasn't a bad smell at all,

41

surprisingly. Ben's memory tickled at him with the smell. It was something from his past.

The homeless man just shook his head. Maintaining eye contact, the man just pointed straight up, like he was trying to tell Ben something. The man looked at where his finger was pointing upwards, and then back at Ben. The intensity shocked Ben.

"Should I be careful in there? Are you trying to tell me that? Are you warning me?" Ben asked. He didn't even need the answer. He knew what the man meant as soon as he pointed up at the building behind him, with one chewed on, broken nail at the top of a very dirty finger.

Ben pulled out a twenty-dollar bill he had in his pocket. He handed it to the man, folding his hands around the money, with his own hands around the homeless man's hands. He shook the hands he was holding, trying to convey his appreciation with his eyes.

The homeless man smiled a broken-toothed smile at him and gestured with his head for Ben to follow the men trying to pull him towards the revolving door. With one last look at the older homeless man, Ben allowed himself to be drawn away.

As he went through the revolving, crystal-clear doors, he looked back over at the piece of cardboard on the sidewalk in front of the building. The homeless man was gone. Ben went one more rotation through the doors, making the chauffeur wait for him in the lobby, but Ben could see no sign of the dirty man anywhere. He had just vanished.

As Ben, now with a cohort of other people around him, ascended to the top floors in the spacious elevator, he put his hand in his pocket, and felt the twenty-dollar bill. He knew that it was the same one he had pressed into the homeless man's hands.

He vaguely heard all of the compliments and fake talk from the people around him and knew it for what it was. But his mind was on the twenty. How did it end up back in his pocket, almost like magic? And who the hell was that homeless man?

His attention drifted back to the suits talking like Charlie Brown's teacher in the cartoons of his youth. "Wwhh wwhh wwhh!"

Five minutes before, he wouldn't have realized how fake all of these smiles were. He was just a paycheck for them. And that was okay, he thought to himself, he didn't write for these people. He wrote for people who would feel his words, and not just read them. Those who needed uplifting, and not just to be entertained.

A little while later, as Ben cautiously read over the contracts on the big glass table in front of him, now very suspicious of the motives of the people in suits around him, the homeless man, now in his eternal form, looked down on him from the place that the Material cannot see the Spiritual, and knew that he had chosen correctly.

These two would do just fine, the entity thought to himself.

Just fine indeed.

Chapter 8

Gwen's ass was numb again. She had pushed on all day since Salt Lake City, south into Western Colorado, and was loving every minute of her drive. The scenery she was seeing outside of her increasingly dirty windshield took her breath away.

Although, she could do without all the bugs splattering against the glass in front of her, she thought to herself as she watched the western face of the Rocky Mountains grow in front of her car.

It was getting darker the further into Colorado she drove. She watched the setting sun in her rearview mirror.

Up ahead, down in a valley of sorts, she could make out the lights of a small town. It was Westcliffe, Colorado, she knew from the maps her father had pressed on her before leaving California.

She had set the goal to get here today and was happy she had made it before it was completely dark. The purple mountains, deep in shadows, in front of her were so beautiful. She felt a catch in her chest. If that was a thing, she mused, chuckling.

Gwen was so happy that she had taken this road trip instead of flying out to Boston.

As she drove into the western edge of the small town, she briefly closed her eyes and felt the still, warm air on her face, from her window still being halfway rolled down.

She drove into the small town, enjoying the spaced-out buildings, and the beginnings of autumn decorations on front porches in the form of scarecrows and a few pumpkins. Many small bales of hay were set out. Many homes had an American flag flying proudly in front of their homes.

She had called ahead earlier in the day, when she had stopped for lunch, and knew that the only room she could get in this little town was at the Antler Inn. She pulled up to the hybrid motel and liquor store and grinned when she saw the gigantic statue of a majestic elk out front.

When she had called earlier in the day, a man answered with a "This is Moose."

She supposed that he was the sole employee of the small motel and liquor store, and except for the man's family, she had been correct. Walking up to the liquor store, she stopped and admired the large statue. The elk was monstrous.

She wondered if they really grew to that size, or if this was an overlarge representation.

The elk was adorned with Christmas lights, and in the fading dusk, they twinkled brightly. The entire scene made her feel happy, but somewhat melancholy.

Entering the liquor store, she walked past an older man bumbling towards the exit, and saw a middle-aged man standing behind the counter, looking at her suspiciously.

"You a little too young to be in here, missy," the man said gruffly.

"I'm looking for...ummm...Moose? I spoke with him on the phone earlier today? I need a room and some directions if that's okay?" She didn't know why she gave all that information in questions. She felt silly and out of her element.

"Well, why didn't you say so? I'm Moose. Or, if you like, you can call me Brian. This is my place. We have a nice room made up for you. My wife just put in fresh towels."

"Thank you. That sounds great. I've been on the road all day." Gwen did feel relieved.

"This way. Just let me lock the door. Give me a sec," Brian said. He walked around the counter, past her, and, ushering her back outside, he locked the door behind him.

"Drive your car around to the right, park anywhere. Not too many visitors this time of year."

Gwen nodded. She got back in her car and drove around like Brian had instructed. As her headlights swept over the doors on the lower level of the motel, they caught Brian and a pretty blonde woman speaking in front of a white door, about a third of the way down the row of identical doors.

Gwen had no idea where the courage to stay in a weird, small-town hotel in the middle of nowhere came from, but she was too tired to worry about it. Her ass was still just as numb as earlier, and she just wanted to eat and sleep. She would think about getting murdered and raped later.

Her wandering, hysterical thoughts put them in that order, as well. She grinned a little at that.

Gwen got out of her car, went around to the hatchback, and pulled her suitcase out. Walking up to the pair, she thought that they made a beautiful couple. She wondered if this was Brian's wife.

"Here you go. Room 107. Best in the place. This is my wife, Rachel, and she will get you all set. We can settle up for the room in the morning when you leave, and I'll give you directions anywhere you need to go, this side of the range."

"Thank you so much." Gwen said as the man turned to go back to the store. His wife, Rachel, smiled at Gwen and beckoned her into the room she just opened.

"Hi there sweetheart. I'm Rachel. Don't mind my husband. He was born gruff."

"Oh, I don't mind at all. I'm just tired," Gwen said.

"There are fresh towels, coffee maker and all that's standard. You need anything at all, just pick up the phone and dial 0," Rachel told her.

"You need anything else before I go?"

"I could use some dinner. Where is a good place to eat here?"

"Just walk right across the street there. That place on the corner is Jake's. Really good comfort food. Just don't mind the boys flirting with you. You're gorgeous by the way. I wish I had your hair," Rachel told her. Gwen thought that she must be a mother. She had a very mothering air about her.

"Thank you so much. I'll check out the diner. I think that's about all I need, except some sleep," Gwen replied.

"Okay, sweetie, here's the key, and like I said, you need anything, dial 0." The woman handed her a real key on a small ring attached to a small white disk with the name of the motel on it in black.

As the woman swept out of the room, closing the door behind her, Gwen plopped down on the comfortable bed, sighing in relief. She was sore all over, and all she had done was drive for the last two days.

Gwen vaguely wondered why the owners had not copied her driver's license or taken any of her information. She figured that this was just the way they did it here. The town was very secluded and was practically the only thing for miles around, except the mountains.

Gwen walked back outside, really enjoying the crisp, chilly air. People were walking around the small main street, and cars drove up and down. She looked both ways and crossed the street over to a clapboard building.

The siding on the building was deep gray and looked like it could fall apart at any time. As she walked around to the front of the building, seeing a porch light up and people talking and laughing, she entered the single glass door, and entered the diner.

Inside, people were sitting and eating, and the noise level was tolerable. There was a lot of laughter, and everyone just seemed really good, in Gwen's estimation. She really liked this small town.

A waitress walked up to her, standing near the front, and asked if she was dining alone.

"Yes, just me," Gwen answered.

"You want a table, or do you want to sit up at the counter, on one of the stools?"

"The counter is fine. Thank you."

The middle-aged, large-bottomed waitress led her over to a row of round stools lined up in front of the bar where Gwen could only assume thousands of breakfasts and dinners had been enjoyed. The stool was padded and felt nice under her.

Another waitress walked up from behind the counter and asked her what she wanted to drink. Being as exhausted as she was, Gwen asked for a Coke. The waitress asked her if she wanted regular, diet, or cherry, and Gwen chose the cherry.

Gwen looked at the other people sitting at the counter. They were mostly middle-aged men, reading newspapers, or talking to each other. There were a few women, and she vaguely wondered if they were the wives of the men sitting next to them. The women seemed to talk just to the other women, and the men to the men. Gwen decided to keep to herself.

She picked up the faded, laminated menu and looked over several options that she felt would add about ten pounds to her small frame. But she was starving.

When the waitress returned with her clear red plastic cup full of ice and dark soda, she had decided on something called "Chicken Fried Chicken."

"Good choice, honey. This is the best chicken fried chicken in Colorado." The waitress winked at her and walked away to give her order to the cooks in the back.

Gwen once again looked around her, and then up at the décor on the walls. It was all very rustic. There were what she assumed were farming implements, and very old-fashioned goods scattered on shelves haphazardly placed all over the place.

She saw a box of detergent that must have been more than fifty years old. There were ancient candy boxes and advertisements for Coca-Cola and Sprite. She also liked the advertisements from what may have been the 50s for several different kinds of cars.

She noticed some old black-and-white pictures of the very building she was sitting in, with several men standing in front, wearing white t-shirts and white pants.

She saw that there had once been a very old-fashioned gas pump out front of this building that wasn't there anymore.

Then she looked at the men in the foreground of the photo. Most had an apron around their waist. The faces were hard to make out as they all appeared the same. Just a featureless set of eyes, a nose, and a thin mouth on all of the men standing together.

Maybe they were all related, she thought.

Her food came to her faster than she thought possible, and she ravenously dug in. It was delicious. Even better than what her mother cooked. She learned very quickly that she was a huge fan of chicken fried chicken. She unabashedly ate everything on the plate, surprising herself.

As she sopped up the last of the white gravy with the remains of her dinner roll, the waitress returned.

"Well, look at you, big eater," she said with a grin.

Gwen smiled back. The food had been wonderful.

"Leave any room for dessert, honey?" the waitress asked her.

"Oh, no, I'm too stuffed. Thank you though. I'll take the check please."

The waitress walked away and returned a short time later with her check. Gwen looked at it and was surprised it was all less than ten bucks. Wow, she thought. What a deal!

She paid at the register standing near the only door leading back out to the street. Getting her change, she handed back several singles and asked if they could give it to her waitress.

Gwen felt overfull as she walked back to the motel. She keyed open the door and set about her normal evening routine. As she got into the comfortable bed, pulling the clean sheets and heavy comforter over her, she was happy.

She didn't remember falling asleep, but as her head hit the pillows, consciousness slipped out of her grasp.

The next day, since she had forgot to set an alarm, she was awakened with the sun shining through the curtains, directly into her eyes. She sat up, knowing that she had slept in.

She hurriedly took a hot shower, eschewed makeup for the day, and packed her things. She ran outside, loaded her suitcase into the back of her car, and drove back around to the front of the long building.

She entered the liquor store once again, and saw the same man, Brian, with a clipboard in hand, counting bottles of liquor. He looked up as she entered and smiled a warming smile her way.

"How did you sleep?" he asked.

"Too well. Thank you. I would like to pay my bill, and can you please give me directions to Bishop Castle?" she said. Walking to the counter, she placed her purse on it. Brian put down the clipboard and walked around to the other side.

"Alright, let's see. Room for one night. That will be 39.99 plus tax. Comes out to 42.50," he said.

Again, Gwen was surprised at how cheap everything had been in this wonderful little town.

She counted out the cash, handed it over, and Brian quickly returned her change.

"Now, Bishop Castle. Love that place. We've watched it being built for a lot of years. Man who is doing all the building himself, Jim Bishop, now, he's a character alright. If you meet him, do not talk politics. He will keep you talking all day, and you'll miss seeing the castle." Brian chuckled to himself.

"Now, it's only about thirty miles. During the winter, we don't go that way because the roads can get shut

51

down quick as you like. But this time of year, it's a really pretty drive. The trees should be changing colors very soon, so you'll get a bit of a sight driving there," he said.

"What you want to do is go east out of town on the main street there. That's 96. It will head straight into the mountains. Like I said, really pretty. The only road that branches off of 96 is 165, and it'll come on you quick, so be on the lookout for it. It branches south, umm, to your right. Can't miss it if you're looking for it," he continued.

"Then, take 165 south about fifteen minutes, and you'll come around a bend and the castle will be right there, on the right-hand side of the road. There'll be cars parked against both sides of the road, so you just park and walk up. Can't miss it," Brian said, almost out of breath.

"Thank you so much, Brian. I hope to come back soon."

"Thank you, yourself. And come anytime. Christmas time is great here. We play a lot of pond hockey, and you wouldn't want to miss that. Most fun you can have freezing your toes off." Brian laughed to himself. He picked the clipboard back up and went back to counting bottles.

Gwen walked out to her car and got in. She needed gas before she got into the mountains. She had seen a 7-11 at the edge of town with a gas pump. She drove there, got her gas and some more snacks, and set off into the mountains. She felt excitement like she rarely ever felt. She knew at that moment that she was for sure more of a mountain girl than a beach girl.

Brian's directions were spot on. About thirty-five minutes later, she was pulling off of the road, behind a line of cars already parked against the shoulder. She worried that her car was sticking out too far into the road, but it wasn't any further out than any of the other cars in the line.

She locked her car and walked along the road to an opening in the trees. As she rounded the short corner, the castle and all of its splendor suddenly opened up to her.

Her breath caught in her chest.

She couldn't believe one man had built all of this with his bare hands. Signs leading into the castle described how many stones had been used to make the castle, and that Jim Bishop had handled each and every stone at least six or seven times. Finding the final resting place for each stone is what had taken so long.

Gwen gawked up at the castle. It was huge. It was capped with a metal dragon head, which she had read spit real fire every evening. Long steps curved up to the upper floors from both front corners.

She couldn't take her eyes off of the large stained-glass windows on the upper floor. They were amazing. The whole time she was looking up at the castle, all she could wonder was how a single man could made something this large and beautiful.

She walked over to a wooden, rustic barn and walked into a small gift shop. There was a white-haired man behind the counter. He was wearing a flannel shirt and dirty jeans. She walked up to him.

"Excuse me sir," she said. "Is Mr. Bishop here at the site today?"

"Mr. Bishop was my father darlin'," the man said. "Just call me Jim. How you do?"

The man held out one calloused hand, which Gwen instantly took and shook vigorously.

"I can't believe what you did here. It's amazing," she stammered.

"Have you been up in the castle yet? Why don't you go explore it a bit and then come back and talk to me," he said as she shook her head.

She nodded and headed back out to the castle proper. She didn't know where to start. So she started climbing the stairs that made up the closest corner of the castle. The steps were narrow and steep, but she didn't have a problem finding footing.

By the time she made it to the second level, she was slightly winded. She was at a high elevation, she knew. The difference in her lung capacity and the thinner air made her scientific mind start clicking.

She entered a dark doorway and wandered through many tight-angled corridors, still marveling at how a single man could set all of these thousands of stones and make something so beautiful. She had a destination in mind. She wanted to see the Grand Ballroom. She had seen pictures of the large, open room.

She knew that several times a year, parties were held in the room, and even a haunted Halloween bash, with the dragon releasing ball after ball of flame throughout the evening.

She wished suddenly that she would be able to be here for the Halloween bash this year.

Rounding one last corner, she saw ahead the doorway leading into the Grand Ballroom. She entered the room more excited than she had been about anything else.

She was surprised that she was alone in the large room. It gave her time to study the beautiful stained-glass windows that seemed to be everywhere she looked.

The floor of the giant room was hard plank wood, but there was no sound as she walked from one end of the large room to the other. The size and splendor of the room awed her.

She didn't even notice when the smoke started billowing slowly around her.

She was standing close to the front of the room, examining the reds and whites in the glass before her when

54

she finally noticed that there was billowy steam surrounding her.

She turned and was instantly terrified that the building was aflame.

But she saw that the fog was a pinkish hue, and not the normal heavy white of smoke. Her brain instantly locked onto what she was seeing and tried to quantify the source. She figured that maybe one of the Halloween smoke machines started up with no one there.

She couldn't figure out how that was possible, but she started walking towards the source of the fog, where it seemed to be thickest.

As she approached the exact center of the Grand Ballroom, the fog started parting. She was looking down at the wooden floor, looking for the fog machine, when a voice boomed in her mind, making her gasp aloud, and grab her head in mental pain.

"GWENDOLYN MURPHY, YOU ARE HERE TO MAKE THE CHOICE."

Gwen looked around her in a panic, wondering where the multi-voiced words slammed into her consciousness came from.

Her eyes found movement and she turned to see a massive figure floating right in front of her. She couldn't believe her eyes. The man (she assumed) had outspread white feathered wings, and was wearing a flowing robe colored a light pink hue. It was almost the same color as the billowing fog surrounding the both of them.

Gwen vaguely wondered where all of the other tourists were.

Her voice sounded small to her ears. She cleared her voice and said louder,

"What Choice?"

Chapter 9

"So, let me get this straight. My mother's last will and testament has been in your possession since I was nine years old, and now that I'm eighteen, you have the legal right to reveal the contents to me?" Ben asked the small, very elderly man sitting across from him.

"Yes, Benjamin. Your mother very specifically laid out in her will that you were not to be given access to, or information about, what she has left to you."

Ben just shook his head and looked around the large office. He had received a letter at his PO Box before he left Texas for New York. The trip initially had been to sign a contract with the new publishers, meet face to face with his new agent, and to do a little reminiscing about his childhood in New York.

All that changed, of course, when he received the letter from a large, prestigious law firm in uptown New York City. The contents of the letter had floored him. He figured it had something to do with *Tower and Traitor* but it had not.

It was from his late mother's attorney, explaining to him that she had left a last will and testament, and the contents of which would be available to him when he came to the office to meet with the small man now sitting and smiling at him across the large mahogany desk.

"Why would she do it this way?" Ben asked.

"Who can say? All I know, is that she left very specific instructions, and we have been managing her estate since she passed away eight years ago. I can tell you; I have enjoyed keeping up with your life. I have been given quarterly updates on your health by your biological father, along with your proclivity for trouble, your growth and anything else I asked for, over the years. Your mother set this all up. And then, when you published your amazing book last year, I knew then what she had known. You were going to do big, big things," the man said with a chuckle.

He then got up out of his oversized chair, holding a folder with stapled papers in it, and came around the desk and sat in the chair next to Ben.

"Your mother left you her entire estate. She had been a very frugal woman. And very smart. Her holdings in particular investments wouldn't have made you rich, in any sense, but it made it possible for us to be able to manage her estate until you could take over everything."

He reached over to a wood box on his desk, about the size of a cigar box.

"This is for you. She left it in my possession only months before her untimely passing."

The old lawyer handed the box to Ben, who felt the first pings of fear and trepidation. He was holding back tears. This was all coming too fast.

Ben opened the box. At the very top was a set of brass keys. They looked like house keys. Ben took them out, looking up at the lawyer, who nodded. Then Ben placed the keys on the desk in front of him and looked back in the box.

There was a tri-folded bit of stacked papers. He took them out, his hands shaking. Unfolding the pages, he saw it was the stationary that his mother had always used for letters and correspondences when he was a little boy.

Once, he had gotten in a bit of trouble for taking some of her treasured paper and coloring on them. She had been upset. She told him that this paper was too expensive for coloring. He remembered her angry face, but then he remembered the huge stack of multi-colored construction paper she had bought for him the same day.

Tears blinding his eyes, he started to read. After the first sentence, he couldn't see to read the next. The lawyer handed him an embossed handkerchief he pulled from his suit jacket pocket.

The initials on the handkerchief read *S.L.*

Ben wiped his eyes, looked back at the letter his mother had written to him, and started to read her beautiful handwriting once again.

"*My dearest Benjamin,*" it started. Ben kept reading, holding the tears inside.

"*I cannot imagine what you have gone through before receiving this letter. I don't know how much time has gone by, but I know that it couldn't have been easy for you. As I write this, you are playing with your army trucks in the front parlor room. The day is sunny, and I promised you that we would go to the beach this afternoon. I can hear you banging the trucks together in there, and you sound so happy. I'm so blessed to have had you. You have made my life whole and complete, and since you were born, I have not needed anything else. I hope that I have been a good momma for you. I'm so sorry you haven't had a father in your life. I thought that I was doing a good job filling both roles for you. When we talk at night, before you go to bed, you always do a really good job, for such a small boy, to let me know that I am doing good. I want to thank you for making my life what it is today. I'm so sorry for whatever happened for you to be reading this letter. My prayer is that you are an adult when you get this, that you are surrounded by your own children and loving wife. But we never know what this life will deal us. We never know what's going to happen. All we can do is make the best of what we have. And today, you, my dear son, are my best. I love you with my whole heart, and I pray that we had years and years together before you read this letter. But if not, if something bad happened while you're still a little boy, just remember two things. I loved you so fiercely. And everything will be okay. You just watch where you're going. Look ahead at where you are going so nothing makes you stumble. You have my strength. You always have. It's okay to be alone, if you have something to love. Don't be like me and not* *have anyone else in your life. But if you are just like me, that's okay too. Find something you are passionate about and focus on it completely. <u>You</u> were that for me. You always were. I love you son. I will always look over you. Now, I have to go get you ready to go to the beach. It's such a beautiful day outside. And I want to stop thinking about death and you being in pain, and I want to go pick you up, kiss your little face, and go enjoy the sunshine with you. I love you my darling dear. Always and forever. Momma."*

Ben read the letter twice. The second time, he felt the tears fall from both eyes, but he kept going. He could hear her voice saying the words to him. For the first time in so many years, he had that mental image of his mother's face again. Her voice echoed in his mind. He smiled.

He could see her thin frame sitting at the old army issue desk in the corner of the dining room in the little cottage where he grew up. She was bent over, concentrating on the stationary pages in front of her, not realizing that she had been gone for over eight years when he would finally read her words to him.

To just him.

He gently placed the folded pages on the desk, on top of the brass keys. He looked back in the box and saw just a couple of other items. The first one was a gold wedding ring.

He picked it up and pulled it out. He knew it. It had been his mother's. From his absent father. While they were so shortly married, his father had given this ring to his mother. She often said it was the second-best thing she had gotten from the man.

Ben didn't know jewelry enough to know if it was a valuable ring or not, but it was the very last thing that was a part of his parents' short union. He treasured the ring. It was priceless to him.

Putting the ring on top of the folded letter on the desk in front of him, he looked at the very last thing in the box. It confused him. It was another key. Silver, with a number stamped into the round end. *1725*.

Ben looked up at the man sitting patiently beside him.

"It's a safety deposit box key. I don't know what the box contains, only that we were instructed to continue to pay the annual rent on it until you were eighteen and could take possession of the contents yourself."

Ben placed the silver key back into the wooden box. He then gathered up all the other things from the box and put them all back together. He closed the wooden box and held it in his lap. He looked back over at the man sitting next to him, telling him to continue with his eyes.

"Ahem, yes, well, as to the contents of your mother's last will and testament, as I said before, she left everything to you, her only child. Namely, the largest asset is the home located on Harbor Hill Drive in Lloyd Harbor, NY. The mortgage was paid off at the time of your mother's death, and taxes have been paid yearly ever since," the man said. Ben was still in a state of shock.

"We were also instructed to maintain the home. Upkeep and all, you understand, which we did. You'll find the home still in tip-top shape, and very valuable, as home values on Long Island have skyrocketed lately," the lawyer said, eyebrows drawn together, as if trying to convey a message to Ben.

"We have actually gotten a few offers since your mother's passing, but of course, we could not sell. You will have that option, and I will leave you a list of the offers we have received."

The older man continued, "Your mother also named you her sole beneficiary on two different life insurance policies. Years ago, we, being the executor of her estate, received the funds from both policies, and have placed them into a trust, in your name, which has gotten a pretty fair return the last eight years. The total in the trust account as of this morning is..." and pulling out a small note page from his inner pocket, he read the numbers apparently written there.

"Ahem, yes, the sum is one hundred and eighteen thousand, thirty dollars and some change." The lawyer reached over, flipped over several pages in the stapled bundle he held and tore loose the last page.

Handing it to Ben, he smiled.

Ben gasped. Looking at the paper he held, he saw that it was a short bank statement, of an account at the First Fidelity Bank, in his name. The account balance was exactly as the man had read off.

Ben swallowed loudly. He had already received his advance and first two quarterly royalty checks for his first book, and that money sat comfortably in a national chain bank. Ben tried to add up how much money he had now, and at almost half a million dollars, he was overwhelmed. He vaguely thought that he may need some sort of financial advice soon.

He didn't realize his mother had left him anything, let alone his old house and a large sum of money. He was shocked and didn't know what to say. He silently said a "thank you" to his mother under his breath.

The man continued: "So, we have the house, which you have the keys to in that box. The life insurance policies, and the contents of both this wooden box, and the safety deposit box at First Fidelity Bank. They are expecting you at any time."

The man slid over a sheaf of papers for Ben's signature, which he woodenly provided. The man then stood up, said something to the effect of offering his services if Ben ever needed anything further, and saying one last goodbye, ushered Ben towards the door, letting him out into the heavily carpeted hallway and closing the door behind him.

Ben didn't see the old lawyer close the door, lean himself against it, and listen to the young man's footsteps echo down the hallway outside his office. A tear streaked down the old man's face, and his shoulders shook. He knew he wouldn't be himself for the rest of the day, so he mentally planned to take the rest of the day, and get home to soak in his own painful memories.

Ben soon found himself on the busy street in front of the law firm office, feeling lost, and not knowing what to do next. He needed to process everything he just heard, felt, and went through.

He hailed a taxi, gave the address to the hotel the publishers had supplied him with.

His nerves were shot, and he couldn't quite catch his breath for the entire drive to the hotel.

As the taxi moved through the busy streets of New York, Ben didn't see anything outside the car.

Instead, he looked down at the wooden box sitting in his lap the whole way there.

Chapter 10

"THE ONLY CHOICE THAT MATTERS, GWENDOLYN MURPHY. THE CHOICE OF LIFE."

The voice reverberated in Gwen's mind. It was giving her a bit of a headache. She didn't know what to do. She wanted to run away screaming. But something inside her was very curious at what she was witnessing.

The Being just hovered, a few feet off the ground, the huge, outspread wings slowly flapping, not unlike a large eagle's wings.

"Please stop shouting in my head. It hurts," she said, boldly. "Who are you?"

The form hovering in the air in front of her became brighter, to her eyes. She fell to one knee, as she shaded her eyes from the bright light emanating from the hovering form. She vaguely wondered if this was an angel. The Being's voice, sounding much quieter in her mind, confirmed her suspicions.

"I am the Archangel Chamuel," the Being said in her mind. The choir of voices the Being spoke with unnerved Gwen.

"I have been here since before the dawn of time. I was there when The Creator spoke this world into being. I was there when The Creator breathed life into mankind. I was given my task very soon after. But different civilizations have called me many different things."

"In your current world, some would call me Cupid. But I have had many other names, depending on the people's beliefs. In ancient Rome and Greece, I was called Aphrodite, or Venus. Other people at the time revered me as Salina, the goddess of dreams and wishes."

The large, hovering angel's voice went on in her mind:

"In that great civilization of the Egyptians, they worshiped me as Satis, the Egyptian fertility goddess of wishes. The earliest Grecian's called me Airli, the goddess of wishes. The Celtic peoples called me Nemetona, the goddess worshiped in Gaul for a thousand years."

"The Greeks and Romans later called me Morpheus. The Japanese knew me as Musubi-no-kami. In Arabia, I was called a Djinni. In Ireland I was called a luricawnes or liprichan. Long years later, in the Golden Age of Rome, I was one of the Fates, or the Moirae," the Being said in Gwen's mind, without moving its mouth.

"In India and Persia, I was known as Kamadeva. On the other side of the planet, in South America, and to the ancient Aztecs, I was Xochipilli. Back to the Orient, to the Chinese, I was, and still am called Yue-Lao, who binds two people together with an invisible red string. They are actually the closest to the truth of what I was made for. Across the world, in other ages, in Slavic mythology, I was called Dzydzilelya, and finally in Norse legends, I was often mistaken for Freya."

"That sounded quite rehearsed," she said, snarkily. She didn't know why her mouth always got her into trouble. But the floating creature ignored the comment.

"The Creator Himself gave me the task that I am now setting before you. You must make a choice. This Choice will usually only come to you once. Choose wisely."

Gwen was now much more curious than scared. Questions were rebounding in her mind, louder than the voice of the Archangel hovering in front of her.

"Is The Creator God? And if so, then He is real? Is He really the Father, Son, and Holy Spirit?" she asked innocently. Never before had she been given an answer that suited her intellect. "Ahh," the angel said, again in her mind. "A great question, and one I'm allowed to answer."

Speaking straight into Gwen's mind, she found it hard to gauge emotion from the words. She could hear him perfectly, not unlike how she could always hear her own voice in her mind when she inner-dialogued to herself. A habit, she thought in passing, that she did all too often.

"God has had many names," Chamuel spoke softly into her mind.

"Even the moniker 'God' is incorrectly used for Him. It's just a capitalized adjective for the ideal of a Celestial Being who created all things. His real name has always been hidden to His creation. Your human brain, with its amazing ability to think up the most incredible things, like art and music, cannot comprehend the complexity of who and what God is. Humans have tried to humanize Him all through history," he went on answering her question.

"The idea of the Holy Trinity, which you just mentioned, is a human construct," Chamuel's voice continued.

"The idea of a Father, a Son, and a Holy Ghost cannot begin to describe His existence. It would be much more appropriate to describe to you, in human terms, that the name 'Jesus' is the Physical Material of Him, the name 'God' being the Will and Power, and the name 'Holy Ghost' as the eternal Spirit of a Being that if you could see but a fraction of him, would melt your very physical material, and shatter your eternal presence. Even that description of the three parts simplifies who God, and his many parts, contains." Chamuel, very un-heavenly-entity-like, made quotations with his oversized, glowing hands, as he said the names of the Trinity.

"But for your comfort, the Holy Three, and a relationship with the Physical embodiment of God, will suffice. Really, I should point out that while a relationship with 'Jesus' is the key to sharing eternity with God, the truth is you must have a belief in the part of God who He gave of Himself to save you from your sins, which separates Him from you, and paves the way for your soul to enjoy eternal bliss with Him," the Being said.

"God, very fortunately, gave you a name, Jesus, so you could have something to latch onto, to understand. Just as the human form of God spoke in parables, easier for you humans to grasp, so too, God gave you a human concept to pave your way to eternal paradise." The archangel paused, looking Gwen deep in her eyes. He continued, voice still loud in her head.

"Can you imagine, a perfectly good Being, giving a piece of His physical self as a sacrifice to forever join you, and your sinful nature, with the rest of who and what He is? He very much gave an 'arm and leg for you'," Chamuel said in her mind, finally smiling.

The Being then chuckled, surprising Gwen, who up until that point, could see no humor in the entity. She was still on her knees, blinded by the light coming from within the Being. As he (and she was assuming it was a he) chuckled to himself at his little joke about the arm and leg, she rose to her feet, shakily facing the glowing form hovering in the air in front of her.

"If all that is true, who and what God is, why is He interested in me?" she asked.

"Ah, now THAT, is another good question. And one I am allowed to answer," the Being stated, still without moving his mouth, as the words resounded in Gwen's mind.

The form, all in pink, shimmered in front of her and seemed to shrink. As she watched, her mouth dropping open, the Being transformed from a giant glowing form down to a middle-aged human man, who seemed vaguely familiar, standing in front of her wearing a very dashing maroon three-piece Brooks Brother's suit and holding a polished redwood cane.

The suit was perfectly tailored and fit the older man well. He also had on a very creamy cashmere scarf. His head was bare, which bothered Gwen a little, and his shoes were very brightly polished black leather flats. He looked quite dapper, and his wardrobe looked expensive.

"I love this form. I have often worn this costume down the streets of your world for eons, blending in with humans, hearing your thoughts and dreams and worries." Chamuel looked down at himself and sighed contently.

Gwen thought that when he said "costume," he was not referring to the obviously expensive clothing he wore. He looked very much out of place in the stone and wood room they stood in, with the pink-tinted, billowing steam still seeming to keep out all other visitors.

As she looked the man in front of her over, she vaguely wondered if they were even still in the Grand Ballroom of Bishop Castle.

"As to your question: A very small part of who God is, at this very moment, is very much interested in you, and the choice I am about to give you. While another whole part of God knows what decision you will make, a whole other part of God is very much concerned with this, His creation, and the children He has created to live in it," the man said.

"All those children, and the happiness and wholeness, as well as the peace He wishes you all to experience, have choices. The ones who He is especially interested in - call them 'essential' to His Plan - He sometimes will give a direct approach, much like this one. Or historically, like the Burning Bush in your history with Moses, so that the Plan meets His requirements in a more, say, complete way," the man/being paused to make sure that Gwen was paying attention.

She was.

"Every moment, God takes His children's choices, and makes beautifully beautiful things come from them. It's actually quite miraculous when you think about it," he said.

"What's this choice you keep talking about?" Gwen asked.

"It's quite simple, really," the Archangel said. "You must choose between life and Love."

"Are you saying if I choose to stay alive, I won't have love?" she asked incredulously.

"You misunderstand, my child. You very well can have life. And you can have love. The Love about which I speak is the Essence of who God is. It's a Love that will complete you, but it's also a Love that if you were to choose it, would end the path you are on for your future, and put you on a path that God chooses. You will exchange a fulfilling Love for the life of greatness you are currently headed towards," the man paused again.

He knew it was a ton of information for a human mind, but this particular human mind was quite extraordinary.

Gwen did not like the sound of the Choice. She suddenly felt quite rebellious. There was no way; not even God would control her.

The thought made her angry. It also made her a little bit sad. She didn't know which emotion ruled out in the end, but she knew her Choice, from deep within her.

"The Choice is easy, angel. I choose life. My life. I'm not ready for a Love that will replace my dreams and goals," she said sullenly.

"I always thought a love should help you meet your goals, not change them completely," she said. She knew she sounded rebellious. She didn't care. Her fists clenched up. She was ready to fight.

Suddenly, she was blinded by a flash of bright white light. She once more fell to her knees in protection. She could feel the electricity in the air around her. Her hair felt like it was standing on end. The room became heavy, somehow.

When she opened her eyes again, looking up, she saw that the kindly older man was once again the giant being, hovering in mid-air, wings outstretched. The voice boomed in her mind once more.

"YOUR CHOICE HAS BEEN MADE AND CANNOT BE UNMADE. AS A FREE-WILL CREATURE,

70

IT IS YOUR PREROGATIVE TO CHOOSE YOUR OWN DESTINY. THIS IS BUT THE FIRST GIFT FROM GOD. BUT, ONCE MADE, THE CHOICE CANNOT BE TAKEN BACK. WE MUST ALL LIVE WITH THE REWARDS, OR CONSEQUENCES, OF ALL OF OUR CHOICES."

Gwen cowered behind her hands that covered her eyes. And then everything was still. She looked up and slowly got back to her feet. Looking around in a panic, everything was as it had been before her confrontation with the Archangel. She again quickly twisted herself every which way, seeing not one thing disturbed in the room.

She bolted from the Grand Ballroom. She didn't even think about stopping to speak with Jim Bishop again. She ran all the way to her car, and sat in it for a very long time, collecting her breath, and her thoughts. She lay her head against the steering wheel until her heartbeat wasn't so loud in her ears.

When she felt calm again, after several more minutes, she started her car, and drove east. By the time she stopped for lunch in Pueblo, CO, a couple of hours later, she was convinced that she had hallucinated the entire encounter.

Chapter 11

Ben wasn't sure what he should do first early the next morning. As he finished his shower and toweled off, he thought back on the events of the previous day, and the confusion and slight aura of pain he had felt as he drifted into a restless sleep.

The truth was, he thought to himself as he got dressed, he didn't have a place in the world to call his own. He had scant belongings and did not currently have an actual address. He wasn't in a relationship and didn't have any family he was beholden to. But now he owned a home. His home. The one he had grown up in before his mother had passed away. The home he thought he would never see again.

But he was extremely nervous to go home. So, he reasoned, he should see what was in the lock box at the bank, which he now owned the key to.

He tucked his wallet into his back pocket, put the keys to his house, as well as to the safety deposit box into his front pocket, and went down to the lobby with his suitcase to check out and ask the clerk to order him a taxi.

Out on the busy New York street, as he waited patiently for his taxi to arrive, he scanned the faces of people hurrying by.

His writer's mind picked out interesting features on people's faces, and in the way they walked and talked. *That man's nose was too big for his face, and mixed with a no-nonsense humor, most people laughed at what he said, and it always confused him. Or, that woman there, she was Hispanic, but told everyone that she was white. He wondered why she hid who she was.* He could never help this part of his thinking. He was always on the lookout for writing material.

The yellow taxi with the white advertising board perched on top pulled up to the curb. He hurriedly got into it, sliding his suitcase into the seat next to him, before someone else could take it.

"First Fidelity Bank, corner of 101st, please," he told the driver. Without saying a word, the Middle Eastern driver started the meter and pulled into traffic.

For the short trip to the bank, Ben felt a sense of foreboding. He couldn't quite place it, but he felt it came from all these new experiences that he hadn't anticipated. Receiving the call from his mother's lawyer during his first stay at the hotel two nights ago had had him on edge ever since.

He still didn't know how the lawyer had known he was in town, let alone which hotel he was staying at. He knew from the letter he had received in Texas that he needed to meet with the man, but deep in his soul, Ben felt like he had wanted to put that meeting off as long as he could. The lawyer calling him out of the blue and pressing the short meeting on him was abrupt.

73

Ben mentally shrugged, chalked it up to things he still didn't understand, and tried to steel himself for what other surprises would be in the safety deposit box his late mother had opened at some point when she was still alive.

The taxi braked in front of the large, obviously old bank, and Ben made a comment about how abruptly the driver had stopped. He handed him cash to cover the fee and a nice tip through the slot in the Plexiglas separating him from the driver, and, grabbing his suitcase, slid out the door on the side of the car next to the bank front.

Ben was cognizant enough of his surroundings to not appear like a tourist. He didn't stand in the middle of the sidewalk gawking up at the turn-of-the-century architecture of the old bank building, but he did notice it in passing. He entered the front double-glass doors with a few other patrons.

The interior of the bank's decor screamed money and class. Classic Roman architecture with gold inlay and lots of heavy marble was the main thing that Ben noticed. As he stood in the entryway of the bank proper, he knew he actually did look like a tourist. But he couldn't help it. He had always had a penchant for classic decor in the Roman, Grecian, and European styles.

A very pretty brunette secretary asked him if he needed help from behind the circular chest high desk next to him. He turned towards her voice, saw a slight look of concern on her face, and walked towards her, before new customers coming in the doors behind him would be bottlenecked because he couldn't move his feet.

"Um, yes," he said, clearing his voice. "I'm looking for the safety deposit boxes, please."

"Yes, one second, and I will call someone to come help you. Please have a seat over there," she pointed to several dark leather chairs huddled around a table covered in bank literature and brochures.

"Can I have your name please?" the receptionist asked as he turned towards the chairs.

"Ben, umm, Ben Reeves," he stammered.

She nodded, picking up her telephone, and Ben moved towards the chairs, feeling somewhat out of place.

He sat there, holding the handle to his suitcase, watching the people coming and going. His writer's mind was making up small stories for each person walking into the beautifully appointed bank.

This middle-aged man was depositing money from his secret hitman career. That woman with the fur wrapped around her shoulders was an heiress who was going to go into a back office somewhere in the bank labyrinth to find out how much her just-deceased father had left her. The young woman with the stroller was stashing money in a secret account to one day be able to run away with the older man who was best friends with her father.

Ben couldn't help his imagination, or the scenarios he saw unfolding in his mind's eye. To be honest, he felt, he was living in his own fantasy. Here he was, about to open an unknown safety deposit box that his mother had left him before she died. It's like she knew it was going to happen and set up this elaborate ruse to surprise him at the age of eighteen. For the last several years, he didn't think he had anything from his mother. At times, he was very depressed about it.

But now, with the discovery of her preparations, he was finding that he had some things from her. The house, the letter, and now, whatever was in the safety deposit box. Ben couldn't help letting his mind run wild with what may be in the box. He was imagining stacks of cash, or family heirlooms that would tell him all about his mother's unknown family. As he watched more and more people enter and exit the bank, he couldn't help but feel self-important, like he was his own long-lost heir, about to uncover the secrets of his origins.

He was still deep in thought when a male voice broke through his revelry. He flinched, and looked up to see a handsome, well-dressed man walking towards him, calling his name.

"Right here," Ben answered, standing up.

The well-dressed man approached Ben with his hand held out in front of him. Ben took it, shaking it, and releasing, all without taking his eyes off of the other man's face. The smile there seemed genuine, Ben thought.

"I was told you are looking for the safety deposit boxes?" the man asked. "Would you like to rent one, or look into one already under contract?"

"My mother had one here from almost ten years ago," Ben answered. He fished the silver key out of his pocket and showed the man.

"Ah, yes, good. You have a key. Please, this way," the man replied, the smile still plastered to his handsome face.

The tall man led Ben over to several desks lined up in a row, each one occupied with a bank employee, Ben figured. Many of the desks had people sitting across from the bank employees, discussing different business and personal matters.

The well-dressed man stopped at the chair behind one of the desks about halfway down the line. He motioned to Ben to take the chair opposite him, and promptly sat down. Ben did the same on the other side of the medium-sized desk. He wheeled his suitcase next to him and placed the key on the clean desk.

"Alright then, let's see." The man started clicking keys on the keyboard in front of him. He looked over at the computer screen, waiting for the proper page to load, Ben figured.

76

"You said your mother opened a box with us, what, ten years ago?" the man asked, apparently arriving at the proper page on his computer screen.

"Yes, her name was Lorraine Reeves," Ben answered. "Two e's."

The man reached over and took the silver key from in front of Ben. He held it up to read the numbers printed on the rounded end. Repeating the numbers under his breath, he typed them into a box on the screen.

"Ahh, here we go. Box 1725. Rented in 1990, under the name Lorraine Reeves, with a second member, under the name Benjamin Reeves?" the man asked, probing with his eyes if the boy sitting in front of him was the same Benjamin Reeves.

"Do you mind showing me your ID, so I can make sure you have access to the box?" the man asked.

"Sure," Ben answered.

Ben pulled out his wallet from his back pocket, took out his ID, and handed it over. The man, whose name Ben now read on the plaque sitting on top of the pristine desk was Guy Brown, looked over the ID, matching the information on it with the computer screen.

Ben took out a small, handheld notebook he kept in his other back pocket and jotted the man's name down. Guy Brown. That was a great name, Ben thought. Ben had a habit of stealing interesting names to put in his writing.

Guy Brown handed Ben his ID back, got up from his desk chair, and asked Ben to follow him. Ben asked if he could leave his suitcase at the desk, and Guy Brown agreed that it would be okay where it was.

Guy led Ben back through an opening made up of prison bars, or so Ben thought they looked, and into a room full of silver lock boxes. Ben recognized the room from several movies he had seen and wasn't surprised that the room looked exactly how the movies portrayed it.

Walking over to one box, still holding the silver key he had taken from Ben, he inserted it into a box with the numbers "1725" printed on the front. He reached into the breast pocket of the dress shirt he wore and removed another key, this one gold, and inserted it into the lock opening on the other side of Box 1725.

He turned first the silver key that had belonged to Ben, and then the gold key from his pocket. After turning the second key, he slid it out, and placed it back into his breast pocket.

Using Ben's key as a sort of handle, he swung the front of the box outward, and Ben could see that it was just a door. Inside the door was a metal box, with the handle on the front side. Guy grabbed the handle, and slid out a long, rectangular box. Putting his second hand under the bottom of the long box, he removed it from the slot in the wall, and took it over to the table in the middle of the large room.

Ben walked over to the box sitting on the table and felt apprehension in his chest again. Guy excused himself, closing the door behind him to give Ben some privacy. Ben watched Guy leave the room and close the door, and slowly turned his head back towards the box sitting in the middle of the table in front of him. Ben thought the box sat there like a spider on its nest.

He gulped loudly, at least in his ears, and took the top of the box in hand. He slowly lifted the box lid, not knowing what to expect.

He flinched when he saw the contents, but not from fear, or surprise. Rather, it was out of disbelief.

His mother's voice echoed in his mind from the beyond, and thinking back to the letter he had re-read several times the night before at the hotel, here she was again. Her presence felt palpable in the small room.

Sitting on top of a pile of what looked like business papers was another tri-folded letter in his mother's handwriting. This letter had his name printed on the front in her classic handwriting. He cautiously took ahold of the letter and again felt a knot in his throat as he started reading her beautiful handwriting.

'*My Dearest Benjamin,*' it started. For the second day in a row, Ben felt his emotions almost overwhelm him. He wiped his eyes on his sleeve and continued reading.

"*A couple of months ago, I set up some instructions with a lawyer in the City who I hope you already met. I hope he didn't pass away as well. That would be a tragedy. I pray wholeheartedly that I am standing next to you as you read this, or at the very least, that you have your family around you. But we make these plans just in case, don't we? I just put you to bed. You were so cute today. You fell off of your bike in the street in front of the house and scraped up your knees. You didn't even cry. You were so curious about why the hydrogen peroxide stung you. I have such high hopes for you Benjamin. I know you will do so much more than I ever could imagine. I have felt these last few weeks that I needed to get all of this prepared. It scares me that we are so alone, but the truth is, son, we aren't as alone as you think. This will be hard* to hear, but I have hope that in the next year or two that you get to know everything I'm about to tell you.

"I found out two years ago, when you were about seven that the family I thought I had lost forever was still around. I have only spoken to a few of them the last couple of years, and while they want to know everything about us, I have kept my distance. Maybe it's a mistake. I'm not sure what to do, but I know that I want you to grow up knowing that you aren't as alone as you think. I have been fiercely independent my entire life, and I know now I didn't have to be. But it's too much of a habit for me now. It's very hard to change, baby. For me, especially.

"The man I hope you get to meet very soon, the man that I am setting all this up with is named Samuel E. Lemons. Funny name, right honey? I know you'll laugh when you hear it. Sam Lemons. I only learned a couple of years ago that this man is my biological father. That makes him your grandfather. It was a very strained meeting when he got ahold of me at work in the City. He told me that he wasn't even aware that I had been born. My biological mother had kept me from him, and when she passed away when I was so little, he never knew about me. Somehow he has ways of knowing things, or at least finding out things, and he was able to use his tremendous clout to get the records from the State that proved to him that I was his. I am still unsure of all of the workings of how he found out, but he proved he is my father with a DNA sample. I gave him one from me, and two weeks later, he faxed me the results. 99.99% match. So, I guess we have some family after all, honey.

"I have kept him at arms-length. I didn't tell him anything about us for a very long time. He tried over and over to talk to me, and I just wasn't ready. He has had no other children, and I don't know the details of how he met my mother. I never knew her, really. I have spent a lot of time wondering how things could have been. A long time ago, I gave up wishing. When you were born, I knew I had everything I ever needed. But I know that I am not everything YOU need, though. You need to know you aren't alone. When you are a little older, I will introduce you to Samuel. Until then, please trust my instincts to keep our distance. I have done everything I could for so long by myself. Your father didn't help much, and I didn't need him to.

"If you are reading this and I am gone, I am so sorry for what you've had to go through. It had to have been so hard. I can't imagine, but I hope that the Lemons' are there for you, to take you in, if need be. When I set up all of these instructions with Sam's law firm, he was very firm in telling me that he respected my wishes, but that it was unfair to keep him from his grandson and his daughter. I know I have been unfair, quite selfish in fact, but I can't help it. I don't trust anyone.

"I am including this letter with some legal documents you will need. My birth certificate is here, as well as yours. The DNA paperwork is here, and there are some old stock certificates that may or may not be worth anything, but that I purchased before you were born. I tend to follow my gut in financial matters, and I think I have done pretty well. You may or may not know much about money. I didn't. But I've learned that if you can be frugal, to live without, and watch the pennies, then the dollars will always be there. Try to remember that.

"I love you my darling boy. I hope and pray that this is all bittersweet for you. That you have been aware of all of this for years. That you and the Lemons' are close, and you have many years of beautiful memories. But I have to make these plans for the just-in-case we always talk about. When you're alone in this world, you tend to *be more careful in taking care of your own affairs and make lots and lots of plans. I love you honey. I'm going to put this in the safety deposit box tomorrow on my lunch break. I hope it's yellow and crispy with age when you read it. I'm going to come kiss you one more time on your forehead and whisper how much you have blessed my life. You are my angel.*

Mom"

Ben took a moment to read it twice. He was in a bit of a state of mental shock. He hadn't even remembered what the lawyer's name was. He berated himself in his mind. That situation had been so intense he couldn't even remember hearing the elderly man's name when he had introduced himself the day before.

So, that guy was his grandfather. And the man had known it the whole time they had been together the day before. Ben was madder than anything. Why didn't the older man tell him right then and there? He thought angry thoughts for a few minutes while staring at his mother's neat handwriting on her personal stationary.

As his mood calmed down, after he used the breathing exercises that his long-time therapist taught him many years earlier, he looked back into the safety deposit box. A stack of papers were loosely laying in a pile. He picked up the stack, and placed it all on the table, and started going through it.

On top, laying like a little nothing of a thing, was his mother's birth certificate. He read her name, Lorraine Pearl Beckman. He knew his mother's maiden name but was now aware that her mother had used her own name, and not her biological father's name. He vaguely wondered how his own mother had eventually felt about that.

She had been born in Connecticut. He had had no idea about that. He felt like he was learning who his mother really was all over again. He was having a hard time processing everything he was learning in such a short time.

He was still reeling from the contract negotiations with the publisher two days earlier, let alone everything that was coming to light so quickly. He felt a mix of fear, trepidation, and a weird sense of invincibility and strength.

That last feeling was new to him. He needed to think more about that, he knew.

After his mother's birth certificate, he saw his own. He had never seen this one either. He had his Social Security card, which the boys' home had given to him when he graduated. But this was new information to him.

He saw the hospital he had been born at. Children's Hospital of New York. He had been born at 3:13 a.m. "That must have been inconvenient," he said out loud to no one, feeling amused.

There was his mother's married name, age, and his father's name. All information he was aware of. His doctor's name was listed last. Dr. Robert I. Liner. That was funny, he thought.

He put his birth certificate on top of his mother's, in a separate stack and looked through the rest of the legal paperwork. The deed to the house, in his mother's name, several paper stock certificates from different companies, and other legal papers he would go over later, he mused.

The stock certificates surprised him in their amounts and the companies they were from. Wal-Mart, Sears, Bell Company. Those he was aware of. He didn't know the math but assumed there were several thousands of dollars' worth of stock here. He figured he had enough

84

money in the bank that he would just hang on to all of these. Use them when he needed.

That was it. He was a bit disappointed when he got to the end of the stack. He thought that he was going to learn some deep dark secrets and uncover riches.

As he looked back over his mother's letter, he realized that that is exactly what happened. This was a whole world of information for him. The scope of shock of what he had learned hit him all at once. He really needed some time, he thought.

Gathering up all of the papers, he left the empty box sitting on the table. He walked back out to the bank proper and sat back down across from Guy Brown. Guy looked up from his keyboard and smiled.

"Get everything you needed?" Guy asked.

"I need to set some stuff up, if you can help me?" Ben asked.

"Sure, I can help with just about anything. And if I can't, I can get someone over here who can."

"Can you look up my bank account information for me, and also, cancel the safety deposit box?" Ben answered.

"Sure thing, just give me your ID back, and I'll see what I can do."

Guy took the offered ID again, placed it at the top of his keyboard, and clicked several keys. He looked at the information on the ID a couple of times, and then turned back to Ben.

"Okay, looks like there is a checking account in your name, with an address in Long Island. What do you need me to do?"

"I would like a debit card for the account. Also, can you set up a savings account for me? That's pretty much all I know about banking," Ben said with a small laugh.

"Of course. We can set up a savings account with a minimum deposit of fifty dollars."

"No, I would like to put everything from my checking account except five thousand dollars into the savings account."

Guy Brown looked a bit surprised but was nonplussed. He clicked some more keys, and then opened a drawer on his side of the desk. He took out a colorful brochure and handed it to Ben.

"We have several account choices, as well as Certificate of Deposits, or CDs, and other investment choices you can pick from."

Ben was a little overwhelmed at all the account details and instruments available to him in the brochure. He nervously looked back at Guy.

"I think I just want the savings account for now. The middle choice. The one with no fees."

"No problem. I will just set it up, transfer the funds, and get you an account printout. We will send the packet of information to your home address, so look for that in a couple of weeks."

After all the paperwork was signed, Ben walked out of the bank holding his suitcase, a folder Guy Brown had given to him to hold all of the important paperwork from the safety deposit box, and a whole heap load of new information in his head that he had to process.

He also had a wallet full of cash that he had withdrawn before leaving the bank. As he stood in front of the bank building, people passing on both sides of him, he felt an overwhelming sense of excitement in his chest.

He was bursting.

He flagged down a passing taxi. Giving the driver the destination he had in mind, his excitement grew.

As the taxi weaved through the mid-day traffic and made its way to the train station in Midtown, Ben could only think one thing.

He was going home.

Chapter 12

Gwen was elated. She was finally among equilateral peers. Today was her third full day on the campus of MIT. Her drive across the country was behind her, and except for that encounter at Bishop Castle, the drive was pretty uneventful. The middle of the country had been a lot more boring than she had thought it would be.

Miles and miles of flat, crop-producing land sped by largely unnoticed. The rest of the trip she couldn't get her mind off of the encounter with the heavenly being. It gave her a small comfort that God was real, but deep in her heart, she believed she had somehow dreamt the entire conversation.

Settling into her dormitory, meeting her beautiful roommate, a girl named Jasmine who was from South Africa, and learning that the cafeteria on campus really was horrible, made her heart glad. She loved it here at school,

88

and except for a nagging homesickness, she felt that she really belonged.

She was taking a harder track of classes than most entering freshmen, but she felt drawn to her early theories about the natural world and how to draw clean energy from it. She was onto something big, she felt, if only she could put all the pieces together.

Her purpose, she believed, was in discovering real, clean, and ready energy. Multiple disciplines of science would help her find the key. She just knew it.

So, she was double majoring in advanced theoretical physics and mechanical engineering. She was going to minor in chemistry as well. She knew deep in her heart that humans had to harness the tremendous amount of global energy in a controlled environment to achieve cold fission.

The field of renewable energy was not a new field. But many in the scientific world believed that cold energy production was "junk science." She wanted to prove them all wrong. It frustrated her to no end to see the beginning of the puzzle, but not yet have all of the pieces.

She had, several months earlier, read an amazing report on the element of tritium. She felt that these tri-fused molecules of hydrogen would answer all of her questions. But how to control the reaction, and turn it into needed energy, at a commercially cheap investiture that was the puzzle. Well, she thought, she had four-to-six years at the most scientifically prestigious university on the planet to figure it out.

She was already thinking ahead to see her family at Thanksgiving. She missed her parents tremendously. She spoke to them every day and could hear the concern in their voices as they asked her how safe she was and reprimanding her to stay on campus and not to go exploring the nearby city of Boston.

Her father had become adept at looking up crime data in Boston and relaying the information to his daughter as an excuse to always stay in the dorms and away from trouble. Luckily, they trusted her to make all the correct decisions for her own life and knew that she would always be careful.

Her first day in the labs and scientific classrooms made her feel like she had really come home. Just as in high school, she started out trying not to make waves. She was coming to an understanding that she just "got" everything the professors were teaching, much more so than the other students.

But here, she decided during her first week, she didn't have to hide her genius like she had in high school. Here, her genius was celebrated. Here, in this place, she could truly be herself.

She quickly found a group of like-minded young people that she could study with, and socialize with, and with her roommate Jasmine, a foreigner, notwithstanding; she was going to take over this school.

Early in her first semester, her mind full of theories and deadlines for papers, she was sitting in one of the common areas for students, studying the effects of fission in a controlled environment, when she felt eyes on her.

She looked up, glancing around, and saw a boy a couple of tables over, looking at her through stylish glasses. She quickly noticed his mop of dark brown, unkempt hair, and general good looks. He smiled, and awkwardly waved. She smiled back and looked back down at her book. She tried to pick up where she had left off, but something about the boy made her mind go blank.

A few minutes of trying to get back into her studies, and she felt a presence across the table from her. She looked up and the handsome boy was standing behind the chair across from her.

"Umm, hello. I'm in your Chem 101 class. I'm Avi," he said.

"Hello, I'm Gwen," she answered. She felt butterflies in her chest.

"Do you mind if I sit and study with you? I saw that you had the *Planet Properties* book open, and I could use some help with some of the theories, if you don't mind sharing ideas?" he asked.

"Well..." she started.

"I promise I won't bother you too much. But I've found it's a lot easier to understand these things from different points of view," he interrupted.

She quickly thought of her response. He WAS handsome, she thought. She had not noticed him in the class he had mentioned, but there were more than a hundred students in that class.

"Sure, no problem," she quickly muttered.

"Thanks. I hope we can compare notes, see if either of us are missing anything."

By the time they decided to get up and leave the commons, to go back to their respective dorms, she felt that she had known Avi all of her life. He was incredibly easy to talk to, and she was starting to really enjoy looking into his deep brown eyes. She felt ugly next to him but enjoyed the way his mind worked. He had surprised her with his grasp of the concepts she was learning. He was easily as smart as she was, and she didn't really know how she felt about that.

As they talked most of that evening, and many evenings after, time just seemed to fly by when they were together. She learned that Avi wanted to be a chemist. He felt that that course of work would help him in discovering new cures and medicines for ailments that were common to humans, but as yet had no cure.

She also learned that Avi's favorite grandfather had passed away from cancer two years prior. She was touched that this event in his life made him want to pursue advancing cures for that illness.

She was touched by his level of caring, and his brilliance for his work. She very quickly became smitten with Avi, and she let him kiss her one chilly afternoon as the leaves of the trees around her were changing into bright, beautiful colors, and she could almost feel the energy in the world from the changing of the seasons.

It fleetingly gave her an inspiration towards energy production, which she quickly forgot about as her handsome Avi leaned in for their first kiss.

After that first kiss, and many others, she almost let Avi distract her from her work. But only almost. She was driven to learn as much as she could, and instead of becoming lost in young love, they both pursued their respective courses with vigor and ease. In the interim, however, they spent as much time together as they could, and it was almost inevitable that their relationship would turn physical.

The night before she was to fly home for Thanksgiving, Gwen was over at Avi's dorm room, having had to sneak in, to study, they both had thought. But things quickly got out of hand, and late that night, in the dark and secretive closeness they shared, she had given of herself the only thing she was capable of giving that early in her life.

They both entered that tryst as virgins, and left having deflowered each other. At first, she approached the affair with a clinical, detached mind, but as it went further, she allowed herself to become enveloped in the sensations and rookie mistakes they had both made, which made them laugh rather than turn self-conscious.

Laying in the dark afterwards, Gwen was smiling up at the ceiling, listening to Avi's heavy breathing next to her, and felt an overwhelming connection with the young man. She just hoped that Avi would look at her the next day the way her father often looked at her mother.

But fantasy very rarely becomes reality. As she would learn in the months ahead, you never really knew someone until you really got to know them with time - and gave to them of yourself, everything.

Chapter 13

The taxi Ben had hailed from the train station on Long Island came to a stop in the street in front of his family home. Ben hesitated long enough for the driver to say something to him. It snapped Ben out of his memories long enough to pay the man and retrieve his suitcase from the trunk of the car.

Walking up the long driveway to the cottage-like home, Ben couldn't quite get his bearings. He felt overwhelmed being back at the home he thought he would never see again and excited that it belonged to him now. He feared seeing the ghost of his mother's memory the most. Not an actual ghost, he thought, passingly. Just the overload of memories he knew would flood him the moment he stepped foot into that house. His house, now.

He walked up to the red door. Everywhere he looked held a different memory for him. They were mostly fuzzy, hazy memories, from the point of view of a very small boy. But they were strong. Using the brass key he pulled from his front pocket, he unlocked the front door, and walked into his childhood.

Everything was exactly as he remembered. No one had moved a piece of furniture. The smells were familiar, yet they weren't. Sunlight cascaded into the front room from the large windows in the rear of the house. Ben looked at the sunlight glaring off of the crystalline water he could just make out through the trees behind the home. The trees had grown, he thought.

He stood in the middle of his memories as he looked around at the pictures on the walls, the carpet where he had learned to crawl and then walk, finally running, and he felt his feelings catch in his chest. He could see her everywhere.

He couldn't help it. He broke down. The tears fell like waterfalls, and he just let it happen. Great sobs escaped his lips, and he let the emotions purge. The tremendous loss, the fear and feeling so alone for so long. It all hit him. He dropped to his knees and just allowed the emotions to spill out.

Sometime later, he didn't know when, he dried his face, wiping his eyes on his sleeve. He squared his shoulders and decided to walk through the house. He wanted to see it all. He didn't know where to start, but he felt it would be easiest to start in his room.

Walking into the sparsely decorated room clearly belonging to a young boy made him smile. There was his desk with the coloring that he had not finished. The bed was made, the room clean. The model planes still hung from fishing line from his ceiling. The star chart poster was tacked to the wall behind his twin bed, showing his short phase of dreaming to be an astronomer.

Everywhere his eyes searched, he saw the proof of so many failed attempts to figure out what he wanted to be as an adult.

He remembered when his mother had bought him the Star Wars bed set that still covered his little twin bed. He had loved it so much. At the time, only the original three movies had come out, years before his birth. He fell in love with Princess Leia, just like most boys he knew.

Ben walked over to his small wooden desk. He doubted if his adult-sized legs would fit under the small child's desk now. He noticed that the red paint of the small wooden desk was cracking with age. *Everything gets old.* He smiled at the thought. Reaching down to the piece of construction paper on top of the messy pile of coloring effects, he picked it up. He frowned.

It was a white piece of heavy paper, and in the middle, he had drawn a big red heart with a black arrow haphazardly shot through the middle. He didn't remember ever drawing anything so girly, he thought to himself. Written on one side of the heart in his childish handwriting was his own name. And on the other side of the oversized heart, he had written the name *Gwen.*

He sure didn't remember ever feeling any feelings for a girl in his class with that name. He placed the drawing back on top of the pile without looking at any of the others. Looking around the room, he just felt a simple feeling of ease. He had spent so many hours in this room. It was the home within his home. Good, solid memories, he thought.

He walked over to the closet and opened the simple wooden door. The hinges still squeaked like they had when he was a boy and could never open his closet to get to his toys when he was in trouble without his mother hearing. The sound brought back a flood of further memories.

His size S clothes were still there, on the hangers they had hung from for over eight years. The toy box at the bottom of the closet still held all of his treasured toys from boyhood. The GI Joes, Transformers, Army men. Even his favorite stuffed bear named Chuck. The bear was sitting on top of the other toys.

Ben excitedly reached down, picked up Chuck, and held him to his chest. The bear smelled musty, but Ben thought he smelled a small hint of his mother's perfume. He remembered it suddenly: Jovan Musk. In the orange box with golden writing. He was sure if he walked into his mother's bedroom, a bottle of the perfume would be sitting on top of her dresser where it always sat.

The idea made him put Chuck lovingly back on the bed where he belonged, turn, and walk down the hallway to his mother's door. It was closed, and as Ben reached for the doorknob to enter his mother's sanctuary, he saw a brief wisp of what looked like steam or smoke come from the gap at the bottom of the door. He was suddenly alarmed.

He threw open the door, and a blast of sweet-smelling fog hit him in the face. He ran into the room, sure that something was aflame. What he saw stopped him dead in his tracks. It was not furniture burning, nor the house on fire, like he envisioned. No, it was much more difficult to explain.

Hovering in the exact middle of his mother's large bedroom suite was what he could only describe as a seven-foot-tall angel. The Being had outstretched wings made of pure white feathers, and a billowing robe hung from its tall frame. Ben thought that the robe should be white. In the pictures and movies the robe was always white.

But this being's robe was a pink color, almost a pastel. Ben didn't know what he thought of that, and he didn't know why he was thinking of the color of the robe at the moment. The juxtaposition in his mind vaguely made him feel whimsical. He assumed this being was making him feel the way he was feeling, instead of outright terror.

They stared at each other for several seconds. Ben couldn't move. Deep inside, he knew he wanted to run. He wanted to check himself into the hospital for seeing visions and things that weren't real. And then the Being spoke:

"BENJAMIN MICHAEL REEVES, YOU ARE HERE TO MAKE A CHOICE."

Ben couldn't quite ascertain the Being's gender from the words spoken into his mind. It sounds like a choir of voices speaking in unison. The experience was quite jarring and seemed to knock Ben out of his temporary paralysis. He started to move towards the door, wanting to run as far as he could from the Being floating a foot off the floor in the middle of his mother's master bedroom.

Something stopped him before he got to the door, however. He turned back to the Being and asked,

"What sort of choice?"

"THE ONLY CHOICE THAT MATTERS. THE CHOICE OF LIFE."

"Are you going to kill me?" Ben asked. His fear returned.

"Of course not. I'm merely here to give you The Choice," the Being said inside Ben's mind, much quieter this time.

Right in front of Ben's eyes, the seven-foot-tall being robed in pink, surrounded by billowing mist and fog transformed down into a slightly short, older man dressed impeccably. The man was dark-skinned and looked very familiar to Ben. He was dressed in a very dark, and well-made three-piece suit and held a dark cane in one hand. He had a cream-colored scarf around his neck.

As Ben looked around the room, the mist and fog dissipated, and the room was back to how it had been in his memory, other than the older man standing in the middle, looking peacefully back at Ben with an amused look on his face.

"Well, please forgive me for the shock. It's not every day you walk into your childhood home and see...an angel, I'm assuming?" Ben said.

"Right you are, young Benjamin. Right you are. I am the Archangel Chamuel. Lesser known than the others, I'm aware. Gabriel and Michael, everyone knows. But I'm as old as they are. I was there at the creation of this universe, and this world, and I watched humanity become what it is today. I have always been here, and I have been called many things by humans throughout history."

"What other names have you been called? Because I'm sorry, I've never heard of an Archangel Chamuel." Ben asked. He could see the older man and angel roll his eyes at his question. Ben vaguely wondered if the Being was asked the same thing every time he appeared to others.

"In your current world, some would call me Cupid. But I have had many names, depending on the people's beliefs. In ancient Rome and Greece I was called Aphrodite, or Venus. Other people at the time revered me as Salina, the goddess of dreams and wishes."

The much smaller man went on: "In that great civilization of the Egyptians, they worshiped me as Satis, the Egyptian fertility goddess of wishes. The earliest Grecians called me Airli, the goddess of wishes. The Celtic peoples called me Nemetona, the goddess worshiped in Gaul for a thousand years."

"The Greeks and Romans later called me Morpheus. The Japanese knew me as Musubi-no-kami. In

Arabia, I was called a Djinni. In Ireland I was called a liprichan. Long years later in the Golden Age of Rome, I was one of the Fates, or the Moirae," the Being went on.

"In India and Persia, I was known as Kamadeva. On the other side of the planet, in South America, and to the ancient Aztecs, I was Xochipilli. Back to the Orient, to the Chinese, I was, and still am called Yue-Lao, who binds two people together with an invisible red string. They are actually the closest to the truth of what and who I am, and the job I am often given. Across the world, in other ages, in Slavic mythology, I was called Dzydzilelya, and finally in Norse legends, I was often mistaken for Freya."

Ben just stared at the Being in awe. That was a lot of history, he thought. The Being was standing there, staring at Ben, waiting patiently for him to respond. "That felt a bit rehearsed. Did you rehearse that?" he asked the Being.

The Archangel ignored his question. So, Ben asked him what was really on his mind at that moment. He was surprised he felt so calm, almost detached.

"So, if you're an Archangel, does that mean that Heaven is real? That God really exists?" Ben asked him.

"Why is that everyone's first question? Don't your soul and mind tell you that God exists? Don't you feel, when you're lying in solitude at night that your thoughts drift to prayer? That even the most agnostic and anti-theology-focused people tend to pray to a Creative Being when in dire straits or in need?"

"I guess so," Ben answered.

"Yes, God certainly exists. In many forms, and in many names. And right now, He is focused on you, and your life. So, I am here to give you the Choice."

"Why me? I'm nobody," Ben asked.

"Ahh, now that is a good question. And one I'm allowed to answer, to the best of my ability," The Angel answered.

"Right now, in this era of human history, and the rise and fall of civilizations, your society is on the precipice of change. That change has happened many times. There are names for it: the Industrial Revolution, the Golden Age, and the Iron Age. Many times throughout your history, a Choice was given. And it has always been given to a select few. If you think back in history, there have been catalysts to those changes. And always, the catalysts have been people. Very specific people. I have been there, throughout time, to give those people a Choice. A singular Choice."

"What is the Choice?" Ben asked. He was starting to feel panic in his gut. He didn't like what this being was alluding to.

"The Choice is simply this: Choose life or Choose love."

"What?" Ben asked. "That makes no sense."

"It does if you were aware of what the term 'life' meant," Chamuel answered him.

"Life is simple," Ben said. "It's being alive."

"There you are wrong. You see, you can be 'alive' without 'life.'"

Chamuel went on: "Life, as God, the Creator, considers it, is being enveloped with Love. You see, you have a Choice as a human. Always a choice. You can Choose Life, or you can Choose solitude. Being cut off from the life-force. That life-force, what God Himself is made of, is Love."

"I'm starting to understand the whole Cupid thing," Ben answered.

The Archangel smiled, amused.

"The Choice is simple, Benjamin Reeves. Say the word, make the Choice, and I will assure you a love like no other. Inside that love, you will find yourself, and you will be the catalyst of the coming changes to Humanity. Or Choose solitude. The changes in history tend to have a way of working out anyway, but it's always easier when you make the right Choice."

"How much time do I have to make this Choice?"

"You have the length of twenty heartbeats."

"What! That's not enough time for something so huge!" Ben was getting angry. He was also wondering when his mind would collapse with all of the changes and information, he had absorbed in the past forty-eight hours. And this Angel wasn't making things easier. He vaguely, in the back of his mind, wondered if the Angel had chosen this specific time to assure that Ben would see that this kind of choice would make accepting all of the other information easier to handle.

"If I gave you time to ponder all of the implications, then the end result would be skewed. These Choices must be made instantaneously, as the core of who you are that already knows the answer would be overruled with your intellect. It's you who must listen to that core. It's the final Gift that God has given you."

"When does the time start?" Ben asked.

"It already has," the angel responded, sounding much calmer than Ben felt.

"This isn't at all fair." Ben almost screamed in frustration.

"There will not be some sudden flash of light, and magically everything in your life changes, Benjamin Reeves. The changes are gradual, they take time, as all such things should. Don't be troubled that you are Choosing drastic changes for today. You must be made ready to

102

receive the blessings, and the consequences, of your Choice."

"Then I choose to be alone. You, or God, or anything else will NOT control my life. I choose to control my own destiny. My own life. I choose ME," Ben screamed in frustration.

Thoughts and feeling swirled all around in Ben's mind. He was confused, angry, horrified at the possible blunder he had just made. But he also felt an overwhelming sense of fortitude. Of being right about his choice. He felt justifiably correct.

The air in the room seemed to grow heavy. Shadows lengthened. Ben felt like he was in the middle of a movie, and the climax was approaching. Everything that was so still a minute earlier vibrated with potential energy. He almost left his hair standing on end. The room seemed to shake with static energy.

The Archangel standing before Ben as an older, very well-dressed, dark-skinned man suddenly grew in size. The pink robe, and the billowing fog once again rolled around him. An instant later, the Archangel hovered before Ben, about a foot off of the floor of his mother's bedroom. The voice boomed loudly in Ben's mind, making him bend over in mental anguish.

"YOUR CHOICE HAS BEEN MADE AND CANNOT BE UNMADE. AS A FREE-WILL CREATURE, IT IS YOUR PREROGATIVE TO CHOOSE YOUR OWN DESTINY. THIS IS BUT THE FIRST GIFT FROM GOD. BUT, ONCE MADE, THE CHOICE CANNOT BE TAKEN BACK. WE MUST ALL LIVE WITH THE REWARDS, OR CONSEQUENCES, OF ALL OF OUR CHOICES."

Ben looked up at the sudden quiet. His mother's bedroom was as it should be. There was no trace that the meeting with the Archangel Chamuel ever happened. Ben looked around him in a panic. Sweat broke out all over his body. His muscles tensed up. There was a buzzing in his ears.

And suddenly, everything was back the way it should have been. He actually looked down at his outstretched hands, making sure he was still alive. He felt lightheaded. He felt tired. He lurched over to his mother's nicely made bed, and fell onto it, not realizing what was happening around him. Just that he needed sleep. He was unconscious before he closed his eyes.

Unknown to him at that moment, two heavenly entities were looking out from the Spiritual Plane, which the material could not see, and both entities were resigned to wait. That was the easy part of being a Celestial Being. Waiting was almost second nature. The shorter of the two Entities looked down on the two souls who had Chosen incorrectly. He smiled. He knew that the strongest-willed humans made the best choices. For they could not see how History would be shaped by their free-will, no matter the choice.

Looking up at the other Entity standing next to him, the shorter one robed in pink chuckled. In a calm, reassuring voice he spoke.

"We chose correctly."

The taller being merely nodded.

Chapter 14

"Mom, seriously, I can do my own make-up," Gwen said with exasperation.

"Shush, honey. This is your big day. You want to look your best."

Gwen looked at the reflection of her mother in the mirror before her. Gwen wore her favorite dark green dress. The dress made her rust-colored hair shine and caused her eyes to glow. Her mother stood next to her, applying foundation to cover the freckles over her nose. The freckles she used to hate as a child.

Gwen continued to look at the reflections in the mirror. She could just make out her father sitting in the reading chair in the corner, already dressed in his best suit. Her father looked much older since she left home six years earlier. She could just make out her brother, Daniel

McCarthy Murphy II, in the kitchen, laughing about something with his girlfriend.

What was her name again? Gwen thought. She could never keep up with her baby brother's many girlfriends. Mona. That was it.

Gwen's thoughts went to the speech she was about to present to the graduating class later today. She was nervous thinking about it. She had already given the valedictorian address eighteen months earlier when she had graduated at the top of her undergraduate class.

That day, her parents were in attendance as well, and she felt even more apprehension than she did today. She barely had made it through that speech. Quoting several pioneers in science and engineering was simple. Interjecting her own thoughts and motivational language into it was a little harder.

She had made it through that speech, and she was determined to make it through this one.

"Stop squinting your eyes, Gwen. For God's sakes honey, don't make your face look any older than you need to. That's how you get wrinkles," Gwen's mother admonished.

"Mom, I'm twenty-four years old and have had exactly one boyfriend my entire life. Who cares how old I look?" She usually didn't give her mother sass, but she was on edge.

Her mother could tell. She stood behind Gwen, looking at her face in the mirror's reflection.

"You know how so very proud of you we are, don't you honey?"

"I know, Mom, and I'm so grateful for you guys. I don't know what I would do without you."

"Oh darling, it's your dad and I who are grateful for you. What else would we have to brag about to the other people at church? God knows, your brother gives us more heartache than hope." She chuckled.

Gwen knew very well how proud of both of their children they were. Her brother was a star athlete at Stanford. He exceled in just about any physical activity he tried. She would laugh at her girlfriends who would come to her apartment on Saturday mornings during college football season just to watch her baby brother play quarterback and drool over him anytime they showed his picture on ESPN.

Gwen was so incredibly happy, but still felt her nerves. Addressing the students and faculty of the Massachusetts Institute of Technology, where she was accepting her PhD in theoretical physics, was a daunting task. She had to be brilliant. Her reputation would not allow otherwise.

When she had received her double bachelor's degrees eighteen months earlier, it had not been so nerve wracking. There was a valedictorian every year. Back then, she had not been such a big deal. But the last eighteen months, she broke every expectation placed upon her. She loosened the strings, so to say, and let her brilliant mind shine. In doing so, she rushed through the PhD program with ease, and even led the charge on the emerging Hydrogen Energy Program she had helped put together. Still a long way away from proving anything concrete, she knew she was on to something.

She was itching to get back into a lab to start working again. She just had not chosen an offered position at many well-funded labs around the world.

CERN was calling her the most often; soon, the Large Hadron Collider would be completed in Switzerland.

She was very excited to see if they could prove the existence of the Higgs boson. It had been the "holy grail" of physics for so long. The media had dubbed it the "God particle." She chuckled at the thought.

She had not accepted a prestigious place at CERN for one simple reason: she felt, deep in her heart, that collision was not the answer. It was too barbaric. Her theories on Super Compression were much more, elegant, she felt.

Her father brought her back out of her thoughts.

"We have to leave in fifteen minutes if we're going to beat this traffic," he shouted to the whole apartment. Typical Dad. Always on a schedule, Gwen thought. But it made her and her mother both chuckle.

Gwen caught her parents' eyes meeting in the mirror. Her father winked at her mother and went back to his paper. Gwen sighed loudly. Avi had never looked at her that way.

She was NOT going to think of that shitbag today! Her mother caught her thoughts.

"It's okay, honey. There is someone for everyone. Your 'someone' is out there right now, sighing loudly like that right this minute," her mother said with a smile.

"I'm too busy for a 'someone,' Mom. I have too much work to do."

Not going to take the bait for another argument over the subject, her mother finished applying the lipstick to Gwen's lips, stood back, gave a satisfied smile, and said,

"Gwen, you are so beautiful. I wish you looked like me, but you're the spitting image of your grandmother on your father's side. Not that she ever liked me much."

Gwen smiled back at her mother. At the age of twenty-four, she now knew she was beautiful. She had finally grown into her tall, lanky body. And while she didn't inherit *all* of her mother's attributes, she held her own, she thought.

Standing up, she admired the way the emerald green dress looked on her frame. She nodded in appreciation, and walked over to the bed, where her cap, gown, and stole lay in a plastic dry-cleaner's bag. Her father stood up, met her at the bed, and helped her get into the gown. As he wrapped her multi-colored stole backwards around her neck, he grabbed her by the shoulders and gently spun her around to face him.

She looked up into her father's not-as-smooth face, with his patches of gray hair above both ears, turning his bright red hair a garbled color there. He smiled.

"We really are so proud of you, honey bear. I have no idea where you got your amazing mind. And you work harder than anyone I know. Take a little break today. Enjoy the moment. You earned this." He gave her a wink. She smiled back, but still looked apprehensive.

"You okay, champ?" he asked her.

Tears threatened to spill. But Gwen squared her shoulders, as was her way, and smiled back.

"I'm okay, Dad. Thank you for everything. I love you."

Her father wrapped his big, meaty arms around her.

"Don't smudge her, you big oaf!" her mother admonished, walking towards them from where she had been adjusting her hair in the mirror.

"Danny, time to go!" she shouted into the kitchen.

"Okay, okay. Sheesh. Didn't we just go to one of these?" her brother yelled back. He would be graduating from Stanford with a bachelor's in Communications the following month.

Gwen was looking forward to flying to California for his ceremony. He was receiving several awards, and the NFL draft was coming up. She knew her big, little brother was as nervous of that as she was of this speech.

109

The speech, she thought. She ran back to her low dresser and found the notecards in a neat pile where she had left them. She did not want to go without her notes.

The black SUV her father had rented, along with a driver, was idling on the street curb. They all piled into the large vehicle, and her father got into the passenger seat, next to the driver, who was wearing a black suit, matching her father's.

They pulled out into traffic and Gwen went over her notes a third and fourth time. Her brother saw what she was doing.

"Hey Gwenny, do you remember that time you drove me to the movies with my friend Austin, and when we got to the mall, you almost ran your car into that rent-a-cop's car? Do you remember what you told him when he came out of his little white car to yell at us?"

"I told him he was in my way and didn't belong there, or something like that, right?" Gwen answered.

"Yeah, but it was a little more vulgar than that. I think it was the first time I ever heard you call someone a 'shit sandwich.' But he DID pull right out in front of you." Her baby brother grinned.

Gwen smiled back, glad that her brother was there. She was so glad they were all there. She had missed them terribly, especially this last holiday season when she couldn't make it home as usual. She had been finishing up her classes, teaching two undergrad classes, and finishing up her dissertation. It had been a very hectic holiday for her. She didn't even realize it had been Christmas day as she walked up to the Sciences Building, and the doors had been locked. A bored looking security guard asked her what she was doing on campus at Christmas.

The memories calmed Gwen down. But only a little. She took a deep breath. And then another. By the time the driver pulled up to the curb in front of Killian Court, where so many people were milling around, Gwen felt calmer.

She steeled herself, and got out of the SUV, holding her father's outstretched hand. He handed her off to her brother as he then turned to help her mother out of the car.

She put her arm through her brother's offered arm on one side, as - *what's her name?* Gwen thought, *oh yeah* - Mona put her arm through her brother's other offered arm.

As a group they walked up the long steps to the large, sandstone building that was called Building 10, or the Great Dome. At the top, Gwen gave everyone a last kiss, and they all wished her well. She waved to them as they walked to the makeshift stage set up as a way to look out over the Court and see all of the matching seats set out in hundreds of rows on the lawns.

She turned and followed the little printed white signs placed into the grass to guide speakers and honorable guests around the stage and over to the rows of comfortable seats in the back of the Great Dome's open courtyard. She entered from the side entrance, and saw so many robed dignitaries, waiting to find their seats while the families and friends found seats out in the sunny Killian Court.

For a few minutes, she was enjoying the lost feeling of being just one of many. Until the Dean of Students saw her bright red hair and yelled for her over the crowd.

She walked over to the older man. He, too, was bedecked in a robe, stole, and cap. His looked much older, and much more used than hers. He smiled at her, asked if she was ready. When she nodded, he directed her to stand at the side of the staging area leading into the interior of the large building, where she would be leading in her graduating class, as was custom. They had all been here

111

last night, rehearsing how they were to enter and exit. She felt ready.

She looked once more at the simple white notecards in her hand. She took a deep breath as all of the other graduates lined up behind her, many of whom were subdued, though a few were making jokes and cracking up. Overall, it was a mixture of excitement and apprehension, and Gwen felt it all.

She smiled at a few faces she recognized, but the majority she had never seen before. She knew she should be relishing these moments. It wasn't every day you graduated with highest honors and were let loose into the world.

The ceremony went very quickly. The keynote speaker was the current Vice President of the United States, Dick Cheney. Gwen didn't particularly agree with this man's politics, but the speech was more motivational than political.

And then her name was called to give the final address before all the graduates would walk across the stage, one at a time. She calmly walked up to the large podium at the left side of the large stage. She looked first at the faculty and school administration sitting on the stage, all looking back calmly at her.

She looked over her fellow graduates, and finally, out at the section of the crowd where she knew her family was sitting. She thought she could make out her mother's white dress. It gave her a sense of peace. She lowered the microphone and began to speak in as strong and clear of a voice as she could.

"Ladies and gentlemen of the staff and faculty, fellow graduates and students, and family and friends. I would like to start by saying thank you all for your continued support, help, and dedication. That alone would be enough to get most of us graduates here today. To my

112

fellow graduates, I would like to urge you, that when all of this is over, that you go back with gratitude and thanksgiving and show your appreciation to those you got you where you are today. As you know, none of us could do this alone." She paused for effect.

"Today, I would like to take this short time I'm given to share with you all, especially the graduates, some truths that I have come to learn lately. I am still very young. I am just starting out in this thing we call life. I, in no way, know everything. But I do know enough, on this day, to share with you a bit of motivation. The motivation that has helped me get to this stage, here, today." She paused, looked back over the graduates, and could feel the pressure of the silence around her, and all of the eyes on her at that moment.

"On this day, as our education comes to an end, and this phase of our lives ends, we need to remember the single fact that this is not the end. It's merely the beginning. This was but taking a step. I believe in my heart that this is a singularly important step. But that's all it is. Merely a step. And it's not even the most important step. Again, merely one of many." She paused again.

"I watched a speech given many years ago that I didn't agree with at the time. The very successful man in the video was telling a group of students not unlike ourselves what the most important thing in the world was. What the man said shocked me. I completely disagreed at the time. But I have come to learn the truth of what that man said."

She paused again, for dramatic effect this time. Looking down at her notecards, she smiled at her handwriting that instructed her to pause for effect.

"That man said to that group of students, at their school, no less, that the most important thing we had heard all of our lives was a lie. He pointed to the students and told

113

them that they had been told, over and over, that education was their most important resource; that it was the singular most important thing that would help them succeed. And he went on to tell them that that fact was a lie. He told those students, sitting AT their school campus, that the most important thing in life was NOT their education. The most important thing, was their dreams."

She took another deep breath. "At the time, I scoffed at the man. Of course our education was what was most important. But after spending almost six years here receiving the very best education in the world, I can tell you now, that I completely agree with that man. Education is merely the possession of facts and figures. It has neither a quantifiable value, nor gives us an intrinsic direction to our lives. It's necessary to getting certain jobs, sure. But education in itself is not a verifiable quantity. It serves no purpose, until the time that it is used to fulfill a dream. In this equation, the dream itself is the most valuable commodity. The dream is the most common denominator. I know many of the faculty here cringe to hear me say this. But it is very true. Many uneducated people have changed the world. And many very educated people cannot find a decent, minimum-wage job. The former changed the world through the realization of their dreams, the latter failed to find one of their own."

She went on, her voice sounding stronger in her ears.

"Albert Einstein, who I have spent years studying, said something that I can't seem to get out of my mind. He said, 'Imagination is everything. It is the preview to life's coming attractions.' And he was so correct in that quote. Education without dreams, without imagination, has no value. You would have basically wasted your time. We are given an education to make our dreams come true.

114

Education is merely a tool. But you must first have a dream."

"The young children who dream of being an astronaut becomes an astronaut. You don't just one day fall into it by accident. The scientist who creates a miracle cure doesn't just stumble on it while mowing the lawn. He first dreamed of the possibility. A man whose destiny is to lead a nation doesn't start out following the crowd. He dreamed first, and made it come to pass. These people had a dream, and using whatever tools they needed, made those dreams come true. You yourselves have seen this time after time."

She paused again.

"That same man who told this group of students this massive, and life-changing bit of information went on to tell them that they should not pursue money or fame. But following your dreams, those simple things are a natural byproduct. The Universal Law of success is clear. Follow your passion. Find your calling. Live your dreams. All those other things we think we want, just tend to happen along the way."

"If I can leave you with anything here today," Gwen said with a loud, clear voice. "Let it be this. As you embark onto this world to make your mark, to set your name *amongst* the Greats, always keep your dreams out in front of you. Like a carrot on a stick, leading you forward. It will take a huge amount of courage. Courage may be all you have to fall back on when it gets hard. When you want to give up. It may be all you have from moment to moment. The truth is-many will scoff at you. Many people who you trust, and love, will try to talk you out of it."

"Persevere! Every great moment in Human History was predicated by a dream. And those dreamers overcame their peers trying to talk them out of it."

Her voice got a little more subdued.

115

"Because once your dreams become reality, those same people will tell you that they knew you could do it the entire time. And finally, realizing your dreams creates more dreams to the ones who come after us. Dreams build on dreams. Goals on to goals."

She was almost shouting as she said the final lines of her speech. The crowd was leaning forward, waiting for her final statement. So, she gave it with everything she had.

"Stand strong against the current and realize your dreams. You have all of the tools you need within you. Now, go make your dreams come true!"

"Thank you."

She walked off stage to loud, booming applause, and so many voices yelling out. She could feel the tears welling in her eyes. She was just happy she made it through the speech without tripping or allowing her emotions to override her voice.

She walked back to the seats and took hers. The other graduates around her clapped her on the shoulders and shook her hands. She looked up with fierce pride, ready to take on the world.

Even before they called her name to receive her degree, she had made up her mind about where she would go to work. She knew it would shock the world. She just had to follow her own advice.

Because at that moment, she finally figured out her very own dream.

Chapter 15

Ben took a deep breath of the fresh, late spring air. He looked around at the students milling past him on the Commons. The tall sycamore trees were in full bloom. The air smelled sweet. Ben was in love.

And as such, whenever he thought back to the weird, strange, and wonderful encounter in his mother's room, five years previously, he figured he had just dreamed the entire thing. He had not chosen love. But here he was, in love like no other. He happily looked around at his school, his home away from home, and where he had met the love of his life.

This was going to be his final month at school. Five years before, as he had gotten his new home settled to his liking and did the many adult things like buying his first car and paying taxes for the first time, he really didn't know what he wanted to do with himself. He was under contract to produce a new, publishable book annually for four years. That was easy for him. What would he do with the rest of his time?

So, sitting at his mother's old army issue pea-green metal desk in the dining room, he made some gut decisions. Writing was easy for him, but he was not yet a master of his craft. The best thing to do, he thought, would be to get a higher education.

So, knowing that Hofstra University was only a few miles away, he applied for the spring semester of the following year, and was accepted into the English-Creative Writing joint degree plan for both a BA and MFA in five years.

Five years later, and after so many wonderful experiences, he stood on the campus where he had become a bit of a celebrity and breathed the air in his final month.

Students walking to and from classes waved to him, and he waved back. Most of them knew him as the New York Times bestselling author of four straight number one books. But a lot of them revered him more as the editor-in-chief of *The Font*, the student-published literary magazine where the best and brightest creative writers wrote poems and stanzas, shorts, and other forms of prose depicting love, loss, student life, and a lot of humor.

He had been the main contributor, as well as the acting Editor for four of his five years at school. He had loved every minute of it.

His first short story, four years earlier, had made him an instant celebrity on campus. It was still upheld as the best piece the small magazine had ever published. And, more importantly, it had caught the attention of a copywriter and contributor a year ahead of him.

Her beautiful name was Neeley Eckhardt, and she was easily much smarter than he was. Over a single cup of coffee, to discuss his next project due several months later for the Big Publishing House in New York, he had fallen completely in love with her.

She was small. Petite, with blonde bouncing ringlets, and two trademark telltale attributes everyone knew her by.

Her perpetual smile, and a penchant for monochromatic clothing.

She only wore black and white, "on principal," she had told him one night laying together in his new bed, sweaty, looking at the fan turning overhead in his mother's old master bedroom.

He never knew that he could feel so at home with another human being. She challenged him. Made him want to be a better man. Made him feel complete. He looked over at her, and marveled that such a beautiful woman would want to be with him. He knew he had better not mess this up.

She also came from a well-to-do family. Her father was a much-respected lawyer in the City, and the first time that Ben had met the family, her father had gone on and on about Ben's grandfather, Samuel Lemons, and how the venerable older man had single-handedly changed the face of tort reform and business law in New York.

It had been difficult to explain to Neeley's father that he didn't have anything to do with his maternal grandfather and hadn't planned on changing that fact any time soon. Her father had knowingly smiled, and just shook his head. "Didn't know what he was wasting," he had said under his breath.

But over the next couple of years, as his books took off, and his name became known in greater and greater circles, Ben grew up a little. He swallowed his anger and pride and had marched resolutely up to his grandfather's office on the day after his second full-length novel had reached the coveted number one spot, and a lengthy editorial had been done on him, with his picture pasted on the front page of the New Yorker.

Samuel Lemons had been joyed to see him, of course, but the conversation had stalled, and the uncomfortableness between the two men was palatable.

The next three or four meetings had gone much better. His grandfather, and his wife, Betsey, whom Ben had met when he was invited to their estate in the Hamptons, became a foundation for Ben that he hadn't known he needed.

With Neeley, and her family, and now his long-lost family from his mother's side, he felt content. He felt at ease. Even his writing had lost its anger-driven edge and settled into what critics called "old Americana mixed with a new generation's view of the world."

He was busy, happy, and didn't think he needed anything else. But at night, sleeping next to Neeley, or alone while she was off on one trip of another, he still felt a small pinprick of unease. Like things weren't as good as he thought they were.

He chalked it up to never having had such a foundation before. He hadn't had the family he had always wanted while growing up, and now he felt a mixture of mistrusting it, and not believing he even deserved it. He was encouraged to see a therapist by his step-grandmother. He tended to listen to the women in his life more than the men. He thought that was a remnant from having been raised by a single mother.

The therapist was helping.

He visited his mother's grave every week. She had been buried in a beautiful cemetery near their family home. The beautiful headstone with her name and dates on it was made from veined white marble. A verse from the bible was inscribed on it. From Psalms 23: "The Lord is my Shepard. I shall not want."

120

Having had no other family, his grandfather Samuel had seen to all the arrangements. He had signed a power of attorney with his newly found daughter, soon after she had set up all the instructions that she had left for Ben.

Ben was glad that her father had been there at the end, to give her a little ease of mind in case anything had happened. The only problem, Ben had found out later, was that Sam had not been able to stop the state from contacting his biological father and granting him guardianship over Ben, and subsequently putting him into the boys' home down in Texas.

Apparently, Samuel had tried, unsuccessfully, for the better part of a year or more to change the court's mind concerning his only grandson. Samuel had to just make do with the quarterly reports of Ben's activities that his biological father supplied, begrudgingly, as it turned out.

Ben often wondered what his life would have been like if Samuel and Betsey had raised him in the high-class lifestyle, they were accustomed to.

All that was in the past now, Ben thought, as he walked towards the Social Sciences building. He would catch up with Neeley after classes that evening for their weekly date night. After having dated for four years, there was a lot of pressure for him to propose marriage.

Her father, and his grandfather somehow mentioned it every time he was in either's presence. He wanted to do it right. He still had the ring his father had given his mother so many years prior. Ben just wanted it all to be perfect. Neeley deserved perfection.

He was also halfway finished with his fifth novel. It had been taking up a lot of his time lately, and he wanted to finish it before he proposed, so that it wouldn't take his mind off of his fiancée.

He had signed a contract with a new publisher, for sums that blew his mind. His first four books had each done better than the previous. Book number four, which he had titled *To Sow a Seed*, had reached the number one spot before it was even released. A movie was being made of it. Directed and starred by George Clooney, no less. His life could have been a whirlwind, but he kept things simple. He had to. For his own sake, and for the sake of those that he loved. Especially Neeley.

He was considered a very hermitic author. He didn't like the limelight, and only went to a handful of signings and interviews. Most of his readers didn't even know what he did day to day, unlike most other well-known authors. He just didn't need all of the attention. He let his writing do the talking for him. He always put his full heart and soul into his writing, and it showed to his millions of fans. He wrote only the truth as he saw it, and the mixture of cultures and viewpoints he was exposed to as a young child gave his writing the perfect classic Americana heart, with the new generation's fresh view of the changing world.

It had made his fan base a varied, multi-cultural and multi-generational mix. He had unknowingly become loved across many types, cultures, and ages, of people all across the world. *If anything,* he had thought on more than one occasion, *that tone of writing sure sold a lot of books.*

His cell phone buzzed in his front pocket as he walked towards the freshman class that he was student teaching. He glanced down at the screen and saw that his best friend, Markson Gray, who everyone called Mars, was texting him.

"Meet me at the Coffee Grounds after your class. I have the answer to your question from last night," the text said.

Ben grew excited. His most recent book was his most challenging, as it was based around an idea he had had one late night while he was taking a walk and trying to figure out where the book should go. It was to be a very scientifically based book, which he was not comfortable with at all, but which his best friend Mars was well versed. Mars was a doctoral candidate in Environmental Sciences.

Ben texted back, "Will be there at 1:30. Better be good!"

His freshman English class went by quickly, and he had only had to answer two questions about being a rich author. His students, most of whom knew him as only a lowly TA, and the others that he interacted with day to day were used to who he was and what he did. On the campus of Hofstra, at least, he didn't make waves like he did anywhere else.

After class, and while driving to his favorite coffee shop, where he did a lot of his writing, his excitement grew. He had asked Mars to do some research for him, concerning an idea that he had had. He wanted to write a fictional account of something that was somewhat feasible. He wasn't necessarily a sci-fi writer, but the book he was currently working on seemed like it.

He didn't understand the science, but he couldn't shake the idea of a cleaner Earth, and how to get there. He knew that the environment had been a huge deal in the media lately, with fossil fuels being scarce, and the global warming epidemic showing up nightly on the news.

He wanted to write a book with a lot of hope for a better future in it, and he knew that in order to do that, he had to fictionalize a human advancement that would change the world. It was that exact question he had posed to his best friend the night before.

The book was loosely titled *Eve's Plight*, and he wanted to do it right.

Walking into the warm, slightly busy coffee shop, with its familiar smell of smoked coffee beans, and sweet pastries made daily, Ben smiled at his friend, sitting at their regular table in the corner. Mars was a giant of a man, with a very gentle heart. He was an Irish ginger, with long, flaming red hair, and a huge red beard. But he was a gentle giant.

Ben had met him in freshman Science, and they had been best friends ever since. It also happened that Mars was a genius concerning comic books, sci-fi literature, and most other nerdy pursuits. They had argued many evenings over beers or coffee about everything from the impact of Isaac Asimov on current technology, to who would win in a fight between Deadpool and Wolverine. Ben loved the giant, redheaded genius like a brother.

"Okay, seriously, I'm not sure if this will work or not, but you'll have to do the research. I can only point you in the right direction," Mars was saying as Ben sat down.

"Hold on, hold on, start at the beginning," Ben answered, putting his bag on the chair next to him.

"Okay, you know how you asked me last night what new technology would change the world for the better in the next decade or two?" Mars asked.

"Yeah, I want to basically have my character discover some advancement that will usher in a, call it a 'global renewal,' so that humanity has a chance of changing, adapting, and basically surviving."

"Well, I think this scientist down in Maryland may have the answer. And she's really hot," Mars said.

"Okay, who is she, what is she doing, and how will it help us?" Ben asked. A waitress came and put his favorite latte in front of him. Ben smiled up at her and received a smile in return.

Getting back to Mars, he thought over his last four books, and how he had a list of names and numbers for

124

people in all pursuits of education and experiences. He was very prudent in his fact-checking, and he always gave credit to those who answered his many incessant questions when he had a bone in his jaw that he couldn't quite figure out from his own research.

"Her name is Doctor Gwen Murphy. She's a theoretical physicist. Bunch of degrees from MIT and the like. Been impressing everyone from day one. Apparently, she's a huge genius and has some theories that even caught Stephen Hawkins's attention. She is working for a government think-tank in Maryland. They are trying to figure out an energy source that is supposed to change the world."

"Energy source, how? Like wind power, or solar, something like that?" Ben asked, intrigued.

"No, this is real science-fiction stuff. Quantum physics and particle theory." Mars was starting to get excited.

"You know that big Super Collider over there in Europe that started up last year? Well, these scientists in Maryland are, like, their opposites. The Europeans think that some kind of answer will come from 'colliding' these particles. The people working for the government, like this Gwen lady, they think that the answers will come from 'Super Compression,' or something like that. I don't really understand the mechanics. I'm an Environmentalist," Mars said with exasperation.

Ben just nodded. This could be it. He was thinking quickly. He was itching to do some internet searching. He drank his coffee quickly, thanked his best friend, made a promise to meet up that weekend to watch the first baseball game of the regular season, and hurried home. This was supposed to be a big year for the Yankees, but he couldn't get his mind off of the technology for clean energy for his book, and how it could fit into the narrative.

Throwing down his bag on the couch, he hurried into his new office. He had twice now added on to the small two-bedroom home his mother had purchased years before. He had extended the home to make it four bedrooms, and added a beautiful office off of the back, with large windows to take in the beautiful, sparkling water at the end of the property.

He had eventually purchased the two lots on either side of his own, making one big lot several acres wide and long. All if it backed to his private beach.

He still remembered walking on that beach with his mother before she had died suddenly, spiraling his life into directions he still couldn't comprehend.

He jumped onto his computer and started doing the searching he had been dying to do since hearing about the scientist in Maryland.

It didn't take long to find the physicist his best friend had told him about. When he saw her picture on the government website, his breath caught. He felt like he knew her. She was stunning. Bright red hair framed a heart-shaped face. She was wearing dark-framed glasses in her photo, but he could clearly see the intelligence in her green eyes.

He studied her picture for longer than he should have. He then read the abstracts of the scientific papers she had authored and that had been published in several highly touted journals. He did some further internet searches for her and found many confounding and conflicting pieces from much more experienced scientists. Apparently she had been making waves in the world of "particle science."

He had to look up what that was.

The more he read, and the more time went on, he was starting to like this scientist. She bucked the system, and she was as young as he was. Their careers paralleled in a lot of ways. He was intrigued by her.

As the sun fell in the sky outside, he didn't hear his cell phone ringing. He was finally brought out of his research and the continuing outlines he was drafting for his novel when he heard a banging on the front door. The sound pulled him out of the research he was doing in clean energy.

He glanced at the clock. It was well into the night. He suddenly remembered he was supposed to have met Neeley for dinner. He felt like a shmuck but knew that she would understand. When he was researching for a book, she knew that he got sidetracked a lot. It had happened before, and he felt like it would probably happen again.

Luckily, Neeley completely had understood before. His mind went to how lucky he was to have fallen in love with such an understanding woman. He figured she was at the door. But she had a key. He absently thought she must have lost it as he walked towards the front room.

The house was dark. He hadn't even turned on lights when he came home, hours earlier.

He was reaching for his phone, still in his bag on the couch in the front room, when the banging sounded on the front door again.

He quickly turned on the lights in the room and hurried over to the door. He opened it to a uniformed police officer. He had not noticed the revolving red and blue lights from the patrol car parked behind his Jeep in the long driveway.

Seeing the patrolman, his heart sunk into his stomach. He knew before the man said a word. All those old feeling from his adolescence came flooding back, all at once, overbearingly. He felt like someone had dumped a bucket of ice water over his head, and he could feel the pinpricks of shock starting at the top of his head and ending at his feet.

"No..." Ben whispered.

Chapter 16

It was storming outside. Hard. Heavy wind was trashing the trees back and forth outside the large office windows. Gwen stood at one, looking in consternation at the dark-gray sky, and it seemed so close she felt she could touch it. Lightning lit up the afternoon gloom, and for a second, Gwen felt like all the answers she had been searching for were at hand. *If only she could harness it*, she thought.

Rain beat against the thick windows and glancing down at the lawns and driveways around the tall building she was in, she could see people hurrying to their cars or offices, bent against the wind, umbrellas with their own minds.

"How could this happen, Gwen? Nothing has been published." Her boss, Stewart Haggerty was talking behind her, but she just heard his voice as a buzzing in her subconscious.

She looked back at the desk on the other side of the room. The book was sitting peacefully on top of the glass, looking for all the world as just another innocent piece of fiction, but it held secrets that she was just starting to comprehend. How did the guy come up with the answers? Answers she only had discovered herself very recently.

She kept asking herself the same questions, like a loop in her mind that she couldn't quiet.

"I don't know, Stewart, but I plan to find out. Does the author have any education in physics? Where did he come up with the answer? Is there a rat in the lab? And why in a fictional story? This would make any person incredibly rich." The questions just poured out of her.

"Easy, Gwen. You know it's not the ENTIRE answer. He just got a lot of the pieces right. But you're correct. Someone needs to talk to this guy."

"I'll do it. I read he lives in New York. I'll go there and ask him myself," Gwen said in exasperation.

"Alright. You are the closest to this. See if he will sign an NDA. Get him on contract. Hell, offer the guy a damn job, I don't know," Stewart said.

Gwen looked over at her boss. He was taking this harder than she was. She looked down at the white coat she wore. How proud she had been when she came to work here right out of college. And now, as they were so very close to the answers she had been seeking since she had even heard of clean energy, here came a fictional writer, no less, with all the answers, laid out in black and white, in a damn love story! She was beyond frustrated.

"Benjamin Reeves. He is a pretty big deal, isn't he?" Gwen asked.

"I don't read his stuff, but I Googled him this morning. Five or six straight big hit books. Two made into movies. Educated at Hofstra. Nothing to set him apart, except his ability to write bestsellers. But this is his first book that has anything to do with science. I have no idea where he got the research, or the answers he outlines in the story. But damn, is he close!"

"I'll go up there. Talk to him. See what I can find out. And if he has talked to anyone here, I say we press charges!" Gwen was enraged.

"Take the trip. I read that this guy is a shut-in. I could only find two interviews on YouTube. He's young as well. About your age. It's weird that a guy with this guy's track record wouldn't be out in the spotlight more. The last article I read on google was that his fiancée or something had died tragically about a year ago. He finished the book right after." Stewart sighed loudly and went on.

"I don't even know if you can find him, but knowing you, you'll be eating breakfast with this guy by tomorrow." Gwen looked over at Stewart, knowing he was trying to be funny, but she wasn't in the mood.

She looked back at the hardcover book laying peacefully on top of Stewart's desk: *Eve's Plight*. She hated the title, as she hated the fact that the author had wrote so nonchalantly about her own discoveries.

She walked resolutely out of Stewart's fifth floor office and back to her own. She could still hear the wind beating against the building. She didn't look forward to being out in the storm, but she needed to get to the airport. She was going about this the wrong way. She knew that. But she was so angry! How could this guy, this author, just write out all of her research? How DID he discover her answers for clean energy, and the use of metallic hydrogen? How did he know that it would take both fission and fusion to get the type of results she needed.

He had even written about the lattice structure of the sphere, and she had only come across that a month earlier! It was like he was reading her mind. This research was under strictest confidence. Top secret. And she had to read about it in a fictional novel!

She was going to get some answers. This Ben Reeves didn't know what was going to hit him!

When she got into her car, soaking wet from her quick dash across the parking lot, she could almost feel the steam lifting from her, and it wasn't because the sudden change in atmospheric pressures from the outside into the inside. She was still fuming. She picked up her cell phone and punched in numbers, long since memorized.

The call was answered with a gruff "What?"

"Madeline. I need you to work your magic." Gwen could hear her long-time friend and frequent wine-and-dine companion on the other side of the phone shuffle papers on her own desk, looking for her keyboard.

"Alright, what do you need to know? I'm not too busy right now. Oh, by the way, what happened to that cute guy at the restaurant last night? Did you get his number?" Her dark-haired, perpetually single friend always asked about men.

"Not concerned with that right now. I need you to get me an address, or a phone number. Benjamin Reeves. He is a writer," she said.

"Oh, I know who Ben Reeves is. He's gorgeous. I've read three or four of his books. I like the one called *Seed*, or *Sowing a Seed*, something like that. Great love story. Why do you need to get ahold of Ben Reeves?" She said all in one breathe.

"He stole my research, that's why!" Gwen nearly shouted into the phone.

"Okay, give me a second. I'll text you what I find. Where are you?"

"Headed to my apartment to pack a bag, and then I'm heading to wherever you tell me, once you find out where this guy lives. I think it's in New York." Gwen said.

She started her engine, and pulled out, windshield wipers on full speed. The traffic was light getting to the outer loop around Washington DC. She was glad. Later in the day, it would be bumper to bumper.

Her friend hung up the phone without another word, and several minutes later, as Gwen exited the loop onto I-270 headed north into Montgomery County, MD, it beeped with a text, giving her the information she needed. Her apartment was in Germantown, and she was for once glad that she lived close to the Red Line of the Metro, so she could take public transportation to Regan Airport, instead of having to park. She wasn't made of money. Not yet, she thought.

Her friend came through, once again. Long Island, New York, she read in the text. Simple plane flight and an Uber. She was going to knock on this guy's door and get some answers!

While she was hurriedly packing a suitcase with what she would need, she got into her head. She didn't mean to, it was just disconcerting that a fiction writer would publish her findings, as fiction, before she could publish the data and experimentation in a respected journal.

She knew the breakthroughs she had had lately would change the world. The more she thought of it, the more she got "stompin' mad" as her father would have called it.

By the time her plane landed at LaGuardia Airport, she felt a little calmer. The two drinks she had had on the hour-and-a-half plane ride probably helped. But she still felt quite compelled to find out the truth from this author. He had to have stolen some key experimentation notes from her lab.

She didn't give any credibility to the fact that someone could piece these puzzle pieces together quite the way this author had. It was impossible, she thought, as she climbed into her Uber and left the airport terminal.

What this guy had written in his fictional story about clean energy had taken her almost four years of constant experimentation and study to come up with. It just wasn't quite reality yet.

The commercial manufacturing of metallic hydrogen wasn't quite in operation, but it was close. She wondered, vaguely, if this author had some inside information on that front. That much, she mused, was possible.

She really wanted to just hear him say that he got some inside information, used it to his advantage, and took some of her credit. Not that she was staking her reputation and career on credit. She really did want to change the world, and make it a much better place to live, for everyone. Her goal of clean, abundant energy would make life for many not as grueling or hard. That was her real goal.

And this writer just up and took her ideas, and put it into a love story, for gosh's sake.

The small Uber pulled up to a long driveway, surrounded by a large expanse of green grass. There were a couple of cars in the driveway, so she hoped someone was home. This guy didn't exactly advertise his home address.

Luckily, her best friend was a fact-checker for the Washington Post, and could find any information about literally anything. She had used that fact to her advantage a few times.

She got out of the Uber, and realized she still had her small suitcase. She hadn't even checked into a hotel first. She felt a bit like an ass, but there wasn't anything for it. She wanted to meet this usurper of information. She wanted answers.

She resolutely walked up the driveway to the rather stunning ranch style home. At least this guy had taste, she thought. Probably a woman's touch, most likely.

She walked up to the red door and rang the bell. She took several deep breaths because she didn't want to jump right into accusations. But she still felt her Irish temper just simmering below the surface.

The door opened and a rather large, redheaded, and bearded man filled up the doorway. She was too shocked at first to say anything. He was the largest man she had ever seen. Even bigger than her father.

"Hey, you're Dr. Murphy. What are you doing here?" the large man asked.

She finally found her voice.

"I am here to speak to Benjamin Reeves, please." Her words sounded like gunshots to her ears. Very staccato and short.

"Okay, okay. He's out back in the shop. Do you want to come in and I'll let him know you're here?" The man held up both hands, acting like she was going to attack him.

"That's quite alright. I will find him. Will you take my suitcase inside though? I'd rather not lug it around everywhere."

"Why do you have a suitcase with you?" He looked perplexed.

"I came straight from the airport." She was getting more frustrated. She didn't want to come across as a crazy lady. This guy could be some sort of bodyguard. She didn't want to seem like a crazed fan. But he obviously knew who she was, which made her much more suspicious.

"Sure, sure. Let me take that, and like I said, he's around back. Just go to the left side of the house and follow the driveway back. The big doors should be open. Just yell for him," the man explained.

She handed over her small black suitcase to the big man, squared her shoulders, and followed his directions around to the side of the house. As she walked down the driveway that meandered next to the lovely home, she saw it ended in a garage with two double doors, both of which were open.

Sound came from within, but mostly she could just hear loud music. It was a song she loved, actually. Blondie, "Dreaming." She had always loved Debra Harry. Big presence in a small package. She based a lot of her life and career around those two descriptors.

She walked towards the sound of the music and heard a loud grinding noise start up, louder than the music. She figured he would never hear her shout over all the noise, so she walked into the brightly lit garage.

She first noticed the cars. There were three of them. All classics, and she was instantly intrigued. She had a secret love for classic muscle cars, and she never told anyone about it. Maybe her father, who shared the love, but definitely not anyone she had dated or had a relationship with. She tended to be attracted to men who had an old-fashioned view on what women should and shouldn't like. It was a deciding factor in more than one breakup.

The first car she saw was a dark blue Mustang. It was a fastback that much she knew. She didn't know the year, or anything about it other than it was stunning. It shone in the bright light. It had a chrome GT500 emblem on the side, in front of the driver's side door. So, at least she knew what engine it had. She knew it was a Shelby. It caught her breath with the potential energy it represented.

She looked over to the car next to it, and saw that it had its hood up, and plaid paint protectors were positioned over the sides of the exposed engine. She still did not see the man she was searching for, but his cars were quite impressive. This one was obviously a 1950s era Corvette. She thought it was probably a Stingray. Her father had drooled over every one of these that they saw at car shows they visited together. Her mother never understood why Mr. Daniel Murphy, Sr. had this love of classic cars, and why his two children were just as wild for them.

The song ended at almost the same time as the grinding noise, and it was eerily silent for a few heartbeats. As the next song started up, the man walked around the third car. He was holding some sort of metal rod in his hand, and at first she just stood like a deer in headlights. He stopped as well and looked at her with a serious look on his face. The quiet between them was going on for too long, she thought. "500 Miles" by the Proclaimers was playing. Another song she loved. He must have it on an 80s station, she thought.

"I thought I would be hearing from you. Figured it would be from a lawyer first," the man said.

She finally found her voice. "How did you know? Wait...I'm sorry. I shouldn't have barged in here. I'm sorry." She lost all the anger that made her come to this point. When she saw him, she had the strangest feeling. She didn't like it.

She just watched the man. He was obviously near her age. Late twenties, dark hair, and he was tall. Very tall. Taller than her. She liked that fact first. He had a beard, but it didn't look kept up to her. He was wearing dirty jeans and a tank top shirt under a blue plaid shirt, unbuttoned and untucked. His hands were black with grease and car dirt, and he had a red rag thrown over one shoulder. She watched as he placed the metal rod he had been holding down on a worktable, covered in tools and odds and ends she couldn't fathom the uses for, and reached over and turned down the old-fashioned boom box sitting at the end of the table.

The silence in the garage was palatable. She nervously clutched her hands in front of her. She was dressed all wrong for this garage. She had on black slacks and a green blouse. She was wearing heels, but she still barely came up to the man's shoulders. She wasn't used to feeling like such a little thing. She was well above average height for a woman, but this man towered over her. She wasn't scared, however. She felt oddly at ease with him.

He sighed. "I'm sorry you're meeting me like this. I'm all dirty. I figured it would be in suits over a dark conference table, with all of the lawyers present," he said.

"No, I wanted to meet you in person. I wanted to know who you stole the information from. Or who sold it to you?" she said. She was aware that she was just standing there, feeling awkward. The man smiled at her. She really liked his smile. But it looked like it was full of pain. She remembered suddenly what her boss had told her that morning. This man had just lost his love. She felt like an ass suddenly.

"I didn't steal the information. I did research," he said, cautiously.

She didn't believe him. One thing she did pride herself on, was being the smartest person in most rooms. She knew that no one but someone like her could have pieced all of the information together. He had even known that the spherical shape of the latticework was optimal for complete compression. There is no way he just came up with that with "some research." She was very skeptical.

"Why don't we go inside, get something to drink? Let me wash up a bit?" he asked.

She looked up at him. He was standing next to another breathtaking car. But it wasn't a muscle car.

138

"First tell me what these cars are. My father loves classics. He would shoot me if I didn't ask about them."

He smiled at her again. Wiping his hands on the rag, and then on his jeans, he walked towards her, extending his hand.

"First, I'm Ben. It's a pleasure to meet you Dr. Murphy. And yes, I know exactly who you are. I have followed your career with a lot of interest." He was charming, she would give him that, she thought as she took his hand. It was large, strong, and felt like it had calluses. She liked his hand immensely.

"You can call me Gwen. Please. And pleasure to meet you as well, I think," she said, adding in the skepticism on purpose.

He just smiled again. They were standing in front of the Corvette.

"That beauty over there is the first thing I bought when I published my second book. It's a 1967 Shelby GT500. I had it painted 'space blue' with the Shelby racing stripes in white. My pride and joy."

He then reached over and tinkered with something inside the engine bay of the Corvette.

"1955 Corvette Stingray. Small block V-8. I saw one of these in a James Dean movie when I was a kid, and it's the only car I can remember my mother saying she would love to have. I call it Lorraine, after her," he said with pride.

"And that beast over there was a gift. 1957 Chevy Bel-Air. Two door, post. Hard top, large block V-8. Painted midnight black with white accented flairs. Those white wall tires and white rims are original. That car is a tank. They don't make cars like that anymore," he said.

She was impressed, but she knew he knew that. It made her hackles rise, and she remembered why she was there.

He ushered her out of the garage, and she stood feeling silly in the driveway while he closed the two heavy garage doors and shut off the lights. After, he took her into the back door of the home. She was surprised that it led into an obvious office. He had pictures hanging on the walls of his books, as well as pictures of two different women. She stopped, and looked at the color picture of a thin, blonde woman on a beach. It was obviously an older picture, but she felt drawn to it.

"That was my mom. Lorraine. At the beach right through those trees there." He pointed out of the windows overlooking the backyard. She looked where his finger pointed and could just make out blue water through a row of tall trees.

"She was beautiful."

"Thank you. Come on into the kitchen. I'll get you something to drink."

She purposely did not mention the blonde woman in the other picture, obviously much more recently taken. She gulped loudly, but it was not the time to ask him about the woman he had lost. At that time, thought, she didn't know that he had lost both of the women in the pictures.

He led her down a spacious hallway and into a bright kitchen. She admired the dark cabinets and darkly patterned granite countertops. She was looking around when she felt the presence of the overly large redheaded man enter from a front room. She looked up at him. Ben saw the exchange and quickly introduced the two.

"We've met," she said sardonically.

"Yeah, Ben, she came to the front door. I told her she could find you around back," said the large man. As she came in the door, he introduced himself as Markson.

"But just call me Mars," he had said.

"I'm going to get washed up. Mars, can you get her something to drink? Wine, water, something stronger?" Ben looked towards her.

"I could use a beer. What do you have?" she said. She noticed the surprise on both men's faces. She loved the reactions she got when she asked for a beer. It would really blow their top if they knew her preferences.

"Umm, I think we have some light beer, but usually we drink lagers. I have a six pack of a new stout I picked up earlier," Ben said.

"I'll try the stout. Thank you."

Ben nodded to Mars, and left to wash his hands, and hopefully change his dirty jeans, she thought.

Mars moved things around in the large, stainless steel refrigerator and came out with the six pack of dark-colored bottles. He used a bottle opener hanging from a piece of leather string on one of the cabinet doors. Handing her the opened bottle, he opened two others.

She took a drink. It was heavenly. Dark, slightly bitter. Cold as hell. This guy had good taste, she thought, quickly.

"So, umm, you found Ben?" Mars asked, awkwardly.

"Yup, found my way and everything," she answered back sarcastically. She was throwing off the big man.

"What do you do? You his bodyguard or something?" she asked.

"Oh no, I'm an environmentalist. I work for the UN Global Compact as a research scientist," he answered. That surprised her. These men were quite odd, she thought.

"How do you know Ben?" she asked.

"Ben and I go back to freshman year. We all went to Hofstra. You know, the university?" he said.

"Yes, I know it. Right up the road, isn't it?" she asked.

141

"Yeah, that's the one. I met Ben when he started dating Neeley. She was my girlfriend's best friend. We all started hanging out all the time. Ben and I became best friends, now I come hang out with him, so he won't be alone so much," he explained. He looked sheepishly down at the ground, feeling like he had said too much.

"I read that his fiancée had died. It was a car accident, right?" she asked. She hoped Ben didn't come back into the kitchen until she learned a few things.

"Umm, yeah. It was a difficult time for Ben. That day, I had told him about your work. He had asked me to look up some stuff on world-changing science that he could put into a book he was writing. That night, and he won't talk about it, but that night, I think he came home and got caught up writing. He was supposed to be with her. She hadn't even been driving. She was in a taxi that got hit by a cement truck. The driver died as well. It was a really bad time. Don't tell him I told you this, okay?" He still looked embarrassed.

"Don't worry. I won't. Is he okay now?" she asked.

"Ben has always been a little quieter than most, so I'm not sure if he's okay or not. He just stays busy. He has another book coming out soon. I think he is just working himself to death. If it's not work, it's the cars. If it's not the cars, it's making homemade knives out in the shop. Always busy." Mars sounded like a mother hen, Gwen thought. But she was touched that this big man would care so much about the dark man she had met earlier.

Ben walked back into the kitchen. He had changed into a pair of starched khaki pants, a button-up blue dress shirt that he still had untucked, and bare feet. She like the look of him, she thought. But then she remembered that he had lost his love not even a year earlier. She felt bad for liking the look of him.

"Now, why don't we chat," he said, picking up the beer that Mars nodded towards. He clinked it with her half-drunk one and took a long drink of his own.

He had two barstools on either side of the large island in the middle of the kitchen. He took one, and Mars took the one next to him. Ben motioned for her to take one of the ones across from him, and as she sat down, she suddenly felt like she was being interviewed by the two large men. She didn't like that, so she took over the conversation before either man could say anything else.

"Alright, ahem...when I read your last book, or at least the part that my boss showed me, it was very shocking to see my own research there in black and white in a book that was a, love story, wasn't it?" she said quickly.

Ben smiled his sad smile at her again. He took another drink from his beer, and she watched as his Adam's apple bobbled as he swallowed the dark beer. He sighed loudly before answering her.

"Like I said, the only information I had about your work was what was online. That just got me started, really. Your experiments with hydrogen as an energy source is just the beginning. From there, I researched the theoretical properties of metallic hydrogen. I read how astronomers think the Gas Giants have a metallic hydrogen core, and it's actually what keeps the gas inside the sphere," he went on.

"So that led to researching electromagnetic fields. They think that metallic hydrogen can be a superconductor at room temps. I think that's pretty awesome. Sounded like the holy grail of elements. Now, I'm not educated in physics like you are, but it was pretty easy to think up using metallic hydrogen as a chamber and a means to create energy," he said.

"Yeah, but how did you get to the perpetual energy production of both fission and fusion? No one had thought of that," she said in exasperation.

143

"Just made sense to me. The sun is mostly a bunch of fusion reactions happening, right? Well I read where they think there's a bunch of fission happening too. I know you can neither create nor destroy matter, so I figured if you could come up with a way to create both types of reactions from the same bit of matter, then one would lead back to the other. The thing I had to really think about was how you could use the electromagnetic field to cause fusion, and then what would cause the fission? So, that's where I went out on a limb and thought that if you did it in a small sphere, or egg shape, bit of metallic hydrogen, you could compress the inner compartment enough so that fusion just happens, and then the bit about using a laser to blast it apart to create fission, I thought, was brilliant. After that, it was just a matter of making it seem plausible," he said, sort of smugly, in her estimation.

"It doesn't make sense to me. You came up with all of this from reading some articles on the internet? How did it come together for you? This must have taken you months to figure out?" She was starting to have to change her opinion of the man sitting in front of her.

"No, took me about a day. I was taking notes on some of the new science discoveries they've been making. Like the proving of the Higgs boson. That Super Collider over there is really something, but it never made sense to me that colliding two particles together was very, umm, easy and clean, you know?" he asked her.

"No, exactly what I thought. I theorized that super compression would be the answer," she said, getting excited.

"Exactly," he said.

"I knew that if you could use the same little bit of something to both fuse and fission, and keep repeating itself, I knew that would work. And it could be small enough that every home in the world could have one of these little eggs," he said.

"How do you know all of this, Ben? Seriously? I have multiple degrees in theoretical physics and I'm just now starting to put these pieces together. The fact that the egg has to be put into a gold-platinum alloy box, well, that's just science fiction there," she said.

"I know, I got the idea from watching Star Wars," he answered with a grin.

She looked perplexed, he thought to himself. He chuckled, and heard Mars chuckle next to him. They both knew what Ben was talking about.

"You know the power generator that Luke Skywalker blows up in the Death Star? I saw that being just a bigger version of this little egg in a box. The laser apparatus coming up from the bottom, and the thermoelectric bundle of wires coming from the top. It just looked cool in my imagination." He was still smiling.

She wasn't. She felt her whole life start to implode. She put her empty beer bottle down harder than she meant to. Both men startled.

She was feeling slightly lightheaded. And it wasn't from the beer. Everything she had been working so hard on, under total secrecy, for more days than she cared to think about, was all just a part of a story to the guy sitting across from her. Their laughter got on her nerves in a way she couldn't comprehend at that moment. She didn't want to be in this house any longer.

"I need to go. I'm sorry I bothered you. I'm going to order an Uber and I'll get out of here," she stammered.

"No need, Mars or I can drive you wherever you need to go," Ben said to her. She hated his patronizing tone. He was just too damn perfect, wasn't he, she though. Her anger was coming back.

145

"No, I can get my own ride. And I can make history with making my own designs and ideas a reality for this world, thank you very much." She was embarrassed. She didn't want to come across this way.

"Look, I'm sorry if I stepped on your toes. It was just part of a story. I write stories for a living. It's all I know. All of that was just a part of the story." He was getting embarrassed himself, she thought.

She wanted to wipe the smug look off of his handsome face. Don't think like that, she thought to herself as she pulled out her cell phone and ordered the ride to a hotel. It asked her a location. She just put in the first hotel she found. She would fly out the next morning, she knew. There was no way, this, this, writer, would steal her work. She felt her competitive nature start a fire in her belly.

"I'm not trying to steal anything from you, you know that, right?" he asked her.

She didn't care. She just thanked him for the drink, and for answering her questions. She knew when she calmed down later at the hotel that she would regret how she reacted to his answers. He really didn't know what he was doing, she thought. And how in the hell did this un-educated guy figure it out? She felt like she was angrier at herself than at him.

Within minutes, her ride pulled up at the end of the driveway. She rejected both men's offer to help her. She didn't need anyone's help. She found her small suitcase sitting next to the front door. Without saying anything else to the men, she grabbed her suitcase, stomped down the driveway, hearing her footsteps loudly in her ears, and got into the car.

She slammed the door closed and sat in sullen silence all the way to the hotel. She refused to look back at the two overly large men, in her estimation, standing in the driveway, looking quite confused.

She would show these men. She would show the entire world. It would be done in her way, not this asshole sandwich's way. Even though he was completely right in what he discovered, she finally thought in exasperation.

The fucker figured it out. She knew she would not be in a good mood for quite a while.

What a fucking fucker she thought of Ben. And that damn smile.

Chapter 17

"Well, that just happened," Ben said to Mars, standing next to him, hands in his pockets. Mars looked up at the sky, sighed loudly, and asked Ben if he wanted another beer.

"I'm dressed now. Let's go get a beer at McGivney's. Talk about what just happened," Ben answered.

A few minutes later, the two best friends pulled up to the corner Irish Pub that they had spent many meals and countless hours talking about the serious stuff. Luckily it was a weeknight and parking was light. Coming here had become their thing since Neeley's death. Not a few tears were shed over dark Guinness, and Murph's bangers and mash was therapy on a plate.

Walking into the dark interior, several older regulars at the bar turned at the sunlight glinting through the open door as the men walked in. There were the regular greetings of vulgarity and recognition. The older men who frequented the establishment, mostly to get away from family duties and nagging wives, loved the two young men. Fun and shenanigans was the nightly course at Murph McGivney's. The two tall men sat at the end of the oak bar, put their arms up on the scarred topper, and ordered two stouts. As was custom.

As the other patrons finished their good-natured ribbing and salutations, Ben looked over at Mars and asked the question that was on both of their minds.

"What the hell was that?" he said as he blew off the foam at the top of his tall glass of the Irish stout the old bartender placed in front of him. He gave Murph a dirty look for the size of foam. It was taller than his usual one finger. Murph just shrugged, slung a white rag over his shoulder and went back to talking to the older patrons at the other end of the sparsely lit bar. At least he had the music turned down this evening, Ben thought.

Mars took a deep drink of his dark beer, sighed in contentment, and looked over at his shorter and darker best friend. He patted Ben on the back a little bit too hard. Ben was used to it, and only spilled a little of his drink onto the heavily scarred oak bar top.

"That, my friend, is what we in the environmental world call a class-A, F-5 finger of God tornado, mixing with a category five hurricane with no warning. She was all piss and vinegar. Pretty though, wasn't she?" Mars looked coyly at his friend.

"I guess so, man. She was mad though. Like I took a leak in her frosted flakes. I get it. I really do. She probably thinks I stole her work. But I just took some ideas and made a story out of it. I didn't publish it in a scientific journal or anything. Saved by the First Amendment, once again," he said with a smile. Mars nudged him a little too hard in the arm. Ben rolled his eyes.

"She was pretty. I guess. Amazing eyes. Never saw that color before. And she has you beat in the strawberry-red hair department. Real old-world Irish. Bet her dad is a beast," Ben said with a smile.

"Come on man, she's obviously brilliant, but kind of egotistical. She is very beautiful, and you know it," Mars said with a smile.

"Okay, okay. But you know I prefer blondes," Ben answered back with one of his own smiles.

One of the older men at the other end of the half-full bar looked down at the two young men and yelled a question.

"Oy. Where are your lady friends? You're both always in here with cute little things that you don't deserve," he said in an Irish brogue. The other patrons snickered or outright laughed. Mars loved these good-natured people but knew that Ben could lose his temper. Mars put his hand on Ben's arm before the smaller man could say anything.

"Hey Harry, and how do you keep that pretty little wife of yours happy?" Mars joked back to the smaller, older man. "She must be about ready for divorce right about now, right?" Some of the people snickered.

The short, older woman sitting next to Harry spoke up before Harry could give a retort.

"Let me tell ye a story young man," Harry's wife answered. "Me and this here bastard been married for nigh on forty years. We married the same day as my blessed sister, Marge."

She continued, looking at the two young men seriously, but both knew a joke was brewing.

"That morning, me and me sister got in a little disagreement on who would be the most disappointed in her own marriage. So we made a pact, we did." The men smiled.

"She bet momma's china set she had got, and I bet the three cast iron pans I got too. We would compare our disappointing lives every year and see who was a'winnin'."

Harry was looking studiously down at his beer, not saying a word.

"Me sweet sister passed about five years ago now. And to this day, I look at that fine china in me cabinet, and I know the truth of it, young man." Her eyes twinkled. All ears and eyes were on the short, graying woman.

"I look at me fine china, and I know. I know deep in my heart, that I won that fucker fairer than fair, and I keep winnin' it every blastin' day!" She took a huge gulp of her frothy beer, and slammed down the large glass.

The bar erupted in laughter, none more than from Harry. He reached over and grabbed his longtime honey and kissed her square on the mouth, in front of God and the world. Both young men at the end of the bar saluted their health, and toasts went around the bar for a good five minutes.

Later, as the banter between the two close friends settled down to casual talk about trivial things, Murph came down the bar and asked if they wanted something off the menu.

"Two plates of your Shepard's Pie, if the lamb is fresh, good sir," Mars said with a smile for the older man.

"Is my meat anything but fresh, young man? Ask your mother," the man said in quip.

The bar broke out laughing, none louder than Mars himself. Ben smiled and looked around, feeling loose and light for once. The darkness had not settled in today, like it usually did. He casually wondered why it had stopped when he saw the tall redhead.

When he saw her for the first time in his garage, and he didn't want to tell Mars this, or anyone else for that matter, but he felt an instant, hot attraction. Like a magnet in his chest. He felt he hid it well. But he felt so shitty for feeling it. He felt it sullied the memory of Neeley.

Looking down into his half full glass of dark beer, he sighed deeply. He was at war on the inside, and he knew no one could tell. He missed Neeley terribly. She had been so much like his mother. He felt at home when he had been with her.

But the guilt almost overwhelmed him when he thought of the woman he had just met. The firebrand redhead. Mars had it down. She really came in like a giant storm. He felt intimidated by a woman for the first time in his life. He wondered if her own emotions were anything other than rage.

He remembered back to the day that Neeley had died. He had lost time doing research and writing, but what he had really spent most of the evening doing, was finding as many pictures of Gwen Murphy that he could online, marveling in her looks, presence, beauty. And Neeley had died because of it.

His conscience tore him apart.

Chapter 18

Gwen was tired. No, not just tired. Weary in her bones, she thought. She looked off of her balcony, down at the expanse of trees in the courtyard below. The leaves were changing colors from green to bright reds and oranges. One aspen tree's leaves were a bright yellow. Even the lovely sight couldn't get her out of her melancholy mood. She sighed, looking down at her glass of Riesling, beads of condensation dripping on her hand.

Eight years of study. Experimentation. Countless hours of research and dead ends. And then her dismal dating life. So many first dates that didn't go anywhere.

The men's faces were fading together. They all dressed well, spoke well, and were utterly boring. Within two minutes she would know. The men were beneath her. Political science majors, economists, one sort-of interesting fellow who was a journalist. At least he had nice stories to tell. Bad teeth though.

She sighed again.

Not for the first time did she think back to that dreamy experience at the castle in Colorado. Maybe she should have chosen a different path. She hated seeing the correlations between her work life and dating life.

It wasn't as if she tried to find fault in every man that she dated. She really did try to give them all a chance. But she felt that many of the men, well, all of them really, fell short of what she wanted in life.

But the truth was, she was just scared of getting into a relationship that would take away from her career, and her passion to change the world.

She looked back at the changing leaves on the trees in the mild Maryland evening. She thought back to her time at college. The fall months in Boston. She missed it terribly. When she and her friends would dress up as different literary characters for Halloween. They would go to Salem and trick-or-treat like they were kids. And they were kids.

She suddenly could smell the New England air. The smoky fragrance of fall. She closed her eyes to the memories. She could see herself laughing as she wore pigtails like Anne of Green Gables. Or her three closest girlfriends and she would dress up like the March sisters in *Little Women*. She was always Meg. She always wanted to be Meg. But the truth was, as she grew older, she was much more like Jo.

Those fall days were magic. Apples, cider, cinnamon. The crunch of the leaves underfoot on campus. She missed her days in Northern California, but she had been made for New England. They understood her heaviness of character there. Her deepness. Her melancholy nature.

She had fallen in love with the weight of the history of the place. She sighed again as she opened her eyes to the

154

Maryland sky above her. It was beautiful here as well. But Maryland represented her failures at her purpose. She hadn't really failed. Not really. She was closer than she had ever been. She felt right on the edge of a precipice, ready to jump. But her frustrations were in not meeting her expectations. But her dreams had begun in New England. She yearned to go back.

She had turned thirty-two last month. She thought she would have changed the world, been married to her soulmate, and had a kid or two by now. None of that had happened. Now, she mostly felt numb.

She laughed as she looked at the small table next to her wicker chair. The spread open paperback she had been reading stared back at her, mockingly. That damn Ben Reeves' newest book. What did he know of life and love, she thought?

And then she felt shame. He knew more than she did. No one could know that she secretly enjoyed his books. She saw behind the writing. She loved the subtle pain behind the love stories that he wrote about.

The stories always worked out, the protagonists always getting the girl, or the boy, of their dreams. But they struggled as well. Gwen liked that. Made the stories feel real.

And he never failed to mention how the two lovebirds looked at each other. Like her father always looked at her mother.

That made her think of home. She would be traveling this Thanksgiving to be with her aging parents through the holidays. She hadn't been home for any length of time for years. She was looking forward to it. But she was not looking forward to her brother's family being there.

How could he have three little children in four years? His beautiful, bubbly wife would be there, thinking she was more intertwined with Gwen's mother than Gwen was. But the truth was, her sister-in-law was just like her mother. They even looked alike.

And Daniel McCarthy Murphy II looked at his wife like her father looked every day at her mother. Gwen's insides twisted.

She didn't want to think of what she was missing in her life.

She was so tired.

Her phone beeped next to the book. She looked at a text from her friend Madeline. Asking if she was still coming over the next day for Sunday lunch. Even Maddy had found her somebody. All Gwen had was her work. And she didn't know how much longer the government grants would last. She needed one more breakthrough, she thought. Just a way to make the metal. She knew it took extreme pressure to make even a quantum sized bit of metallic hydrogen.

A team in France was close. Something to do with the shape of the diamond anvils needed to make the necessary pressures. She sighed again and answered the text. She would be there the next day. Maddy was almost eight months pregnant, and John was her constant companion, and husband.

Gwen smiled at the last time she saw the pair the week prior. John had the look of a lost, confused puppy perpetually plastered to his handsome face. Maddy constantly complained that she had never even felt her ankles before, how could they hurt and swell so much now?

Gwen set her phone back down and put her earbuds back into her ears. She picked the phone back up and pulled up her music lists. She pressed play on her playlist titled "old school peace" and as the first song began playing in her ears, she smiled. "Dreaming" by Blondie. She remembered hearing it blast away in that garage, when she had first seen Ben Reeves. A tiny bit of anger crept into

156

her chest but looking down at the mutely colored book cover on the table next to her, the anger was replaced, once again, with melancholy.

She finished her wine, and picked the book back up. She was surprised how he always mixed in faith and spirituality in the story in some ways. It made her think of the angel again.

She should have chosen the other way.

The following Monday, as she was walking into the office building near the NIH campus in Silver Springs, her phone beeped in her purse. She ignored the phone until she got to her office. Once she was settled behind her desk, with the computer booting up, she looked at her phone.

It was a text message with a link another colleague had sent her with a French URL. Her computer beeped at the same time, and as she looked up from her phone to her computer screen, her boss burst through her office door.

"Have you seen the news, Gwen? It's big!" Stewart was almost yelling as he ran into her large office.

"Apparently. Everyone in the world is beeping me at the moment, Stewart. What happened?" she asked.

"They did it, is what happened Gwen. The fuckers did it. Paul Loubeyre and his team made metallic hydrogen. You were right about the diamond anvil cells. The design is called toroidal. You were right all along. And now the bastards did it," he said.

She looked at the link. It was an archive of articles called *arXiv*. She had heard of it.

The enclosed pictures taken of the claim for metallic hydrogen were stunning. And yes, they proved what she had written about months earlier. This claim did not upset her.

They did not have the necessary equipment here in the States to do what the French team had done. But now she had the leap forward that she needed. Now, she could really go to work.

She looked up at Stewart's excited face. She felt excitement herself. Maybe it was finally time to do all those "changing the world" things she was expecting of herself. She found a new energy looking at the microscopic pictures on her computer screen.

The bright, shiny circle of material in the center of the three separate pictures would change her life. She knew it. Stewart knew it. And soon, the world would know it.

She grinned. She stood suddenly, grabbed her white coat off of the coat rack next to the door to her office, and walked right past Stewart to get to her labs. She had work to do.

Stewart smiled at her retreating back. He knew what this meant to her. And as he watched her walk resolutely away, he felt inwardly that he was getting close to his own life change.

He would tell her how he felt about her soon. This may have been the chance he needed.

He walked out of her office with a new spring in his step. He didn't care as much about the breakthrough as he did about her. And he was ready to tell her how he had felt for the last eight years.

He closed her office door with a soft click and walked down the white hallway in the other direction from the woman who held his heart.

He didn't even realize that he was whistling out loud.

Chapter 19

Ben hated book signings. He would avoid them all completely if he could. But his contract stipulated that he attend at least three, of his choosing, in the upper 48, after each publication. He hated this.

He had made one rule very early on in the contract. If people wanted to see him, talk to him, he wasn't taken a damn selfie with the fans! They were always upset at the first rule when they got to the event. No cameras! So much grumbling, but he didn't care. He didn't want his damn picture plastered all over the internet.

He usually chose his public appearances close to home. He traveled quite frequently for studying and researching his book locations and tried to get a vibe of different places in the world. He didn't want to be a two-dimensional writer. He wanted truth in his stories.

But this book signing was different. He was in San Francisco, and he had not come to California much at all in his life. He felt like he needed to make this trip, but he couldn't put his finger right on the reason he felt that way. But he had also made a promise. He never took those lightly.

The car pulled up outside of the Four Seasons Hotel. As always, he got out of the car and took a moment to look around, feel the vibe around himself, and breathe in the slightly salty air. The city was loud, but it wasn't New York City loud. And it was a very bright summer day. It wasn't as hot as the East Coast either. He actually liked the feel to the city around him. That surprised him.

He knew the bookstore where they were holding the signing was about two blocks away. Alexander's Books. He had been there a few times in the last couple of years, mostly out of a curiosity. The owners had always asked him to come do a reading and a signing, but he had always begged off, giving one excuse or another.

He couldn't do that this year. His last book had been set in San Francisco, and while he had been here a couple of years previous, for research, he had made the promise that brought him to the City by the Bay this time around. He was actually looking forward to the day.

He took his suitcase and computer bag from the driver of the black, darkly tinted SUV idling at the curb, and walked into the poshly decorated large lobby. Nodding to the doorman dressed all in black, who held the glass door open, he walked over the thick stripped blue and white carpet and appreciated the modernistic

160

appointments contrasting with the wood-colored walls and light-colored furniture scattered in different sitting areas.

He looked over at the bar area, closed this early in the day. Last time he had stayed there, the bartender had made him a smoking old fashioned, which he looked forward to again that evening. Last time he was here the drink had perfectly paired with a buttery ribeye steak from the kitchens. He always remembered good food, and good mixed drinks. This hotel had, in the past, been one of his favorite memories.

And while he hated public appearances, he really did enjoy this part of the job. The travel, staying in beautiful places, being treated well. It was a stark contrast from his boyhood in West Texas.

He walked up to the light wood-colored front desk, noting it was the same color as the walls of the lobby. The woman behind the desk, dressed all in black, looked up at him and smiled. She was a very pretty brunette, with great teeth, Ben thought. He noticed the splash of dark blue on her left breast. A handkerchief, silk, setting off the drab black. He approved.

"Mr. Lemons, always great to have you back," she said with a smooth voice. He always used his mother's maiden name when he traveled. He had another author friend who reserved rooms under Disney character names, but he couldn't quite get over cringing if they addressed him as Mr. Duck.

"Thank you. Nice to be back. Lovely weather."

"It is. We have your room ready for you. Management sent up a small 'thank you.' Jimmy will take your bags for you, and if you need anything at all, please ring," she said with a smile. She waved over an older man to take his bags, and he allowed the stooped man to take his rolling suitcase, while he kept his computer bag over his shoulder. The older gentleman was dressed sharply in

161

a full black uniform and was wearing an old-style driver's hat on his mottled and balding head. No words were exchanged as Ben followed the slow man to the bank of elevators.

As they walked into the large, two-roomed suite that Ben had reserved for himself, he handed the older man a folded ten-dollar bill, and when the older man was gone, he walked over to the large windows. Looking over at the close-by buildings and down on busy Second Street below, Ben breathed in the lovely smell of the room and was at peace.

He turned back to the very bright and white room and saw the gift from management on the round table between the white couches near the windows. A small bottle of his favorite bourbon, red wax seal intact at the top, and a white, heavy thank you card. They both sat next to a small basket holding several cheeses and sausages, still wrapped, and a sleeve of white soda crackers.

He picked up the bi-folded card, saw several scrawls of signatures, and smiled. A very nice gesture. And for them to remember his favorite spirit was a lovely touch. He would enjoy it, as well as the snacks, later tonight.

For now, as he walked into the other room in the suite, he opened the suitcase that Jimmy had placed on the low table meant for such and unpacked. He would be here for three days, and he wanted to be comfortable and enjoy as much of the city as he could. Luckily, he had packed a tweed sweater and jeans, and he knew this would be his uniform as he went on his customary walks.

A couple of years earlier, he had started taking daily walks. He didn't know why he had not always done that. As he had walked further and further every day, he got a bit addicted to being outside, walking, and being in his memories and plans. Any time he traveled, he always researched places to walk wherever he could.

162

He had read about San Francisco's many parks and looked forward to enjoying the cool summer days exploring the walking paths of the city's famed stretches of public spaces.

Finishing up unpacking, he looked at his watch. The three-hour time difference from the east coast made him feel that it was later in the day than it was. He had a couple of hours before he was due at the bookstore at 2 p.m., so he decided to take a little nap.

He stretched out on the comfortable king size bed, laying on top of the plush white bedspread, and took several pillows and threw them on the floor. As his head hit the single pillow under him, he closed his eyes and fell asleep a lot faster than usual.

He dreamed. Waking, an hour and a half later, he would remember his vivid dream for the rest of the day. It was poignant and strong.

In the dream, *he was in a field. The field was made up of prairie grasses and several differently colored, small flowers. The field was ringed all around by tall, fully leaved trees. The first thing he had done in the dream was look completely around himself in a full circle and saw no breaks in the trees.*

He started walking. He didn't want to walk into the trees, but the large clearing was spacious enough for a bit of exploring. He walked through the mid-calf prairie grass, feeling it tickle his legs. He looked down and saw that he was wearing a pair of khaki shorts, and a pair of tan leather deck shoes. No socks. He looked further up his body and felt and then saw a soft, untucked white collared shirt, with white buttons down the front. He felt strong. He felt peace. As he looked ahead of him in the field, soft music started to play. If came through the air as if he was in a concert hall, but it was quieter, and wavered up and down with the soft breeze. He could make out violins

163

accompanied by a piano. He recognized the song. Pachelbel's "Canon." He loved this song. He savored the feeling that it was the music caressing his face and body, rather than the gentle wind.

He felt the warm sun on his face. He looked up to it, seeing birds flying through the air, dancing to the music. He looked back down, focusing on where he was walking. He was almost to the center of the large clearing, when he first heard water flowing, and then saw a quickly moving creek cutting the large clearing in half. As he walked up to the bubbling water, watching it move swiftly over rocks and past the sandy shores, he noticed that the creek was just too large to jump across. Somehow, the way he felt, and the way he was dressed, he knew that passing over the creek was impossible. It was more of a feeling of truth that he just needed to stay where he was, on his side, and enjoy the sounds of the music and watch the water turn white around the rocks.

He sat down on the soft sand, next to the water, and waited patiently for something. He didn't quite know what it was he was waiting for, but it felt right to sit there and just enjoy the day. He closed his eyes again and angled his face towards the bright sun directly overhead. The music meandered with the breeze, the grasses swayed behind him, and the sound of the rushing water soothed him. Keeping his eyes closed, he felt complete serenity. When he slowly opened his eyes, he was looking at the opposite bank of the swift water. And he saw a woman.

She was dressed in a white, gauzy dress. It looked light enough to be caught in the breeze and blow away. The fabric pressed to her thin frame, without being obscene. She was tall. The hem of the wispy dress didn't quite cover her feet clad in brown leather sandals. As he watched, the woman stepped into the shallow water at the

164

edge of her side of the bank. She didn't seem to mind the obviously cooler water moving over her sandaled feet.

His eyes traveled up her thin frame and his breath caught in his chest in anticipation of seeing her face. She was wearing a wide-brimmed straw hat, and she was looking down at the water. He couldn't see her face. What he thought at first was medium-length blonde hair transformed in front of his eyes into long, curly red hair. He still couldn't see the woman's face. The wide brim of the hat just covered enough that he couldn't see her face. It was frustrating him. He tried to speak. He tried to tell her to look up so that he could look at her beauty. Everything else about her was perfect in his opinion, and he yearned to see her face. He knew it would be the face of an angel. But she never looked up.

He got to his feet, cupped his hands around his mouth, and tried to shout at her. But no sound issued from his lips. And the woman never took her eyes off of the fast-moving water rushing over her feet. As Ben looked around to figure out how to cross the short distance to the other side, the water started growing wider. Ben didn't feel himself moving, but suddenly he was twice the distance he had been in a second. And a heartbeat later, he was twice as far from the other side as that. The woman never looked up.

The music grew louder, the breeze turned into a gale. And Ben never saw the face of the perfect woman on the other side of the now mile-wide water. As the music reached a crescendo, and the winds blew Ben away.

He came awake with a jerk, looking around in a panic, not remembering where he was for a second or two. The hotel. San Francisco. He brought his hands to his face, remembering every detail of the dream. He felt like crying. He was so frustrated, and it had just been a dream. His phone's alarm went off, making him flinch. He reached over to the phone on the side table next to the bed and switched off the incessant beeping. He looked at the time. He had a half hour to get to the bookstore, two blocks away. Just enough time to shower and change.

He walked to the bookstore. It was a beautiful day and the streets between the hotel and the bookstore were full of people walking to various places. The absolute differences in this city and his city on the east coast was jarring. The sidewalks were not quite as packed. People here wore so many different colors of clothing and styles he hadn't seen anywhere else, that it was jarring. There were only a few men in suits, carrying briefcases.

The walk was cool. He stayed in the shadows from the tall buildings around him. He could hear traffic behind the buildings he walked in front of, but it seemed further away than it was. He knew Mission Street was just on the other side of the buildings of his block, but he couldn't see the heavy traffic.

He approached the street in front of the tall bookstore. Looking at it, he marveled that it did as much business as it did. The bookstore was in a four-story gray building sandwiched between a larger building on the left, and a shorter building on the right. There were fire escape balconies made from wrought iron over the face of the thin, tall building, and the ground floor was covered in glass.

Ben looked at a crowd gathered in front of the building and wondered how he was going to get into the blocked-off front door. No one had noticed him yet, as he walked towards the front of the building. Most of the people in line were looking down at books, or cellphones, or talking to each other.

Ben ducked his head and walked over to the large man standing in front of the glass door. He took off his sunglasses and the man recognized him. Without saying a

166

word, the large man nodded his head backwards, towards the door he was covering.

Ben moved next to him, opened the door, and entered the ground floor of the bookstore. He could hear whispers from the line of people as he ducked inside.

The store was empty except for a tall, thin man setting up chairs. The usual shelves of books he remembered had been moved to each side of the deep, skinny room. At the rear of the room, behind what looked like about fifty chairs set next to each other in rows, was a tall lectern. A thin microphone rose from the top of the lectern, and Ben knew that in just a few minutes, as the room filled up around him, he would be reading the first two chapters of his most recent book into that microphone.

He was nervous, as he always was in these situations. He wrote his books to be read by readers, he thought. Not for him to read aloud to others. But he knew the residents of this city would love the first two chapters of the book.

It was set right here in SF, and he knew from the reviews the book had received that he had captured the magic of the West Coast city perfectly.

He walked over to the tall man. The man looked up, recognized Ben, and almost tripped over a wooden chair to meet Ben at the center of the large bottom floor. He pumped Ben's hand a little too hard, and as Ben looked up into the tall man's face, he felt gratitude. One of the problems with being a hermitic writer, is that he did not often get to see the impact his storytelling had on others.

"Wow, Ben Reeves, what a pleasure man. True pleasure. I'm Grayson. I've worked here for five years. I've read all your books," the taller man said all in one breath, without releasing Ben's hand.

Ben smiled at the exuberant man. Finally getting his hand back, he looked around at the room. He noticed three fixtures at the front of the room holding copies of several of his books. The biggest was of the newest book, and they sat on a table in front of a life-size cardboard cutout of himself. He liked that picture of himself. He thought he looked a bit like Benedict Cumberbatch in it. His arms were folded in front of him, and he looked seriously at the camera. He wore a black turtleneck sweater, and he thought he looked very British. He loved the look.

Looking at the assembled chairs, and the lectern in front of the rows of chairs, he asked Grayson if he had the copy of the chapters he would be reading. Grayson nodded, and went over to the cash register table and came back with a leather folder.

Anyone who set Ben up to read his own writing knew that he did not read from an actual book of his. He always asked for typed out and printed full-size pages in a folder.

His eyesight wasn't as great as it always had been, and this helped him not squint at one of his own books. He knew anyone listening from the audience wasn't hearing the words so much as seeing the man who wrote them. He did not want to disappoint his fans.

Ben walked over to the wooden lectern and told Grayson to start letting the people waiting outside in. He watched and smiled and nodded at several of the fans taking their seats. There were about fifty chairs, but he knew that that wouldn't hold the number of fans coming through the door. He also knew the bookstore staff was prepared to handle so many people, and the employees were ready to stop the line when the ground floor filled up.

Ben was suddenly glad for the microphone as he looked over the heads of at least two hundred people, crowded into the space behind the chairs, which had quickly filled up first. Everyone knew the rules, and there was not one cell phone out, or camera pointed at him. He was thankful that he didn't have to say anything about that rule.

He had realized a couple of years previous that people weren't even mad about him not wanting his picture taken anymore. Now, it had become a part of his persona, and like a badge people respected, and then even started appreciating, this became part of his mystery.

He knew now, that if he were to tell people that it was okay to take pictures, they would be more than upset at the change. He had wanted to state just that to a couple of crowds like this to see if any of his fans would take out a camera. He doubted they would. It would be against the single truth they had of him in their minds.

He again smiled at the faces looking up at him. He was used to the women looking at him like he was the perfect man. He caught several men with the same look. He wasn't perfect. He couldn't even make dating work out. He was too set in his ways.

But he wrote about men who could be perfect. Men who worked hard at the important things in life. And he wrote women who were real. More than anything in his prose, he wanted to tell the truth. He had received good reviews for most of his career for that very thing. Telling the truth.

It inspired and motivated him in his writing. And his readers knew that fact.

The room quieted as it filled up and the front door was closed. All eyes were on him. He tapped the microphone lightly and heard the echo of the noise from the speakers in the ceiling. He cleared his throat.

The performance was always the same. No introduction. No words spoken but those that he had written himself. He looked down at the first typed page of the book he had named *Shall Become a Thousand*. He glanced back at the crowd to make sure they were all paying attention. He knew that those with copies would follow along as he read.

The crowd of colorfully dressed and quite differently type people looked at him in excitement. He started to read the words into the microphone. He got lost in his own story. His voice was strong as he started to read out loud for all his fans in the small space. His voice was loud through the room.

He read:

"Gabriel Fairchild? Is there a Gabriel Fairchild here?" The rotund black woman with the leopard print colored glasses perched on her large nose called into the large room. The glasses were held to her head with a short gold chain. She yelled the name into the room again, too quickly for social acceptance. Gabe looked up from where he sat and raised his hand like a second grader being called on to answer a math problem on the blackboard.

" Ri-right here," Gabe stuttered quietly. The woman saw him and motioned for him to approach the desk she was sitting behind. Tall, bullet-proof glass separated her from the rest of the waiting room. Gabe didn't take his eyes off of the woman's face as he shuffled towards her. He held in his hand a perfectly clean and crisp manila folder. He gripped it tightly as he approached the loud woman behind the glass.

She thought the man walking towards her window looked scared. He felt the fear that she could see on his face. She looked him up and down, noticing the lanky, greasy blonde hair falling to his shoulders under a flat twill hat. His clothes looked dirty and slept in. She couldn't place an age on the man behind the large, black horn rimmed glasses. He looked a little homeless. She mentally shrugged his appearance off. She had seen

170

hundreds of people approach her desk with the same look on their face. There was wildness in their eyes. She understood that all too well.

"Please present your claim form and signed ticket to the man standing there," she told the nervous man and pointed. They both watched as Jose, the over large security guard, approached the man, his hand held out, other hand unconsciously hovering over the black pistol on his hip.

Gabe flinched and looked over at the large, dark man approaching him. He held the manila folder tighter to his chest. Gabe looked back at the women behind the glass. And then looked back and forth between the two employees several times. Jose saw this and smiled. He, too, had seen this very scene played out many times. He looked into the homeless man's eyes and smiled again.

"It's okay sir. We are just going to verify the claim form. You can sit back down while we take it in the back." Jose had often had to placate nervous, panicked people in this man's situation. It always started out tense here. The celebrations came later.

Gabe handed the security guard the manila folder. He didn't take his eyes off of the folder as Jose walked with it to a solidly built wooden door, with a keypad next to it. Jose pressed in a quick series of numbers, and the door opened for him. Jose walked though, and the door shut behind him with a loud bang. Gabe flinched again. No one looking at him could tell it was all an act.

Gabe nervously sat down and wondered at the life that was going to unfold when the contents of the manila folder were analyzed by someone unseen behind that big door.

He reached up and made sure people were looking at him as he scratched the fake wig under his flat cap. He looked around him at the other people sitting nervously

171

*around him. His glasses had no lenses in them, and Gabe's
perfect eyes saw the real emotions on the faces of other
people waiting for their winnings. He felt no such
emotions. He knew exactly what he was doing.*

*He had planned this day for so long. And it had
finally happened. His bald head itched under the wig, and
he dug his fingers into the fake hair once again,
scratching his head as he absentmindedly fantasized
about what he would do first with the millions of dollars
he had just won.*

Ben stopped reading and looked up at the crowd,
seeing them leaning towards him as the words of the first
chapter of his newest book bounced around the tightly
packed room. He felt pride at knowing he had everyone's
rapt attention. And so, he kept reading for the fans.

About a half hour later, he sat behind a short table
the bookstore staff had set up where the lectern had stood.
As fans and readers lined up to get their copies of his books
signed, he looked around in-between fans setting their
copies in front of him. He knew several eyes were on him,
watching his every movement, watching his mouth as he
thanked his fans for reading.

But he felt like he was being watched. By more than
just his fans waiting for their minute or two of time with
him. He felt eyes on him, and a tightness between his
shoulder blades disturbed him.

He wanted to wrap this up quickly and get back to
the hotel.

Much later that evening, after he had signed
hundreds of copies of his books, and had walked back,
alone, to the hotel, he changed into the sweater and jeans
he had packed just for his walks. The first park he wanted

to visit he knew was too far to walk to. It was across the city, near the water surrounding Alcatraz.

So, he called down to the front desk, where a different voice than the woman from this morning answered. He vaguely remembered her nice teeth. He asked for a car from the man who had answered this time, and the new front desk attendant informed him that the car would be waiting in the covered valet area in five minutes.

Ben took a bottle of water from the small refrigerator in the living area of his hotel suite and headed back downstairs. The music in the elevator reminded him of his dream again. In the busyness of the day, he had almost forgotten about the dream.

It all came back to him as he exited the elevator and walked through the lobby, to his waiting car. It was a black Lincoln sedan this time. He got into the back seat, as the driver held the door open for him. The driver quietly closed the door and walked around to the driver's side. The car bounced a little as the large man got behind the wheel. He looked into the rearview mirror at Ben and asked in a British accent where Ben would like to go. Ben gave his directions, and the car pulled out into the early evening traffic.

It was silent for the entire car ride. Ben felt tired, as he was on East Coast time, but he needed to walk. Needed to clear his mind from both the frustrating dream, and the feeling of otherworldly eyes on him at the book signing. He thought of both, simultaneously, as the car drove towards the Golden Gate Bridge.

Pulling off of 101 right before the bridge traffic, the car pulled into a busy park, and Ben could see his destination through the trees. He placed his now empty water bottle in a cup holder behind the front seats. He asked the driver to wait one hour for him, and as the driver

173

nodded, Ben exited the car and walked towards a tall, rotund structure in the middle of the park. He could smell bread baking. He thought it was sourdough. It made him happy and nostalgic for no reason.

Walking through the very large Roman pillars surrounding the tall structure in the middle of the park, Ben marveled at the architecture, as he usually did. The columns were very large and made a tunnel towards the Palace of Fine Arts at the middle of the park.

That rotunda was surrounded on one whole side by a shallow lagoon, and Ben spied white swans floating in the tepid water. Several plants flourished in the dark water, and Ben looked around at couples and groups of people enjoying the dusk. No one seemed in a hurry. Everything was slow. He smiled.

He walked towards the very tall rotunda of the Palace and saw that he was alone as he walked under the bright dome. There was an echo to the space. He looked up at the ceiling of the dome, seeing the golden colored honeycomb structure made from white marble. It was breathtaking.

Ben walked to the very middle of the tall structure, keeping his eyes on the beautiful ceiling high above him. And as he noticed the short, beautiful statues high up on the sides, he saw that they were all the Archangels.

He had not known about the statues from his reading of the place before his trip.

They surrounded him, all looking down, and as he spun in a circle, looking at each of the statues, his hearing went out, like he had slowly dunked his head underwater.

He couldn't hear any sounds of the city, or people walking around the structure. The echo was gone. He closed his eyes as he felt, rather than saw, the fog gathering around him.

When he opened his eyes he saw who had been watching him at the bookstore, and who had sent the dream that had bothered him all afternoon.

He knew without words the truth of both things.

"Hello Chamuel," Ben said with a smile. "I knew I'd see you here. It's been a long time."

The tall, hovering Archangel looked down on Ben from the middle of the brightly lit rotunda. Pink tinted fog rolled around both of them. Ben knew that everything outside of the fog had stopped. Or maybe it was the other way around. Maybe everything inside the fog was what was stopped.

He felt the pressure that had been inside of him since waking from the dream dissipate.

"GREETINGS BENJAMIN. I'VE COME AGAIN TO GIVE THE CHOICE." The archangel's multi-chambered voice boomed in Ben's mind.

"Easy, Angel. Can you change to the small man you were before? My neck hurts looking up at you like that," Ben said.

In front of his eyes, just as before in his mother's room, the large, floating being seemed to shrink down into a dark-skinned older man, splendidly dressed, and smiling a beautiful smile.

"Okay, why do you keep coming into my life like this, Chamuel? Why me?" Ben asked.

"Oh, Benjamin, do you really think that once God has you in His View, you can get away so easily? You have been watched. And the journey that you have been on for so long, is not at an end my friend. You must, once again, make The Choice," the angel said while looking deep into Ben's eyes.

Ben looked away. He looked up at the Palace once again. The Angel stood, patiently, in the center of the rotunda, watching Ben's every movement. He tried to ignore the command from the angel.

"Beautiful spot for meeting me. Did you pick this yourself? Or do you just appear wherever you like?" Ben tried to change the subject.

They both looked up at the rotunda, the small statues of all of the Archangels, the splendor of the setting. Both seemed moved by the beauty of the evening, and the stillness within the rolling fog.

Ben felt an ease coming off of the angel, like he was standing with his best friend, completely at home. Ben assumed that was an effect of being in the presence of an actual angel.

"There are nodes, if you will, on this world, which attract travelers. Call them Crossroads, Benjamin. This is but one such Crossroad. God led you here, and I was sent to give the Choice. Now, unless you have any more questions, I have things to be about. Please Choose. Life. Or Love."

Ben looked the small man deep in the eyes. He smiled wistfully back. He was not one to be controlled. Not when he was a kid. And certainly not now. He saw no reason in it, and seeing no motivation to change his choice, he waited for Chamuel to ask him to make the choice once again.

The Being smiled and reached out his arms in questioning. Ben smiled in return.

And then he made his Choice, when it was given, once again.

Chapter 20

"No, sing with me! I love your voice," Gwen shouted over the radio as the wind blew through the windows of Stewart's SUV.

Stewart looked at her and grinned, stupidly. He looked back at the road in front of him. But he did not sing along with Gwen. The road was I-95. They were driving north.

Gwen sat in the black leather passenger seat next to him, her wild red hair blowing all around her heart shaped face from the open window next to her. She spat out a hunk of her beautiful, shiny red curls, grinned, and started singing along with the Bruce Springsteen song playing quite loudly from the stereo of the large vehicle.

She has every right to be happy and let loose a little, Stewart thought to himself. He smiled inwardly again. And she was finally his.

Two years ago he had quietly, over dinner, told her in a very scientific, matter-of-fact way, just how he felt about her. How he had felt about her for almost a decade, he admitted. She never saw it coming.

She knew that he had been a self-professed bachelor. He was forty-one years old and had never had a serious relationship. He grimaced as he thought about it. He was a slave to his work. To the science.

And then Gwen came sweeping into his drudgery-style life, like a bright fire, exposing his shadows. He worked side by side with her in the labs for years. Smelling her light perfume, seeing her beautiful face every single day.

He had been in agony over her for so long.

Even meeting her parents every time they had come to DC to visit. He liked her father immensely. But he didn't think that Daniel Murphy, Sr. liked him as much after Gwen informed her family that she and Stewart were together.

Stewart was a bit older than her, and while she had been his employee, Gwen's parents saw him as a mentor, a protector of sort. He could imagine their unease when his intentions had become romantic.

But over the last two years, things had been smoothed out, anger had turned to acceptance, and all was well with the world.

Stewart thought over the reason for this vacation. Looking back over at the love of his life, hair whipped around by the mid-Atlantic wind blowing in the cab of his

SUV, he was overcome with gratitude. They had come so far.

And then she had made the final discovery, only three months prior. Their decade-long struggle wasn't for nothing. Not now.

So, here they were, released from the labs for two precious weeks, and she had wanted to share her love of New England with him. He, too, wanted to share something with her.

Gwen, too, was happy. As she sang her heart out to "Born in the USA," she felt peace, giddiness, happiness, and relief. All rolled into one.

She looked past the strands of her red hair blowing in her face to the trees outside the car. Whizzing by her open window, the sound the trees made as they flew by the speeding car was like a train, bound for heaven. Her mind drifted to deeper things. The beliefs that she had recently started studying.

When your career life, your love life, and your family life were all humming along nicely, you started looking to your faith life, she thought.

She stopped singing, letting the next song on the 80s station play without comment. She always listened to this station when driving. "80s on 8." She loved it. And she secretly waited impatiently to hear Debbie Harry's voice sing through her speakers. But Stewart didn't know about that.

She had just finished reading the essay titled "Nature" by Ralph Waldo Emerson. The juxtaposition of finding deeper faith in nature, as well as our internal power, spoke to Gwen's intellect.

So, when Stewart had asked her a couple of weeks ago where she wanted to vacation now that there was a lull in the lab work, she didn't hesitate. New England.

She hadn't been back north of New York since college. And now, more than reliving memories, she wanted to go where Transcendentalism was born. Ever since her experiences in Colorado, years ago, she knew that there was a deeper meaning, a much larger world, then she, even in her genius, knew about.

And, as she looked over at Stewart, driving with both hands on the wheel, at 10 and 2, she smiled. He made her happy. She wasn't delusional enough to think that Stewart was the perfect man for her. But he was a good man. He was smart as hell, gentle, kind.

No, he didn't know anything about classic cars, or how to change a tire. Her father had instilled those qualities in her, to look for in a man.

But Stewart was always prepared. He always had a plan. She wasn't intimidated by Stewart. He was a good partner. But sometimes he was too damn gentle.

She smiled anyway.

She wasn't alone, and she shared so much with the man. Her work meant everything to her, and he was one of the biggest parts of that. So, she was happy.

Soon, they were driving up the New Jersey Turnpike on I-95. They would get up to Boston before they stopped for the night. She was excited to show Stewart her memories at MIT.

He had earned his education across the country at Stanford. Which was why he was a little starstruck every time he got to spend time with her little brother, the breakout football star of Stanford.

But Stewart was still a brilliant man. He had struggled for so long in the world of theoretical energy science before she had been hired to help him. Together, they had discovered the answers that the world had needed for so long. She briefly chided herself as she thought that thought.

It had really been the author, in a random book he had written years ago, that had ushered in the critical last steps. That fact still rubbed her the wrong way. And the fact that she still waited excitedly for each of his books to come out for sale upset her as well.

But none of that mattered. She was right here, right now. And she was happy. Why did she keep repeating that thought, she wondered, like she was trying to convince herself? But she WAS happy.

The road trip was going along smoothly. They stopped at a roadside relief area for a bathroom break and to get lunch. Stewart had ordered an oversized piece of pizza, and Gwen, uncharacteristically, ordered a hamburger and large fries. She was going to enjoy this trip, damn it.

She drank down a large Dr. Pepper, smiling at her boyfriend, as he tried to eat the large slice of pizza without folding it like a damn American should know how to do. She laughed and explained how to eat it cleanly.

He grinned at her sheepishly, folded the triangle of amazingness in half, and took a large bite. She winked at him and looked around at all the travelers moving around their small table in the food court of the travel stop.

So many people, she thought, who needed what they had discovered in her lab in Washington DC.

Clean, abundant energy. For everyone. All over the world.

And it would be cheap. No government of the world would be able to control this science. There would be no taxes on this.

She was excited at the prospect of ushering in a brand new world. And as she thought of those possibilities, pushing fries into her mouth in a very unladylike manner, she thought back on her earlier thoughts of how this whole "life" thing worked.

She knew in her own research and reading of very old doctrines, she was on to something in that field as well. If she told anyone her thoughts, they would marvel that she had to have so many deep things going on at the same time.

Well, it makes me, me, she thought. The fries were wonderful. She reached for more salt. Damn it, she thought, she deserved to enjoy herself.

A short time later, as the SUV bounced over the George Washington Bridge, moving into the borough's surrounding New York City, she looked out the side of her window at the tall, gray skyscrapers of the city across the river. She suddenly remembered the last time she had come to New York.

It had been to get some answers from Ben Reeves.

She quickly shut down that mode of thought. She was NOT going to think of Ben Reeves on her first vacation with Stewart. Stewart deserved her undivided attention.

So, she took her eyes off of the city passing by on the right side of the bridge and looked over at her man. Driving through the traffic, hands at 10 and 2. She sighed.

He was handsome, she thought as he carefully wove the large vehicle through the traffic. They didn't have to talk. She enjoyed the quiet between them. It was so easy with this man.

Later, as they passed out of New York State and into Connecticut, she fell asleep. And dreamed.

She sat in an old-fashioned library. She could smell the dusty and yellowed pages of the leather bound books around her. In her lap, she was holding a heavy book. The script on the pages was faded, and in a font she didn't recognize. It looked ancient. She closed it and held it in her lap.

She sat in a very comfortable red leather chair. She placed the heavy book on the table next to her and stood. She started to look around at the room she was in. Standing in the middle, she looked up and saw floor after floor of books. They went so high she couldn't see the top. The room was a tall cylinder. Each floor of overstuffed bookshelves above her were held back with black, wrought iron, waist-high barriers. The iron was shaped in very interesting curlicues and formed pictures. She saw running foxes in the grating. Children playing. A hunting scene in one. It was beautiful, she thought, as she looked up as far as she could see.

The room was completely round, and the books rose around her on all sides. She did not see a way out of the room. She looked down and saw that she stood on hard, wide, wooden flooring. The wide planks were gray with age, and worn smooth by countless feet, she surmised. She still felt at peace, even though she was trapped in the tall room.

She heard a scratching sound and spun around. There was an ancient phonograph. She hadn't noticed it before. The large, bell-shaped tube started producing sound from the record spinning on the flat surface below it. The song was haunting. She knew this song, she thought. She couldn't help but to start swaying to the melody.

The notes were crystal clear. "Sound of Silence." There were no words, but she knew them by heart. It sounded to her that it was being played on a five-chord zither as well. It was mournful.

She closed her eyes and swayed to the chilly music. She felt the skirts of the long, flowing dress she wore brushing her naked legs underneath. As the notes intensified, and repeated on the refrain, she opened her eyes and stopped dancing.

She had an urge to look inside a book. A magnetic need. A hunger. The music drove her.

She hurriedly walked over to the closest bookshelf, stacked high with large, ancient tomes. She wondered, fleetingly, if she could lift the heavy books. The music behind her intensified in volume. The notes were ringing though the round room until she felt the books would start falling from the shelves above her.

She reached for a red book. The spine was divided into thirds by thick, golden lines. She ran her hands over the raised lines. She couldn't read the title. Or the author. She could feel a frustration start building from not knowing what was happening, what she was feeling, or why the music was so damn loud.

She pulled the heavy book from the shelf and tried to pick it up. It fell out of her hands and landed on the gray floor with a loud thunk. She furrowed her brow and reached down to open the cover. As she flipped through the yellowing, heavy pages, her frustration grew.

Every page was a picture of two people, close together, holding hands. They were in the forefront of the picture, and there was a colorful background.

But every single picture was fuzzy. Out of focus. As if she were looking at it without her glasses. She squinted, but still could only make out the outlines of the pair in the colorful pictures. But no details.

She could tell that one of the figures in the forefront of the pictures was a lot taller than the other, but that was the only detail she could make out. She flipped through every page, and every page was the same. The picture never changed.

She reached up and pulled down a black-spine colored book on another shelf. It, too, fell to the floor. Dust puffed up from beneath it. She hurriedly opened the cover and quickly searched all of the pages.

It was identical to the other book. Every page a blurry, full page-sized picture of a couple, standing close together, features completely blocked to her eyes, one figure taller than the other. She screamed in frustration and started pulling down book after book, all with the same results.

There was no truth! There was no knowledge! Nothing to learn.

As the books fell around her, the notes of the song playing on the phonograph reached a crescendo, each note a ringing staccato, loud in her ears, the room around her shaking.

Books started falling all around her, a rain of books. Each falling open to the same blurred-out image on every yellow page. She felt like Alice in Wonderland, things getting curiouser and curiouser.

She screamed in frustration, grabbing her head with both hands and came awake with another scream, soundless in her throat.

She jerked in the passenger seat of Stewart's SUV. He was humming to an Enya song playing on the radio. Another song she recognized but didn't particularly like. She was confused where she was, at first, but settled when Stewart reached over and put a hand on her jean-covered leg.

"You were snoring honey. I didn't want to wake you. We are almost to Boston." Gwen wiped drool off of her chin, and smiled at Stewart shyly.

She looked out of the window at the darkening sky. The lights of the city twinkled in front of the vehicle. She was coming home, she thought.

She closed her eyes, remembering the dream in extreme detail, and felt her heartbeats slowly settle down. She was unnerved for some reason.

It had just been a dream, she thought.

The next day, after they left the quaint little hotel in downtown Boston, they drove northwest. They had plans to go to Concord, and then onto Salem. Make a circle through the day. They were both towns that she had fallen in love with.

She especially wanted to show Stewart the Alcott home in Concord, called the Orchard House, as well as the Old Manse. She remembered the poem that Nathaniel Hawthorne's wife had scratched on a back window over her child's rocking bassinet. She had used the diamond in her wedding ring to make the inscription.

Gwen had never shared that with anyone else, and she hoped that Stewart would appreciate it. Appreciate the history and the fact that these people had just been regular people as well. But they had changed the world in their own way.

The green trees around them were full of leaves in the summer heat. She wished they had made this trip in the fall. There was a better feeling to the area later in the year, she thought. A beautiful dying out of the heat and joy of summer, and a mournful moving into the cold months.

The wind would change directions, coming out of the Arctic Circle. Heavy snows would be right around the corner, and the magic was palpable.

But she would take what she could, she thought, as they drove into the small community of Concord.

They stopped at the visitor's center downtown and found pamphlets of the notable things to see. Museums, eateries, historical monuments.

This small town held such an overwhelming history of change and vision. It was like all of the greatest American thinkers were situated in the small black hole of Concord, Massachusetts. She loved the place.

She felt her mind expand in the New England sunshine.

As they pulled into the parking area of the Old Manse, she thought, not for the first time, that the old buildings were smaller than she thought they should be, to hold so much history.

Looking at the vulgarity of parking lots, tourist signs, and information booths, she wanted, once again, to have seen it a hundred years before. When it was a home, rather than a museum.

She sighed as they walked up the steps to the old home. It was still lovely she thought, grabbing Stewart's hand, and walking into the cool interior of the home. She spied the gardens to the left of the gray-clapboard home. She smiled at the bright colors of flowers and plants.

She had been there several times, and as the guide explained about the fire buckets hanging near the side stairs, she let go of Stewart's hand, told him that she wanted to walk around the monuments in the rear of the property, and that he should enjoy the tour of the home.

He agreed, told her to be careful, and turned back to the guide explaining about how each citizen of the town was a fireman of the time. If a home or barn was burning, every citizen would grab the metal fire buckets and join the brigade.

Gwen walked back into the midday sunshine. She walked around the side of the Manse and started down the path towards the North Bridge.

She knew the history by heart. How the "shot heard around the world" happened on that bridge. How the war for freedom from the British started right here, on this hallowed ground.

She looked around and realized she was unusually alone on the property. The times she had visited before, Minuteman Park was always packed with people and children. But, as she walked towards the river, she was completely alone.

Odd, she thought.

She stopped at the tall monument before the bridge. She read the inscription, words from Emerson, dedicating this site as a historical relic of American freedom.

She looked around at the tall, green trees, heard the sound of the water rushing under the suspended bridge. It wasn't the original bridge. But it was close.

She put her hand on the tall stone monument and said a quick dirge under her breath. It was a tradition of hers, and only hers.

She walked onto the short, wooden bridge. She stopped in the exact middle and breathed in the light breeze. The smells of the trees, the heat of the sun, the chirping of the birds. She didn't hear the sound of traffic from Monument Street behind her. The trees were thick around the river.

She looked down at the slowly moving water, seeing her reflection looking back up at her. The blue of the sky over her head was bright on the surface of the dark green, slowly moving water.

As she looked at her own reflection, red hair spilling down around her face, the blue of the sky disappeared. Her hearing became muffled. She looked up in fear. It was like she had stuck cotton in her ears.

She looked around quickly. No one in sight. She held up her hands to her ears, expecting to feel something.

As she looked down at the wide wooden planks of the bridge, wondering what had happened to both her sight and hearing, she saw the tendrils of pink fog gathering around her feet.

Suddenly she felt okay.

She looked up, turned around in the middle of the North Bridge, and he was hovering right in front of her. She smiled. The Archangel smiled as well.

"Chamuel. I knew I would see you again one day. It's been a long time." Her memories went back to the stone castle far away in both time and distance.

"DAUGHTER, I HAVE COME TO GIVE YOU THE CHOICE."

The words echoed once again in her mind.

This time, she thought to herself, she was ready. She blurted out her answer before the angel could change, or speak, or move.

"I choose love Chamuel. I choose love. With all of my heart," she said excitedly. Her thoughts went to Stewart.

"PARALLEL CHOICES MUST BE MADE. BUT YOUR CHOICE HAS BEEN MADE. WE MUST ALL LIVE WITH THE CONSEQUENCES OF ALL OF OUR CHOICES," he said without moving his angelic lips.

Gwen shaded her eyes as she looked up at the large being, white wings outstretched. She didn't understand that last statement, but she had made her Choice. She was ready, she thought. Oh, she was so ready.

Her hearing returned in a rush. The birds, the wind, the running water. It all came back suddenly.

The world started moving again, and the pink fog was gone along with the Archangel.

She smiled and skipped back to the Old Manse. Her heart light. This time, she hadn't even felt the lightheadedness she had the first time she had met the Angel.

She smiled as she passed a small family, walking the opposite way towards the bridge she had just left.

All was well in the world, she thought.

All was well in her world.

Chapter 21

Gwen sat at a small table, across from Stewart, inside one of her favorite diners close to Lexington, MA. She was telling him more of her history in the area.

About how her small group of friends from college would travel this area, stopping at all the small roadside delis, antique shops, and other New England oddities. He laughed at all the right places as she told the stories, completely comfortable. He ate delicately, cleanly.

Sometimes she felt like a pig in front of Stewart, but it was a sweet feeling. He was a really good man. And, thinking back on the choice she had just made with Chamuel, she was glad to be here with this man, sharing parts of her soul with him.

He understood, was patient and wise, and seemed to enjoy her. Her heart was glad.

They drove east into Salem in the middle of the afternoon. It was as beautiful as she remembered.

She had given Stewart some ideas of things to see, but he surprised her. He told her that he had set up a little thing, and he wanted to show her something. She was shocked. Stewart was not a spontaneous man. She liked the fact that he always had a plan.

So, she agreed to go along with him, as he expertly drove the narrow streets of the town she loved best from her early years in the area. She constantly looked over at the man behind the wheel as he drove the car, and it drove her crazy, wondering what he had up his sleeve. He just smiled and patted her leg.

They drove right past the Witch's House and Museum in downtown Salem, as she tried to point it out to him and get him to stop.

He just shook his head and smiled a secret smile. They drove past several of her favorite pubs in the downtown area. And then she figured out where they were going as he pulled onto Derby Street.

They crossed over the busy Hawthorne Boulevard. She saw it up ahead.

The House of Seven Gables.

She knew their destination before he pulled into the small parking lot next to 115 Derby Street. She was so excited. Stewart must have seen the Hawthorne book in her home. She read it at least once a year.

She looked over at him, appreciating the man she loved. He smiled, told her to move her butt, and they walked into the well-lit reception area. She loved this place.

She could see water through the windows.

But Stewart didn't stop in the front of the visitor's center.

He didn't stop to read the history of the home, or of the Hawthorne story.

He took her by the hand and moved to the rear of the visitor's center, through the heavy glass back doors to the courtyard.

Many times she tried to get him to stop moving, so she could explain an important part of the site to him.

But he was driven. He just pulled her along.

Stepping back out into the sunlight at the rear of the site, she saw the well.

It stood in the middle of the courtyard that separated the House of Seven Gables from the ancestry home of Nathaniel Hawthorne, which had been moved from further down the street to this location.

The courtyard was shaded, and quiet.

This was her favorite part of the grounds. The covered stone well stood silently in the middle of the brick-floored courtyard. She looked around at the short, stunted trees that surrounded the small space. The trees always looked sinister and spooky to her.

At Halloween, this courtyard was the site of amazing parties. She had been to two of them herself, dressed as a character from a different classical book each time.

She ran her hands down the banister leading from the visitor's center down to the courtyard.

Stewart pulled her down the short flight of stairs. She wondered at his oddness. He was acting weird.

Stewart took her out of her mental wispiness. The courtyard was empty. Again, she felt out of place due to being alone in areas that were usually always full of people.

Stewart took her by the hand and led her under the trellis surrounding the well. Gwen could smell the harbor. The sun was bright, and the courtyard didn't hold its normal spookiness for her.

But Stewart was acting strangely.

He led her next to the well. He turned to her, looking at her face. They were of the same height. It had bothered her in the past, but today it was sweet, she thought. There was a buzzing in her ears.

She almost didn't catch Stewart's words.

"Gwendolyn Marie Murphy, I have loved you from the first day we met. You swept into my peaceful life like a forest fire. I am a better man because of you," he said to her, looking into her bright eyes.

She gulped loudly, finally understanding what was happening. Her heart soared, and she thought back to the bridge with the Angel. This was happening a lot faster than she imagined, she thought to herself as she watched Stewart's lips move.

Her mind was in a million places.

"I agree, Stewart," she began. But he put a finger to her lips, quieting her.

"Gwen, it would be the most wonderful thing to have ever happened to me..." he started, as he slowly lowered himself to one knee.

He held one of her hands with his. With the other, he reached into his shirt pocket and pulled out a diamond ring. She recognized it immediately. It had been his mother's, and his grandmother's, both women she had met and adored.

She was surprised that they had given Stewart the ring that had been in his family for so long. She was speechless. The moment seemed to stretch forever, and she didn't want the mood to break.

She closed her eyes as he said the rest of the proposal.

"...if you would be my wife. Would you marry me? Please?" he finished. He was happy that he didn't stutter.

She was shocked. So many things went through her mind as she looked down at his handsome face. But she was sure. Very sure.

"Yes," she said.

Excitement swept over his face, looking up at her.

Stewart stood, wrapped his arms around her, and pulled her in to kiss her. It was so sweet, she thought. She pulled back from his kiss as he put the ring on her finger. It fit perfectly.

She looked back into his handsome face as he looked boldly into her green eyes. Brown eyes shining into bright green.

A comparison of sorts.

The depths of souls straining for recognition, falling short of equality. But it was okay to them both. He smiled. She smiled back.

At her answer, she heard a commotion all around her. The house staff was carrying and moving down a wrought iron table, two chairs.

A young man swept a white cloth tablecloth over the table and plates and glasses soon followed.

Gwen was so impressed with the planning that Stewart must have put into this. As everything was settled, the newly engaged couple sat down over white wine, charcuterie, and shy looks at each other.

But in her stomach, she knew the truth. He did not look at her the way he was supposed to. The way she had always fantasized about.

She mentally shrugged, squared her shoulders as was her way, and chose to be Stewart's wife.

Chapter 22

"Well, what am I supposed to do about that? We weren't exactly close, Steven," Ben said into his cell phone while he was on a walk around his neighborhood.

He was up to eight miles a day, and usually could walk that in under two hours.

"Ben, listen, he didn't have any other family. After his wife died a few years ago, the only people he knew were you and his nurse, what's her name...it's here somewhere. Oh yeah, Suzann. Anyway, he left you everything. Not that you need it, but it's all there. The firm has a board of directors, and last I heard, they will happily buy you out."

Steven was a partner in his grandfather's law firm, and Ben had used his services several times in the last decade in intellectual copyright matters.

"Steve, in the last ten years, I have seen him maybe five times, total. And it was always a guilt trip about how he didn't have any family or friends and it was just so sad. I don't know why he wanted anything to do with me."

Ben was trying not to breathe heavily into the phone as he got past the five-mile mark. His left knee acted up every time he walked now, and the orthopedic brace that his doctor had given him helped through most of his walks. But he knew that stairs were the worst part now.

He was distracting himself. He didn't want to feel bad now that Samuel Lemons was dead. He still had the funeral to get through, later in the week.

"I don't know buddy, but it's a lot. You need to figure out what you want to do. I have most of the papers here, but Mark Brown has the rest. When Sam retired, Mark took over the helm, and he will be the one to tell you what the firm wants to offer for your share."

"Alright, tell Mark that I will be at the funeral on Saturday at St. Patrick's. We can talk after or on Monday. But I have a deadline coming up and this is a big book for me. I can't dilly dally," Ben said.

He heard his lawyer snicker.

The knee really did hurt. And he knew he didn't want to think about how he would be the only person at Samuel E. Lemons' funeral who had not worked for the old man.

Thank goodness no one had asked him to say anything about his grandfather, Ben thought to himself.

He had no idea what he would say.

"Alright man. Hey, by the way, I got a call yesterday about you. I'm still your attorney of record for the books that you did for Every House. Including the energy one, what was it called?"

"*Eve's Plight*," Ben answered.

"That's right. Anyway, this was from some guy in DC. Says he works for the government, and that they needed to speak to you about that particular book.

197

Something to do with giving you credit for something. Anyway, he wouldn't be specific, and I told him that I would put you in touch. I wrote his home number down here somewhere." Ben could hear papers shuffling around on the man's desk. He was a notorious packrat.

"Ahh, yes. Guy's name was Stewart Haggerty. Works for the Department of Energy." Steve then gave a quick phone number.

Ben asked him to text it and hung up the phone.

That was a weird conversation if he had ever had one, he thought to himself as he wiped his forehead with the workout towel he always had slung over a shoulder during his daily walks.

Well, not the weirdest call he had received this week.

The first weird call informed him of his grandfather's death two days prior. A worker at the hospital, or at least he thought the man had worked for the hospital, had phoned him while he was working in the back office of the home he kept expanding. The room he had added on to his house with the big bay windows that looked out at the ocean.

While he got the news, he had looked out of the big paned windows at the clear view of the beach and sparkling blue water. He was so glad that he had had all those tall pine trees removed a couple of years back.

Now his view was unobstructed.

He had hung up without saying much and went right back to working. He had felt bad for that, just as he felt bad now for not grieving, or really thinking about Sam. He had told the truth to Steve about how much he had seen his grandfather ever since he graduated from high school. It was a shame that had grown over with scars so that it became a memory, rather than something he had to deal with now.

The second phone call he had received this week was from his new publisher. The editing and marketing departments had joined forces and had wanted him to go a different direction with his newest book, but he still had not written one word of it. He was stuck on how to start.

It was a bit out of his wheelhouse of heroic love stories, with strong male and female characters. But he had never had writer's block before, and it unnerved him. He didn't want to deal with it right now.

What he did have to deal with was calling Stewart back. He knew exactly who the man was.

He had read an article online two years previously that the man had married Gwen Murphy, the scientist who had caused so much craziness in his own life.

The article had large, colorful pictures of the wedding, and he couldn't help but feel a lump in his throat as he saw her bright red curls, done up in a bun, and the tight white dress. She was laughing at something the man she had married said in one particular photo, and Ben felt gentle satisfaction that the man was the same height as her.

It was just another thing that Ben put out of his mind. She had been a pill. Good luck to Stewart, he had thought at the time.

And now he had to call the man back and try and sound normal.

Ben kept walking despite his knee and turned the corner on the street on which he lived. And as he walked around the large juniper bushes at the end of the long driveway leading to his large home, he saw a familiar black SUV parked in his driveway, behind his own Ford. He smiled and hurried the last few steps home. The damn knee was burning when he walked through his red front door.

"Mars, you asshat, what are you doing here..." Ben started. He stopped the vulgar language when he walked into his living room and his longtime best friend looked up from the couch where he was sitting next to his wife, Jane. Jane was holding the baby. Ben smiled an apology at her, and heard rustling coming from the back bedroom.

"Is Benji in the back?" He asked. Mars just nodded, smiling himself.

Ben rushed to the back, and grabbed the young boy coming out of the guest room where Ben knew he had been playing with Ben's model airplane collection. As Ben wrapped the tall four-year-old in a big bear hug, the redheaded boy squealed with delight. Ben was incredibly close to his young namesake. He had already set up a trust fund for the boy's college. Ben regretted not having his own children by now, but Benji was a suitable substitute. He needed to remember to call Steve and set up the trust for little Jessie. She was already almost a year old. He felt like a bad uncle.

"Alright you two, get in here!" Jane called from the front room.

"Yes ma 'm!" the two Bens answered her. They smiled their secret smile at each other.

Ben carried his small godson back into the living room and deposited him in his father's lap. He told everyone he had to take a quick shower, but he wouldn't be more than five minutes.

Showered, changed, and hair combed, Ben walked back into the living room, and took the sleeping little girl into his arms. Jane smiled at him and kissed him on the cheek. He handed the baby back to her mother after kissing her softly.

They had not seen each other in almost a month. That was the longest time spent apart for all of them since Mars had married Jane five years earlier.

"How was the trip? Did you bring me a present?" Ben asked with a grin.

Mars sighed, looked over at his lovely wife sitting beside him, and grinned. "Told you he would ask," he said.

Jane just smiled and reached into her purse. She had to juggle the sleeping baby in her arms, but her husband soon helped. She pulled out a small white box and handed it to Ben.

"Yes!" Ben said. "I love presents."

Little Benji came over to where his "Uncle Ben" sat on the opposite couch in the bright room and climbed up into his lap. "Open it, 'nkle Ben," the boy said.

Ben smiled at the boy, shifted him in his lap, and opened the small white box. It looked a little like the small boxes that ring boxes would come in.

He moved a piece of white tissue paper out of the way and looked down on a flat, slightly twisted piece of chrome-colored metal. It was incredibly shiny, and Ben knew he would see his reflection in it if he held it up to his eyes. He curiously touched it with one finger, moving it slightly, and looked back up at his best friends in the whole world in confusion.

"Umm, thanks for the, umm, piece of metal?" he said.

"You educated idiot," Mars grinned at him.

"It's a piece of a famous sword worn by Robert the Bruce in his campaign against the Crown," Jane answered for her husband.

"There's a certificate of authenticity under the foam," she pointed.

Ben was impressed. He had found out years earlier that he was of Scottish decent, on his father's side of the family, and since he learned that, he had become obsessed with the history of the small country. It also was one way to feel close to the family that he had never met or heard from. He hadn't reached out to the long-lost family either.

He knew that his biological father had passed away years earlier, but that wasn't as important to Ben as where he had come from before his crap-ass father had put Ben inside of his mother and split, leaving them both.

"Holy cow, guys, that's amazing!" Ben said. "Thank you so much!"

"Welcome!" Benji screamed into his eye. Ben had to wipe his eyes from the boy's exuberance.

Ben squeezed his godson and put him on the couch next to him, letting him play with the piece of metal. He made sure it wasn't sharp before handing it to the young redhead.

"Tell me about the trip. Tell me everything." Ben looked over at the two closest people in his life. He was immensely happy they were home. He had missed them terribly.

Ben listened to them both give details about their month-long work trip over to Europe, and especially the time they had spent on the Emerald Isle and the UK. Both Mars and Jane worked for the UN as environmental scientists. They both worked tirelessly to change the world's policies on the increasingly serious global warming crisis.

He had twice visited the Western European region that the pair had traveled to with the kids, but he wanted to go back. He had felt drawn to the area both times. The beautiful couple sitting across from him had been a part of a month-long summit for policy changes concerning the non-decomposing plastic trash in both of the largest oceans in the world. Something about the warm water current, or something.

Ben wasn't as educated in their passions as they both were.

He tried listening to the warnings of both over the years, but he lost interest.

The baby started fussing. Ben offered to take her, but Jane told him to talk to Mars, and she would just go feed little Jessie.

She stood up with the bundle of pink blankets and walked into the kitchen. Both men watched her walk away. Mars was more in love with his wife every day, and Ben loved her for being the perfect woman for his best friend.

"So, what's new? You seem off."

Mars looked over at his decades-long best friend with concern.

"Nothing. The new book is in a jam. I'm having a simple case of writer's block. Oh, and my grandfather died," Ben answered honestly.

"Mr. Lemons died!" Mars said. "When?"

"On Monday."

"You okay? How are you feeling?" Mars asked.

"I'm fine. He left me everything. Pretty much doubles my worth. But I don't need it. Thinking up a way to use it for something meaningful, in his name," Ben said wistfully.

"You can give it to me!" Mars smiled. Ben ignored his comment.

"Also, I almost forgot. Do you remember Gwen Murphy, the scientist?" Ben asked. Mars nodded.

"Her husband called my lawyer yesterday. Wants to speak to me."

"What's it about? Does he know how much you're in love with his wife?" Mars chided.

Ben didn't smile. He had often thought about the tall redhead, but he knew she was in the stratosphere, with him on the ground, admiring her fire from the crowd.

He didn't even think she read his books, but for some reason, he had a larger population of redheaded powerful women as characters in his love stories than he liked to admit.

He often wondered why it was that particular woman, and why she had affected him so.

"Steve said it was something to do with that book I wrote that upset her so much. Something about some kind of credit for it."

"Well, don't ask about his wife. I remember when you showed me the article about her wedding. She looked really happy. Even if the guy looks like a Poindexter." Mars grinned again.

"I'll call him this afternoon. Right now, I want to keep catching up with my favorite people in the world! I missed you guys," Ben said.

"We missed you too buddy. Especially Jane. If she can't talk books with you, she has to settle for me, and I always disappoint her," Mars said. Ben nodded in agreement, and Mars threatened to punch him. They both laughed.

As Mars and Ben, and a tired Benji, walked into the kitchen to find some lunch, Jane looked up from where she was laying out a board of charcuterie. Ben's favorite. Somehow Jane always found the best stuff to snack on in his pantry. Most of the time he didn't even realize he had bought all the stuff she routinely pulled from different parts of his kitchen. He suspected that Jane snuck into his house and brought groceries when he was out. Mars looked over at his longtime love and winked. Ben was sure she snuck in. His heart soared as he spent time with this family. His family, he corrected himself. He loved these people fiercely.

But then his mind went to the impending phone call with Stewart Haggerty. He already hated the guy. He put it out of his mind and focused on the people around him eating the meats and cheeses that Jane had found somewhere. Benji loved these kinds of snacks. Ben winked at his godson and Benji winked back using both eyes. They all laughed.

"Alright mister, what's been going on with you? And are you dating anyone since we went to Europe?" Jane asked Ben. He rolled his eyes. She asked the same thing almost every time they were together. He just smiled at her and gave the same answer he always did.

"Oh no, my dear. You know I'm waiting for you. Always have, always will," he said with a wink, using both eyes.

She smiled at him and put her arms around her big husband. They were all so close, Ben didn't know what he would do without them. They were the only family he had, and the truth was, they were the only people he needed. He had a plan to spoil his friends with the money, which they didn't know about yet.

He was excited to give them a fully funded grant that he had set up, to fund their work for the foreseeable future.

And that's also why he didn't date. He didn't trust women, and he certainly didn't want to date anyone who knew who he was.

He was always afraid their expectations would be too high because of the relationships that he constantly wrote about, but which he knew, he couldn't sustain himself. He didn't have it in him.

So, he looked at the four people that he loved most in the world and continued to chitchat with them for the rest of the early afternoon. As the sun started lowering outside, Mars announced to his small family that they had to get their butts on the road. Their house, which was about twenty minutes away, needed cleaning. Benji moaned, Jane joined him, and smiles were on every face. Ben hugged them each, especially Jane, who whispered in his ear that she loved him.

He whispered the same back to his female best friend. But there was nothing to worry about. Not even Ben would ever come between Jane and Mars, and Ben loved her for it.

Later, as he stood in the driveway and watched the big redheaded man who meant so much to him load his children into their car seats, he felt a bit of apprehension in his chest. He needed to make that phone call.

He waved as the small family backed out of the driveway, and he kept waving to his godson in the back window until the large car disappeared behind the large juniper bushes at the end of the drive.

He squared his shoulders and walked back into the house. He went to his office, sat down in front of the computer where he had written so many words. He hesitantly picked up the receiver of the phone next to the computer and dialed the number he found from his lawyer's text message. It rang twice, and was answered by a beautiful, singsong voice.

His heart dropped into his stomach.

"Hello?" Gwen said into the phone.

"Umm, hi, hello. This is Benjamin Reeves, calling for Stewart Haggerty," Ben nervously said into the phone. He didn't know how badly his voice shook.

"Oh, Ben, hello. This is Gwen Haggerty. How have you been?"

"Fine." His voice sounded gruff to him. He took a deep breath, and tried again, gentler: "I'm fine, Mrs. Haggerty. How have you been?"

"Please, call me Gwen," she said. "Honestly, I feel like a bloated opera singer. You know, the one who ends the show? Anyway, I'm seven months pregnant with our daughter. I can't see nor feel my knees." She sounded happy.

Ben felt miserable.

"I was returning your husband's call to my lawyer," he reminded her.

"Stew is out right now, but I'll fill you in on what's going on." She paused. "I'm glad that you called, Ben, and I could be the one to talk to you."

Ben's emotions caught in his chest. He spun his chair so he couldn't see his reflection in his dark computer screen. He didn't want to see the look he knew was on his face.

Ben heard something in her voice, that made his breath catch, but he didn't give it credence. He remembered: she was in the stratosphere compared to him.

She cleared her throat. Took a deep breath. Ben could hear it through the phone.

"As you know, when we met years ago, I was working on the exact science that you had so eloquently described in *Eve* and I was upset because you fictionalized my work. That wasn't your fault, but since you published the work, pretty much how it has come to be, the authorizing committee as well as the accreditation groups want to rename my discoveries. I'm going to tell you something that the rest of the world is unaware of at the moment."

"Okay, I'm listening," Ben said. He felt suddenly nervous.

While she talked, he turned back towards the desk and booted up his computer. He used the mouse to get to his desktop, and found the folder labeled simply "Books."

He then opened the file for *Eve's Plight*. He wanted to remember what it was that had shaken this woman up so much.

207

"Early next year, we are going public with our discovery, and our research from the last twenty years. We have used your fictional description for clean, renewable energy as the bedrock of what we have mastered. We did it, Ben! Well, you did it first, but my team made it a reality. We are going to change the world."

Her voice suddenly sounded energized and almost crazed, he thought. He couldn't believe that they had done it. This really would change the world, as it had in his story.

"How do I fit in with this?" he asked her.

"The device resembles exactly the way you described. I tried to do it a hundred different ways, but your way was the only one that worked. I still don't know how the hell you knew," she said.

She went on before the catch in her voice would register to him, but it registered all the same.

"We named the device the 'Haggerty-Murphy Egg,' but credit is due where it is due, and the accreditation group wants it named the 'Reeves-Murphy Ovum.' I actually like that a lot more. Since you came up with it before anyone else, and I revolutionized the creation of commercialized metallic hydrogen as well as the tritium process, I get credit as well. And the fact that it IS an egg, well, that's why that's the name. What do you think?" She asked.

Her voice changed once again. He felt it almost sounded nervous.

"I think that's brilliant. Usually I would beg off the recognition, let you guys have it all, but you know what? I'm still proud of that book. It was my first bestseller. So, I'll take it. What do I need to do?" he asked.

He could hear her smile through the phone.

"I'm glad, Ben. You deserve it. I know that now. I was so mad at first. Fiercely mad. And I'm sorry about how we ended that meeting, by the way," she said.

"Think nothing of it. So, what can I do?"

"When we go public, there will be, of course, a press release, and lots of pictures. We are putting it off until next year so I can have the baby and get some last-minute little things taken care of. But think of it, Ben. The Reeves-Murphy Ovum. How perfect, right?" She sounded happy. He was glad.

"Let me know what I can do in the meantime. I'm working on a new project, but as I'm sure you're aware, writers don't usually have much going on." He laughed.

"Perfect. I will be in touch. Take care Ben. I'm glad that you called," she said.

She hung up the phone. He placed the receiver back in the cradle and stared at it for the longest time.

Her voice, and the whirlwind of emotions he could always hear in it, brought back a lot of old feelings. Feelings that he thought he had squashed.

He felt melancholy suddenly. His mood got heavy. He felt like he had really missed out on something and he wasn't sure what it was. He went into his room and took out his black suit for dry cleaning. He still had to pay respects to his grandfather at the end of the week.

He looked forward to being back under the beautiful eves of St. Patrick's Cathedral in New York. The architecture of that wonderful church always gave him hope. He remembered the stained glass windows.

But he knew that he was trying to distract himself from thinking of Gwen. That damn woman was in his head all the time, and he had no idea why. He wondered if he had an obsession over her. He worked very hard to stay to his internal rules.

And thinking of another man's wife was definitely against his personal rules.

But he couldn't help it. He even pictured her pregnant and knew instinctively that she looked more beautiful than at any other time.

He hoped the baby had a head of bright red hair from its mother and wouldn't look anything like its father. All of his life he had never been a jealous man.

Until now.

His melancholy deepened. He spent the rest of the evening sitting in his comfortable leather executive chair, in the dark, facing a blank page on the computer, drinking Jameson and water, and wondering what exactly he had missed in life.

He thought of San Francisco.

And wondered if he had made the wrong choice, once again.

Chapter 23

A loud scream broke the unusual quiet of the hospital room. The scream was followed by several pants and heavy breathing for two minutes. And then another scream.

"Honey, just breath. Push when they say. We've done this before, champ." Stewart tried to sound calm.

"You tell me to breathe one more time and I will keep this kid inside, so help me God!" Gwen was covered in sweat. She looked down at the OBGYN between her legs and hated everyone. Why had she decided to have her second child without pain blockers? It would have made things so much easier. Just one little shot in the epidural space in her spine.

Her daughter's birth, two and a half years prior, was so much easier with the shot. Goddamn holistic childbirth!

She looked over at her husband and suddenly hated him for suggesting it. And she hated herself for agreeing to it, in the spirit of health and happiness.

She also knew that she probably wouldn't have any more children. So this was her only chance to do it like the women who came before her. But at this moment, those women could suck eggs! This fucking hurt, she thought to herself in between pushes.

She tried to keep breathing through the pain. But looked threateningly at her husband, daring him to say another damn word.

"That's it, Momma, a couple more pushes and the little guy will be here." The doctor was too damn calm.

Why wasn't everyone panicking? Gwen thought they should all be more in a panic.

She felt like she was tearing right up the middle. She screamed again.

And then it was over.

She lay back on the pillow, head drenched in sweat, her eyes closed, and legs still in the stirrups.

She felt Stewart let go of her right hand, which he had held all though the labor, and then she heard the sweetest sound in the world. Her little boy's first cry.

Gwen started to weep. She opened her eyes as they placed her son on her chest. And then she saw all the strawberry-colored hair, slicked down with fluids, but unmistakably bright red just the same.

She kissed his little head, as he quieted. This skin to skin contact between baby and mother was so important, and Gwen wanted it to last as long as it could. She could feel the tears again.

She looked over at Stewart, saw the pride on his face, and smiled through the tears.

"He's beautiful honey. So beautiful," Stewart whispered.

He placed his hand on his son's little back. It was a beautiful moment. And just like they had done with their daughter, Ellie Marie, Gwen named him on the spot.

Stewart had allowed her to do it this way, as she had always dreamed. She had refused to even speak about names when she was pregnant with Ellie. And now, she repeated the tradition with her son.

It made her fiercely protective of her children, and so very proud of them. And, as they both had bright, strawberry-colored hair like their mother and grandfather, she felt like they were much more of her, than Stewart.

She felt a bit of regret for feeling that way, but she couldn't help it.

"His name is Sean. Sean James Haggerty. It just fits," she said, looking up at Stewart. He nodded and smiled at her.

She hoped in her heart that having their new son would bring her family back together again.

She didn't have long to think about it because the doctor was ready for her to push the afterbirth out and get stitched and cleaned up. She saw through the new, lesser pain she was feeling as Stewart moved away towards their son, and over to where the nurses were cleaning Sean.

They would be weighing him, and wrapping him in his first swaddle. Stewart never looked back at her the entire time.

Much later, as the room darkened because of the lengthening shadows of the late afternoon, with little redheaded Sean James, asleep in his clear roll-around crib, she looked over at her husband, who was reading a trade magazine on the vinyl couch on the other side of the recovery room. She thought back on her earlier musings, about having Sean and how his birth could bring her little family closer together.

Over the last few years, as the technology that they had developed had become public, and the intense interest in clean energy rose from infancy to full fact, she had become so damn busy being the figurehead of the movement.

She was gone most of the time to one Senate hearing, or media campaign to another. All over the world, news of her discovery, no, hers and Ben Reeves, had made a complete and total change in social and economic circles. As she knew it would.

What she didn't know, was how busy she would be setting up the workings all over the world, and the subsequent discoveries in so many other areas because of it.

So, as Stewart had stated so many times when they were alone, she was leaving him behind. He was in her shadow, but come to find out, he had felt that way for so very long.

She had had no idea.

He had been her boss, after all, but she hadn't realized how much ownership she took in the technology. She had, in fact, left Stewart way behind.

And now, he took great pride in being a father, and doing everything for their daughter, and doing so for their son now. She felt in some ways, that she had sacrificed her family for her work. No matter that it would, and had, changed the world for the better, she had not been a great parent and wife through the work.

She had so many regrets. But Stewart had stepped up and had taken care of everything she didn't have time to take care of. She thought he had changed his purpose for his daughter, and for Gwen as well.

But maybe now, with their second child, and some of her responsibilities delegated to others in the new company that she had started, she could re-focus on her family. Maybe now, they could be a team again, a unit, a powerhouse of a couple.

She looked over at her husband, felt great love for him, and a new purpose, but he never looked up at her. She swallowed what she was going to say to him. She didn't want to provoke anything. She hated the fear the most. But it was a daily constant. No one had ever told her that she would have so much regret, fear, and uncomfortable emotions in the creation of her little family.

There was a knock at the door and when she said "come in," her parents, Ellie, and her brother, Daniel McCarthy Murphy II came bustling into the dark room.

It was soon a jovial, and light environment because of her family, and she felt better. Looking over at her precocious toddler of a daughter meeting her new baby brother for the first time, her eyes met her own brother's eyes, and something passed between them. They had never really been close, but he was family. He gave her strength. As did her aging parents.

Sean was soon awakened with hunger and a dirty diaper, and her whole family rejoiced in the little Irish boy. He had a good set of lungs on him that was for sure. Gwen did not see her husband slip out of the room.

The next day, the entire family left the hospital. Gwen was wheeled out to the minivan in a wheelchair. She was still very sore, but very happy. She loved having her parents and brother here with her. They supported her and made her laugh. Two things she sorely missed.

Stewart drove the minivan to their home, bought right after their marriage, and both of her children would grow up in it. Her father drove their rental car behind the van, with her mother and brother.

Gwen was looking forward to having them there to help with both children as she recovered her strength and could walk without flinching again.

215

When they got settled in at the large house in Montgomery County, Maryland, her mother declared to everyone in the kitchen that she was going to stay "until Gwen is back on her feet."

"Mom, thank you, but you don't have to stay. We can hire help if we need it. Stewart is well able to handle the kids while I rest." Gwen tried to talk her mother out of staying. Gwen wanted to work things out with Stewart and wouldn't be able to with her mother hovering like she was known to do.

"Not at all, honey. I don't have anything pressing at home, and I want to spend time with my new grandbaby. I'm staying, and you won't talk me out of it," her mother, who was still in excellent shape declared with a smile.

Gwen's father just looked lovingly at her and shook his head at Gwen when she tried to raise another argument.

Later, alone with him in the study, her father looked down at Gwen, who was holding Sean in a swaddle, and rocking him. He smiled at her, and she smiled back.

"It's good to have you guys here, Dad. I missed you," she said.

"We missed you too, sweetheart. And we are so very proud of you. We see you on TV all the time. I don't understand what you did, but I know it was really big," he said with pride in his voice.

"Thanks Dad. Yeah, it's really big. But I think that it's hurting my family."

"Stewart seems really disconnected, that's for sure. Are you okay, honey?" He asked her, sitting in the chair opposite her.

"We will work it out Dad. We always do," she tried to reassure him.

They talked late into the evening about trivial things, and when he left her to go to bed in the guest room with her mother, he bent down and kissed the top of her head. He didn't have to tell her anything more. She knew who her father was. Even as he had gotten older, and his body started to bend in age, he was still the strongest man she knew.

She smiled up at him and wished him a good night.

The next day, her father and brother left for the airport. Her dad had to get back to California for work, and her brother kept talking about how much he missed his wife and children.

He kidded Gwen that she always took him away, but inside, Gwen knew that her brother needed a small break, and loved her as much as he could. She had always drawn strength from the men in her family.

Over the next two months, daily life with a small child and a new baby settled in. Gwen was very happy to have time to spend with her family. As her mother took over the house and directed both Gwen and Stewart in all things domestic, Gwen grew impatient to work things out with her husband.

By the time her mother flew home, after eight weeks, Gwen was very ready for her to go. Not that she didn't love all the things her mother helped out with, but Gwen wanted the house empty so she could get comfortable to talk out and get past the tough stuff she had felt from her husband for so long.

The day after they had all piled into the new minivan that Stewart had purchased before Sean was born and took her mother to Regan Airport in Alexandria, she put the baby down for his early day-nap and set Ellie in front of an educational video she loved, and asked Stewart to come into the office to talk.

Stewart came into the office with the attitude that he had adopted the last several months emitting from him. She sat in the chair behind her busy, yet organized, desk and he took one of the chairs against the far wall and drug it over in front of her desk. He wouldn't meet her eyes. Gwen was one to get to the bottom of a problem, and she was more than tired of the gulf that had opened up between the two of them. But she was nervous.

"Things haven't been the best around here for a while, Stewart," she started. "I want to clear the air and get to where we were before I got pregnant with Ellie." Stewart nodded, and looked down at his hands. He started fiddling with his fingernails, and Gwen had to clear her voice to get him to look at her.

"What happened to us, honey?" she asked him in a softer tone. He looked up at her, and there were tears slowly falling down his face.

"I'm going to tell you something that I've needed to say for a long while now. But it will hurt you. And I never wanted to hurt you, Gwen," he stammered.

"Whatever it is, Stewart, we can work through it. Just like we used to when we shared a lab, worked together, spent all of our time together," she said.

"I miss those days. I really do," Stewart replied.

"Well, I'm here to listen. I know things have been more than hectic, but I want to clear the air between us. Even the children can tell there's something wrong," she said. And then she quietly gave him time to frame his words. She tried not to fuss with anything on her desk while he sat there, tears streaming down his face, trying to say what he needed to say.

Finally, he took a heavy breath, wiped his eyes and nose on his sleeve, and looked her in the eyes. She was an island of calm. Whatever he had to say about her, she was ready. She was ready to put in the work to get her happy family back. She steeled herself to hear that she needed to spend more time at home, less time pushing the breakthroughs that were happening every day, and she was on the go daily, pioneering change.

She was ready to hear that Stewart was tired of doing all of the family duties and wanted his wife home more. She was ready to make the changes for what mattered. Her family, and the happiness she found in that.

So, she squared her shoulders, ready for whatever her husband needed her to do. But she was not ready for what he told her next.

"Gwen, I love you for all that you are. When you swept into my life so many years ago, it was like a storm clearing out everything in its wake," he started. She wanted to say something, but knew she had to stay silent. Let him talk it out. And she had to make the changes he would ask for.

"When I was your boss at the labs, I still held onto my dignity and self-esteem. I still felt like a man and was still in charge of things." His voice got a little louder. She knew he was passionate about what he was saying.

"Ever since the final breakthrough, ever since you gave the world what you had spent twenty years building, you have left me behind. Not that I was ever your equal. I was okay to give you your credit because of your brilliance, and still receive some credit for directing the lab. But when you left me behind, the world left me behind. You didn't need me anymore, and living in your wife's shadow is the most, umm, eviscerating feeling there is." He looked back down at his hands.

Her heart hurt for her husband. He always seemed so strong, but she could see the wide cracks in him now.

She suddenly remembered something her father had told her, years before. He said, "Never marry a weak man."

She suddenly wondered if she had.

"I was happy to stay here at home and take care of Ellie, watching you on the TV, giving interviews watched by millions, given laurels, given the whole world as you changed it. I was happy. For a time. But then I realized that you have never needed me like I needed you. You don't need anything. You have the power to take on the world and make the world better for it. I'm just the guy who gets to carry your purse and change your child's dirty diapers."

Now she was starting to see the problem.

She was still very quiet, but her mind was moving in a thousand directions on how to fix this problem. She started to feel the empathetic emotions build in her chest for her husband.

"When you got pregnant with Sean, I was happy that you were going to be forced to slow down, take time to work on this family, and be my wife again."

"Stewart, I was never NOT your wife..." she started.

"Let me finish, please," he interrupted.

She nodded, lay her hands, palms down on the desk in front of her, and looked him in the eye. He breathed deeply again, settled deeper into the leather chair he was sitting in, and did what she always did. He squared his shoulders and prepared to tell her the crux of the problem, so she thought.

"Gwen, I can no longer feel like this. I feel like a failure around you. How do you compare to the sun? I feel so emasculated every single day."

"So, what can I do?" she asked. She was getting a little frustrated but remembered what she told herself. To listen to him and make the changes he needed.

"I just need to get this out," he said. Several minutes went by as he collected his thoughts. There was really something on his mind, Gwen thought. But she gave him the time. The baby was asleep, Ellie was watching her show, and the phone wasn't ringing for once.

"Six months ago, I started having an affair," he finally said. He looked right into her eyes as he said it, not embarrassed, not ashamed. He looked emboldened, she thought. A bucket of ice water fell over her. She felt both heat and cold start at the top of her head and wash down over her entire body. She had never felt such a feeling.

He continued.

"We met at the grocery store, and swapped numbers for a playdate. She has a son the same age as Ellie. When we got the kids together at the park, we started talking. She looks at me like a woman should look at a man, Gwen. She thinks very highly of me and makes me feel good about myself. Things just progressed from there. I'm in love with her now." There, he had gotten it out finally.

Gwen had a million accusatory things she wanted to say. She wanted to scream that he had used their daughter to cheat on her. That he was less of a man because he had betrayed her. That he didn't deserve her, and he was a piece of shit.

But she knew the truth. He wasn't the man for her, and he had never been. He was right: she had never respected him as a man. Only a companion. She cherished his friendship more than his inability to take care of her. She had always felt like she controlled their entire lives, and she could see the truth in what he said. As furious as she was at him, she couldn't blame him. She had left her husband behind long ago. His cheating wasn't her fault. She knew that. But she HAD caused it. She felt the first tears fall and looked at her husband through the blurriness of her grief for her family. This was an ending that she had not seen coming. And she knew that there was no fixing it.

"Okay, Stewart. I get it. I don't even blame you. What do we do now?" she asked.

They were both openly weeping. But in a lot of ways, she suddenly felt free in her chest. A feeling she hadn't had in a very long time.

She wanted to scream and yell and throw things. She wanted to hurt this man who was hurting her. But looking within, she had known that this was coming.

She knew it the day Stewart had proposed. He never did look at her the way he was supposed to. She was suddenly resigned. It was over, and she had tried to ignore that fact for a while now.

She stood up, walked around the desk to her husband, and he flinched away from her. That tore at her heart. But she reached down and put her arms around Stewart. She held him like that for what seemed like an hour.

She kissed the top of his thinning hair. She got on her knees next to his chair and kissed him on the lips one final time. They looked at each other through their tears and knew that they still loved each other.

But not in the way a man and wife should.

"We will always be friends, won't we?" she asked.

"Always Gwen. Always. You were always too good for me. But you gave me your love. I just wasn't the man strong enough to carry it," he said.

She smiled at him, hugged him again, and stood. She squared her shoulders, wiped her eyes, and walked out of the office.

She had wanted to ask him about his new woman but couldn't quite take that just yet. But she was happy for him while mourning her family. This was going to get complicated, she knew.

But it was time to focus on her purpose in life and put her marriage behind her. She would have time to grieve it later. Right now, the baby was crying from his nursery, and Gwen needed to figure out where to go from here.

And she needed to call her parents. They would understand.

She remembered little remarks from them both about Stewart and her marriage. She had ignored them, but now the remarks all came crushing in.

She stopped in the upstairs hallway, hearing Sean crying from his room, hearing the TV downstairs playing a song about science to her daughter, and her husband weeping in the office behind her.

She hung her head, letting the sobs take her. After two minutes of her chest heaving, she wiped her eyes, sniffled the snot coming from her nose, wiping it on her sleeve, and shook her head.

This would not break her.

She took care of Sean, sitting him in his rubber chair to feed, and pulled out her phone. She dialed her father first. She needed a man to tell her everything would be okay.

Something she had never had in her marriage.

As her fingers dialed the familiar numbers, she suddenly, and out of the blackness of her subconscious, wanted to dial another number. One she would have had to look up, but one she knew was in the history of her home phone from a couple of years prior.

Where did that come from? She wondered.

Her father's voice on the line made new tears fall down her cheeks.

Chapter 24

"Wait, what? Say that again, Steve," Ben said incredulously into his cell phone. He was sitting in his office. The news that his lawyer had just given him making him almost see stars in surprise.

"The Nobel Prize, Ben. For both you and Gwen Murphy!"

Ben couldn't believe it. He had just gotten home from more travel for interviews and questions about what they were now calling "the new energy" and he was tired. But this bit of news jolted him awake.

He felt bad that his own writing was suffering from all of the energy attention, but in a way, as well, he was enjoying it. But he was only an ancillary for it. The famous face behind the idea.

Gwen was the real drive behind the marketing and informational propaganda for "the new energy." He was just there to add credence to the ideas, and to take credit for the single day of research he had done nearly twenty-five years prior.

He felt like a fraud in the rooms of scientists and researchers who looked up at them as they traveled for speeches and demonstrations all around the world, but he was confident enough in his own contributions to the cause.

"Are you serious? Why?" he asked into the phone.

"Well, it's really two different prizes, so they tell me. Gwen is winning the prize for physics, and you are winning for literature for *Eve's Plight* since that is the book that marshaled in the changes," Steve said excitedly.

"Well, that's really something, isn't it?" Ben was still stunned.

"It sure is, old friend. Congrats. You deserve everything you get. I really mean that," Steve said, lowering his tone.

Ben was touched. But he also knew that he wasn't the driving force behind the emerging technology. He was basically the idea guy.

Gwen Murphy was the real hero. He tried not to think of the tall redhead. Especially about the article link that Mars had emailed him the night before, giving the details of her divorce to Stewart.

Ben was trying his best to not feel something about that.

He wondered briefly, from this last two-week trip he had made with Gwen, why she hadn't said anything about her divorce, but realized that she may have thought he already knew, since it had been public for a little while.

But when he, himself, didn't say anything about it, he assumed she happily didn't want to talk about it as well.

He hung up with his longtime lawyer soon after and decided to go on a walk. He had a date that night, and he wanted to burn some travel calories before he met Rachel at the restaurant.

A couple of years prior, just as he was really settling into bachelorhood, Mars and Jane had set him up on a blind date with a fellow scientist friend they had. The date had gone fairly well. But his suspicions were confirmed that women who read his books automatically deduced that he would fit the same mold as his many strong male characters. He didn't.

He was uniquely deep, and pragmatic. He wore his emotions on his face at all times, and most of the women he then dated after that first encounter were pushed away by his abruptness and lack of playing the game. He was blunt to a fault, and always wanted to discuss the deep aspects to life.

He was finding that most single women his age just wanted to go on adventures, not talk about deep emotional things, and to be taken care of. He was slowly but surely getting sick of dating again.

But, he had promised his best friends that he would keep giving it a shot. The most recent woman had stayed with him for almost three months, and Rachel seemed to like him. He was still somewhat on the fence about his own feelings.

She was a short blonde woman, and he wondered if he enjoyed dating her because she reminded him of Neeley. Both in looks and temperament.

He couldn't quite put his finger on it, but he wondered if it all led back to his own mother. He needed to talk to his therapist about that. Ben thought that he had solved those issues years earlier, but he wondered why he was still attracted to the same kind of woman, and how he could break that cycle.

Also, he had tried not to think of Neeley for several years, but she kept encroaching on his peace. He sighed as he tied up his walking shoes and set out into his neighborhood.

It was a beautiful late summer day. The breeze was from the water side of his neighborhood, and he could smell the salt in the warm air. He was always at peace here where he had grown up. It had been too many years for him to still see the ghosts of his youth. Now, it was just pleasant memories and peaceful feelings.

He enjoyed knowing that everyone around him knew who he was, what he did, and gave him space and, more importantly, a lack of attention. Ahh, he thought. New Yorkers.

Nobody else in the world so causally ignored you, no matter your celebrity status.

He surprised himself this day. He walked a total of twelve miles and still felt great. The knee was doing a lot better since he started getting cortisone shots, and his mental status was really good as well. It had been for quite a while.

He got back home and started getting ready for his date that night.

Rachel was an okay woman, but Ben knew that she probably wasn't the one. As a writer of mystery and romantic relationship fiction, he had researched and studied how relationships were supposed to work. He knew all the angles, theories, and ideas for successful marriages, or whatever form people's relationships took.

So, he tended to overthink when he was in a new one.

Years of therapy and now trying to dip his toe into the dating world had made him comfortable being alone, but still wanting more. He knew that. And he was okay waiting for it.

He thought on all these things as he showered, dressed in a pair of pressed khaki slacks and a button-down dress shirt, which he rolled up the sleeves, and kept untucked. He styled his hair, happy that at the later part of his forties, it was full and thick, and showed a lot of gray, but he knew most women liked that.

He was happy. But he was missing something in his life that he felt for years that he didn't need. His life felt like a funnel, spinning, and spinning down to something significant and big.

And in a lifetime of very big things happening for him, he was excited at the prospect. He looked into the mirror, having to wipe it with a washrag to make it clear from the steam from his shower, and knew that if the Archangel ever appeared again, he would make the opposite choice from the two he had already made.

He didn't want to think too much about Chamuel, because he wasn't quite ready to give up control to a God who wanted something from him. As he left his house for the drive into the city, he wondered if he had already given God what He wanted in the energy development he had helped with.

But as he pulled onto the highway into the city, he knew that there was a lot more for him to do. He felt renewed. He knew, deep in his heart, that he was strong enough for whatever it was.

So, going towards his date with Rachel, he felt an optimism and joy for what lay ahead. He was ready.

He drove up to the posh restaurant in his 1967 Shelby Mustang GT500. It was buffed, waxed, and looked amazing under the bright lights from the overhang leading into the restaurant. Chico's. It was new, and it almost impossible to get a reservation.

He wanted to impress Rachel with this date, as their five or six other dates had been in the park, a walk, and a day at the beach. He wanted to show her this side of him as well. And as he exited his car, handing over the keys to the valet and warning against scratching the muscle car, he liked that he could show a woman that he had so many sides. He was a complicated guy, and at his age, he was happy about it.

He also knew that the right woman would appreciate that in him.

Again, he had done all the research and knew that he was a rare kind of male. He gave a fleeting thought that maybe he was more like the strong men that he wrote than he gave credence. He was again feeling great as the maître d' showed him to his reserved table by a lovely window near the lit fireplace.

He looked down at the thick white tablecloth, the many glasses, and utensils, and was happy to show this side of life to Rachel. He wondered if he could make it work out with the woman.

He was happy that she was a research doctor for infectious diseases at the largest hospital in the City. She did her own thing, was independent to a fault, and was quite lovely when he thought about her. He smiled and looked forward to her arrival.

He ordered a whiskey and water on the rocks and sat back waiting for his lovely date.

An hour later, as the waiter came over to him and inquired for the fifth time if he was ordering, and if not, they needed the table, Ben angrily threw his white cloth napkin onto his empty plate, swung back, and drank the rest of his second whisky like a shot, and laid a hundred dollar bill on the table.

He took his cue, looked into the judgement in the waiter's eyes, and stormed out to the valet stand. When he heard the roar of his Mustang GT500 from half a block away, he felt slightly better. Even if a woman stood him up without a call or text, he was still Ben Reeves, he thought, angrily.

But he soon chided himself for the thought.

No one cared that he was Ben Reeves. Especially a blonde doctor who he would have to ask why she had stood him up, and if the reason weren't good enough, he would block her from his life.

He got behind the wheel of the supped-up muscle car and gunned the engine down the busy street of New York City. He turned the radio up loud, with Nirvana blasting from the almost sixty-year-old speakers.

He only had one thought as he gunned the engine towards home.

"Fuckin' Rachel."

God must be preparing him up for something truly amazing. Why else would he keep having so many problems dating or finding the One meant for him.

He wondered if there was even such a thing.

But in his romantic heart, he knew. Yes, he thought, as he headed back home.

He knew.

Chapter 25

The phone rang. Gwen yelled to her assistant, Tiffany, to answer it, as Gwen was changing Sean's diaper. It rang again.

"Tiff, can you get that please!" she yelled. The ringing stopped as the young woman picked up the line in Gwen's home office.

As Gwen latched the second tab securing the diaper around her one-year-old son, Sean squirmed enough to almost fall off of the changing table. Gwen smiled down at her amazingly handsome son and knew that he was getting a little too big for the changing table. She vaguely wondered if she needed to start changing the growing boy on the bed in her room. There would be more room.

She finished dressing the little redheaded boy and picked him up for a kiss and hug. Sean wiggled in her arms, squealing into her ear.

"Ms. Murphy, it's another journalist. Wants a quote about your partner and the company," Tiffany yelled to her from the office. Gwen knew that the twenty-something skinny brunette would be smacking gum into the phone and rolling her eyes. But she was amazingly efficient at directing Gwen's hectic life, both work-wise and home-wise.

Gwen put Sean into the playpen in the children's playroom next to the nursery, patted her daughter on the back as she played with dolls on the floor, and walked into her beautifully appointed office inside her new townhouse.

The tall, three-story brick-front was about five miles from the home she had shared with Stewart until their divorce. She loved this new place. But she missed her old house. A year since they split, Stewart had stayed in the home, and moved his new love and her child in about six months earlier.

Gwen was happy she had her own space, once again.

She took the handheld receiver from the eye-rolling young woman and answered it as she sat behind her busy desk.

"Hello, Dr. Murphy here," she said into the phone.

"Hello Dr. Murphy, this is Jill Bryant from the Washington Post. We are running a series on powerful women in the DC area, and we wanted to highlight you first. How does that sound?" a woman with a deep voice said abruptly from the other end of the line. Her voice portrayed that she was a woman who was used to getting whatever she wanted, Gwen thought. She smiled.

"Tell me more about the angle of the piece please," Gwen replied. She had gotten into the habit of not talking to journalists since they had run scathing articles about how her work had driven her husband into the arms of another woman a year prior. Just because it was true didn't mean it had to be public, she thought.

"We know that you are leaving this week for Stockholm to receive the Nobel Prize in Theoretical Physics. We wanted to get a couple of quotes on how it feels to win the prestigious award, how it feels to finally see your hard work over the last twenty-five years come to fruition, and where you think your company and your technology will be in five to ten years," the woman said all in one voice. Gwen assumed she was recording the conversation.

"Are you recording at the moment, Jill," Gwen asked the journalist.

"Not yet. But if you aren't opposed, I will start it now. Do you mind answering a couple questions?" she asked.

"That's fine, Jill. I have about ten minutes. But I have a rule to only answer questions from the media if I am allowed to see the article before it prints, please," Gwen said to the exasperation she could feel coming from the other end of the line. Gwen smiled again.

She loved taking a little bit of control back from journalists like this. Men were worse, she knew. She was never one to be the "little woman" they all wanted her to be.

Thinking about men made her slightly less nauseous than it had over the last year or so. She wasn't ready to think about that quite yet.

"That's fine, Dr. Murphy. Fine, fine," Jill answered distractedly. Gwen knew she was starting the recording, and also getting out some pre-written questions. Gwen was becoming an expert at handling the press.

"Dr. Murphy, your clean energy technology has been called 'the advancement of the millennium' from several scientists and experts. Do you think that it will continue to make the global impact that it has been touted as doing? Is it sustainable?" The journalist asked first.

"Yes, Jill. I started the idea of a clean, renewable energy source with the goal that it would be small enough, cheap enough, and available enough, that the entire world would benefit from it. But it's not just about producing heat and electricity. It's all the other advancements we have made in other areas because the energy is available in places where it wasn't in the past," she answered back.

"You are referring to the terra-forming operations in the desert, where they are growing grain from desert sands, aren't you?" she asked.

"That technology is amazing, yes. They are hydroplaning desert sand and making almost a billion acres of desert into cultivated land to grow hardy crops for the entire planet. It will be the Middle East's new 'oil boom.' But I'm also talking about the minimizing technology that will allow our clean energy to be used in clean vehicles, especially large-haul trucks, and trains. And just an over-all ability for faster magnetic tube travel, clean energy use in manufacturing, and giving sustainable jobs to replace the ones lost to ending the reliance on coal and natural gas production," Gwen said.

"That really does sound like a global game changer. But how do you feel, personally, that this work has taken away from your own life and family?" the reporter asked, slyly.

"Well, nothing has been detrimentally broken. My ex-husband has found his own happiness, and our children have gone from one unhappy home to two happy ones. I think that that is all positive progress, and it didn't 'take away' from my life," Gwen said strategically.

"You're not going to give me anything juicy to print, are you, Dr. Murphy?" Jill laughed into the phone. Gwen liked her blunt honesty.

"Afraid not. I want to show the world what this work has meant to me, as well as the others on the team that created it," Gwen answered.

"Speaking of, we have gotten word that you have hired famous writer Ben Reeves as a consultant and a member of the board at EnergyOne, the company you created to hold the patents to the energy technology. We know he was the man who first thought up the idea of the energy source, but he is just a fiction writer, why would you need him as a consultant at your scientific firm?" she asked slowly.

"Mr. Reeves is a brilliant man, and as you know, a Nobel Prize winner himself. We are lucky to have him on our board, and as a consultant. He is more than just a fiction writer. You have to understand, Ben took one day, just one day, with a little bit of research to come to the same conclusions that teams of scientists took years figuring out. Why wouldn't we want him working for us?" Gwen said more than she meant to, but every time Ben Reeves was mentioned, her mind went fuzzy.

"Did it have anything to do with the ridiculously large donation he made to your technology cause, when gave you the seed money to start EnergyOne?" This reporter had done her homework.

"Let me tell you this straight. From what Mr. Reeves told me himself, when his grandfather, who he had never really known, passed away, and left his entire fortune to Mr. Reeves, he didn't know what to do with the money. He also didn't need it, as you are aware. He is quite successful on his own. He told me, when donating the funds, that he would rather his mother's family money go towards something life changing, than to line his own deep pockets even more. You can quote those words, because that is exactly what he told me," Gwen said. She went on.

"But, rest assured, Ben Reeves did not 'buy' his way onto the board of directors of my company. He earned his spot the same way I did. With his own merit, and from his work when he was much younger. He just did it a lot differently than I did. In fact, and I'm going to say this slowly, I don't know if we would have created the technology the way it ended up, if it wasn't for Ben's contributions to it. He described and wrote about the idea to the extent that, it was the only way we could have made it work. And you can guess, I wasn't happy about it. I tried a thousand other permutations of formation, but it only worked the one way. His way."

Gwen hoped she hadn't stepped over the line. She would really like the line of questions to get away from Ben Reeves. She almost stated that to the journalist, but knew if she did, Jill would dig even more into that subject. Gwen wasn't ready for that.

"Getting back to your ex-husband, Stewart Haggerty. He has taken another managerial position at the National Institute for Standards and Technology. Do you think he wanted to get away from the energy sector because of you?" Jill asked. Gwen thought there was probably a better way for the reporter to ask that but tried to ignore her own growing frustration. She was getting this question more than she liked.

"Dr. Haggerty worked as tirelessly as I did on the clean energy technology. It's as much his baby as it is mine. His personal reasons for getting away from energy research and moving into nanotechnology are his own. I have no opinions about his career change. His new area of scientific research has as much application potential as my own. I don't blame him for the career shift, and I don't think he made a bad choice. But you'll have to ask him the 'why' of his move. It's not my place," Gwen said.

After that response, the two women spoke more about the applications of Gwen's own technology, the upcoming speech she was to make in Stockholm, and ended up with Jill asking after the children and the changes that Gwen had to make in her own busy schedule to maintain the balance between career and family.

Gwen was happy to answer those questions, and left the conversation feeling good about the article. She hoped, and even told Jill, that she wanted to focus on the potential and strength of her work, and how a woman could make it just as far in a man's world as any man.

As Gwen hung up the phone, she felt peace about the article. Jill had promised to email her a draft before it was printed in the next edition of the Sunday paper.

Gwen spent the rest of the day playing with her children and taking a few more phone calls from work colleagues and friends about the upcoming trip to receive the Nobel.

It still hadn't hit her. Not fully.

She had learned about the Royal Swedish Academy of Science's selection of her and her work in theoretical physics almost a year prior and had at first felt horrible that she alone was receiving the Nobel.

Stewart and the rest of the team deserved to be on that stage with her, but she knew that was impossible, and she also knew that it was her own drive, work ethic, and ideas that had made it possible.

She would give credit in her speech, she knew, but after almost a year of focusing on it, she finally accepted that she deserved the medal. She was confident in her contributions to the work.

But she was going to spend a lengthy bit of time in her acceptance speech thanking and giving credit to the entire team. A lot of them would be the room, and she was happy about that.

Ben Reeves would be in the room as well. That made her more nervous, and she didn't know why.

As the day lengthened into evening, and the children were put down for the night, she curled up on her bed with a glass of wine and a book.

She started reading the new fictional novel, from a woman who had only written one other book. She was good, Gwen thought. But she was no Ben Reeves.

I have to stop thinking about the man, she thought to herself. It was difficult to focus on the story unfolding in the pages before her.

She took a drink of wine, and pictured the tall, dark-haired writer as he had been more than twenty-five years prior, when she had burst into his workshop.

And, as she saw Ben in her mind's eye, like a jolt from the universe, her bedside phone rang. She looked at the caller ID. And just like a conjuring, she thought, here was Ben calling her.

The phone rang again, loudly, in her hand.

She took a deep breath and answered.

Chapter 26

"Hello," Gwen said into the phone.

She sounded breathless to herself, as if she had run a mile and then answered the man on the other end.

"Dr. Murphy, this is Ben Reeves," his voice was still deep, slow. Gwen had learned during the meetings that she and the board of directors had with Ben; that she really liked his voice.

"Yes, Ben. How are you? And call me Gwen, please," she said. For some reason, every time the two talked, she had to tell him to call her by her first name. She vaguely wondered why that was.

"I'm really good. Thank you for asking. I'm sorry to call so late in the evening, but I wanted to ask you a question. It's embarrassing, really. But I didn't have anyone else I could think to ask," Ben said with a chuckle.

"Of course, Ben," she answered. "What can I help you with?"

4ot Chosen | Joshua Loyd Fox

"Well," Ben said. He sounded sheepish. "It's about the ceremony on the tenth."

"Yes, of course. In Stockholm. What do you want to know?" she said.

"Well, I'm all set to go. I think I know how it's all going to go. I'm not worried about the logistics. The people at the Swedish Academy have been great in letting my people know what to expect, and what I'm supposed to do. I have watched several of the past years' ceremonies on YouTube. I guess what I really need to ask, if you don't mind, is about my speech." He sounded nervous to her.

"Well, Ben, I'm not the writer here," she laughed. He laughed in reply, but she knew that he wouldn't have reached out if he wasn't really worried about this.

"No, I know. I'm sure I can write something incredibly moving and sincere, but I don't know if it would be right, you know?" he asked.

"Okay, Ben. I'll help if I can. What's the problem?"

"Well, Gwen, to be honest with you, I think it starts with thinking I don't really deserve this," he said.

There was a pause. She knew he wanted to say more. But she felt like she needed to dispel him of his thought process.

"Ben, do you know how the selections are made?"

"Only from what I read online. I know that nomination forms went out to a bunch of people last year. Other than that, no, I don't know how they do it," he responded.

"Right. Last September, hundreds of nomination forms went out to people. Those people are the existing prior Nobel Laureates in Literature, presidents of writing bodies and organizations, universities, professors, esteemed colleagues, and anyone who is anyone in both American and European literature."

"Wow. That sounds like a lot," Ben said.

"It IS a lot, Ben. And for a reason. Every one of those esteemed professionals are allowed to nominate one person, or piece of literature. And they cannot nominate themselves. And then, all of those nominations go back to the large, deciding committee at the Swedish Academy for review. And it's never who gets the highest number of nominations. There are whole papers written on each nominee. And they do not publicize nominees for fifty years," she told him.

"Wow. Really?" he said.

"Really, really, Ben. So, if you are lucky enough to be one of the almost 900 laureates since 1901, you got there for a reason. They do not hand out the medals lightly. That's why the prize amount is so high. You had to make a significant impact on ALL of humanity to receive a nomination, let alone the prize," she finally said.

"I feel like I'm saying 'wow' too many times," he laughed.

"So, Ben, if I may be blunt? You are going to Sweden because you damn well deserve to," she replied.

There was another long pause. She heard his sniff away from the phone. She wondered if she had made him choke up. The thought of that was really nice, for some reason. He came back on the line seconds later, sounding composed.

"Okay, thank you. But I still have a question about the speech," he said.

"I can't answer anything about your own speech, Ben. But let me give you one piece of advice. You are a storyteller. A very good one. I have read all of your books. So don't give a speech. Tell the story. Tell them your story. Of how you got from wherever you came from, to where you are now. I'm sure it's an amazing story," she told Ben.

Another long pause. She could hear the man thinking. What could he be thinking about? She thought. Their conversations seemed to be made up of long pauses. Again, something she liked, for some unknown reason.

"I think you're right. I never thought of that. I was writing a speech thanking everyone involved and was just going to speak to what we hope to do in the future," he finally admitted.

"That's all well and good, Ben, but everyone does that. Be different, because you are different."

"You've read all of my books?" he asked. She gulped loudly. There goes her mouth.

"Umm, yes. Well, I thought I should when we wanted to approach you for the board position," she quickly replied. She could hear the lie in her tone.

"Oh, okay. Well, thank you for reading, and thank you for the advice about the speech. That's exactly what I needed. You're a pretty smart lady, Gwen Murphy," he laughed again. She felt her face turning red. Hundreds of people had told her that she was brilliant throughout her life, and this man's flippant remark made her blush about it for the first time. What the hell was wrong with her?

"I'll let you go. I hope you have a great night and I will see you on the other side of the pond this weekend. Oh, one last thing," he said.

"Yes?" She answered, still blushing.

"While we are in Stockholm, would you like to grab a drink? Just to talk shop about EnergyOne?" he asked.

Her heart beat loudly in her chest. What the hell WAS wrong with her?

"Of course. Yes. Sure. That sounds amazing," she stumbled with her answer, but he didn't seem to notice.

"Perfect. Great. I will give you a call while there or speak in person. That is always better to me," he said.

"Sounds great. I would rather talk in person as well. I'm old-fashioned like that," she replied.

"Good. Me too. Goodnight Gwen. Thank you for taking my call," and with that, he hung up his side of the conversation.

She held onto the phone and stared at the blank wall on the other side of her room. A cascade of thoughts went through her mind. A mixture of memories of him in his workshop, greasy, easily smiling twenty-something years in the past, and thoughts of the man now, with gorgeous salt-and-pepper hair, still tall and strong. She reached for her wine glass, almost knocking it to the floor because the phone was still in her hand.

She put down the phone loudly and picked up her wine glass. She drank deeply from it and kept staring off into space. She was nervous as a schoolgirl for some reason. She couldn't put her finger on it, but Ben Reeves made her feel little and huge at the same time. She had never been intimidated by anyone in her entire life, except maybe her father. But Ben Reeves made her nervous.

And as she thought about the man, she knew that he also made her feel important.

He had done it twenty-five years previously, and he did it now. He was amazingly accomplished, yet he had called her late on a Thursday evening for help with a speech.

A speech for the damn Nobel Prize in Literature. She took another long drink of her wine, finishing the glass.

She wondered how much trouble a drink in Sweden would be for the organized, controlled life she had created for herself since her divorce.

Right before sleep took her, she wondered just how dangerous Mr. Benjamin Reeves was to her.

Chapter 27

Benjamin Reeves, the most recent Nobel Laureate in Literature, and Gwendolyn Murphy, also the most recent Nobel Laureate in Physics, sat at the dark bar.

It was a two-hundred-year-old pub that Ben had read about, and where they had agreed to meet after the Nobel ceremonies.

The pub was dark, with the only light coming from behind the bar, shining down on a long, scarred mirror, and several candles scattered on the tables and across the long, wooden bar top. It was Christmas time in Stockholm, and they both appreciated the wonder and heaviness of the season, and especially the day they had just shared.

Gwen was still wearing her dark green ball gown. She had kicked off her matching high heels, and her stocking covered feet were slightly cold, but felt better after a day of her toes being pinched. She had both covered feet sitting heavy on top of the wooden cross beam of the rather comfortable bar stool she sat on.

Ben was wearing his black, very well-fitted tuxedo, the bowtie untied and hanging around his neck, and his heavy jacket on the stool next to him. He had taken her heavy winter coat off of her and placed it under his own on the stool. She was rather comfortable in the pub, and every time the door opened, and the twinkling sound of the old bell sounded, she smiled slightly.

Ben, too, was comfortable, but was very tired. It had been an extremely busy day. He was happy to have this little bit of relaxation with Gwen, where neither had spoken much because of the solemnness of the day. As Gwen glanced slowly over at Ben, he distractedly took off his tuxedo jacket, sighed contently, and placed it on top of the growing pile of garments on the stool next to him.

Both were silent. Both were reliving the day that they just witnessed firsthand, and the events that led them to having this drink together. Gwen went from looking deep into her glass of dark beer to again glancing over at Ben sitting next to her. Benjamin Reeves was only a foot and a half away from her to the left. She sighed, and went back to looking at the bar top, where both of their gold medals lay, Alfred Nobel's face etched on the surface of both, looking like an American president on a coin.

She sighed, picked up her glass, and took a long, deep drink of the deliciously dark and very malty beer. Both had their elbows up on the bar, and both were deep in thought, but still felt together.

She liked very much that Ben wasn't an over-talker. She respected that when he did talk, which he could passionately, she found, he always seemed to have something to say. He wasn't so much a strong, silent type, but rather, a slower, studious, and very intelligent observer. Gwen liked that, a lot.

Gwen set her glass back down on the circle of wetness where it had just rested, trying to make sure to place the glass exactly where it had been before, to keep the circle intact and by itself. But she missed, and now she knew when she picked up the glass again, there would be two circles, intertwined.

Ben, as well, went from looking into the light from behind the bar reflecting in his three fingers of very fine Kentucky Bourbon with a splash of water to looking at the two medals placed haphazardly between the pair of them. He picked up his glass and drank deep at the same time that Gwen did the same. When he put his glass back onto the deeply scarred wooden bar top, he saw that Gwen had placed her left hand on the bar.

She was drumming her fingers on the old wood. He looked over at her distracted face, saw her deep in thought, and knew she didn't realize that she was tapping her fingers. Tap, tap, and tap.

He looked down at her hand, picked up his glass for another drink, but didn't bring it to his lips. He just kept looking at her long, pale, slender fingers, tapping.

Her fingernails were blunt and unadorned with color. He liked that for some reason.

He put his glass back down and reached over with his right hand to still her fingers. But when their hands touched, a spark of something went between their skins, where it touched.

She swung her head over quickly, seeing his strong, large hand cover her own, and realized that she had been tapping, a nervous tendency, and thought she had annoyed him. But his hand stayed on top of her own. His was darkly tanned, contrasted with her pale, thin hand. She liked the comparisons.

But his hand was so warm, and it stayed on top of hers longer than it took to silence her tapping. She realized that her hands had felt chilly all day, as usual. But the heat radiating from his hand warmed her left one instantly.

With just a touch of his hand, he was warming her all over.

She looked up into his tired eyes, and he was looking back into hers. She felt suddenly naked before his gaze, like he could see all the way into her deepest recesses, and she saw the look of acceptance in his eyes. She gulped loudly. And her breath caught in her chest as the pressure of his heavy hand settled heavier on top of her own strong, yet feminine hand.

She couldn't take her eyes away from his, and the background of the dark, slightly crowded bar faded in her eyes. The voices around her disappeared like a volume knob on a stereo slowly being lowered until there was no sound.

She only saw his face. And the look that he was giving her.

They were both so very tired, but it wasn't just the day they had shared. It was the life they had both been running through, searching for so long.

And as he continued to look deep into her, his hand starting to slowly rub her own, and she saw what she had spent so very many years searching for.

This man was looking at her.

He was looking at her the way she had always fantasized. Like her father looked at her mother. It was the look she had noticed so many times, but never directed at her. Benjamin was seeing her. All of her. She almost passed out.

Hours earlier, at the start of that day, she was in her hotel room, getting ready for a very long day of ceremony, and was nervous about her speech. Her mother was in the room with her, and she felt like she had on both her wedding day and her long-ago graduation day. She expected her father to walk in at any time and tell her how beautiful she looked, as he had done at both events in her past. But her father was in the room next door, playing with Sean and Ellie, and keeping them both busy while Gwen mentally prepared for the day. Her mother didn't need to say a word, for once. She was very aware of what this day meant.

They had all flown together the day before, and even the kids were jetlagged. They had not had a chance to see much of Stockholm from the airport to the hotel, and even today, Gwen wouldn't get a chance.

Her father was going to take the kids to a couple of Christmas celebrations around the city, as well as shopping at a few outdoor Christmas Markets. Gwen had brought her assistant, Tiffany, to watch the two young children during the ceremony, and the following banquet.

She knew it was going to be a long day for everyone, and she was happy that she had help, as always. She vaguely worried about her father taking the kids into the cold of the city, as it had heavily snowed the night before, but she knew that at least Ellie would love the winter wonderland of Sweden in the snow.

She adjusted her hair in the large mirror and glanced up and saw her mother looking at her intently. There was a tear on her mother's cheek.

"We are so proud of you, Gwenny. You know that, right? For everything?" her mother asked from over her head and at the reflection of Gwen in the mirror.

"I know, mom. Thank you guys so much. And thank you for being here," Gwen answered.

"We wouldn't miss it for the world. We aren't getting any younger, but how often does your only daughter win a Nobel Prize and change the world in the same day?" she asked with a smile. She sniffed and wiped the tear away.

"Still, I know it's hard on Dad to travel like this. I worry about you two," Gwen said.

"Oh, hush. We are okay, even if we are older than dirt," her mother answered and shuffled away to handle her own dress.

Gwen was again pleased that she had the family support that she had. Today was going to be hectic enough without thinking about how much she would have worried and not been able to focus without her family's help.

She was also thankful that the young assistant, Tiffany, had gotten over her fear of airplanes to fly with the family. Gwen, also, tried not to think of the fact that Stewart had decided to not make the trip. It would have been a lot easier with him there, but he had told her that it was too difficult for him, as he had always dreamed of a Nobel for himself and he couldn't quite handle watching her win the medal, without him.

She told him that she had understood, but deep inside, she really hadn't. She was bitter at her ex-husband. But there was nothing she could do, so she just decided to put it behind her for this day.

Gwen adjusted her makeup a final time, stood and smoothed out the deep green ball gown she wore. She knew her feet would be killing her by the end of the evening inside the high heels she wore. She reminded herself to take them off every chance she could. Luckily they were strapless, and she could just slip them on and off.

She loved that they perfectly matched the deep green of her ball gown.

She knocked on the connecting door, hearing squeals from her young daughter through the wall, and her father opened the door wearing jeans, a heavy flannel shirt, and solid boots.

At almost seventy-five years of age, she was glad that her father had taken care of himself as he had. But she suspected it was more to do with her mother's constant pressure to exercise and eating right that did the trick than his own choices.

She loved her parents intensely and was as proud of them as they were of her.

She gathered her daughter into her arms, careful not to wrinkle the silk of her dress, and kissed her daughter soundly on the cheek, nose, forehead, and top of her bright red hair. Her daughter laughed and wiggled out of her grasp. Gwen was daily surprised at how big her daughter was getting.

Gwen then bent down to her son, who was still rolling around on a blanket on the floor near the connecting door and picked him up for his own face kisses and a hug. He was turning into a very serious young boy. He looked at her with a very piercing look, she felt, for an eighteen-month-old boy. She kissed him one last time on his little nose and he finally grinned.

Gwen turned to her father, hugged him tight, and told him to be careful, and to let Tiffany do all the lifting. With the snow, she was fearful they wouldn't be able to push the double stroller they had brought with them. But her father told her not to worry, kissed her on the forehead, and as they pulled apart, he winked at her and told her to break a leg.

She smiled again at her father, remembering so many memories of things he had taught her, and before she could get overwhelmed with emotions, pulled apart and gathered up her mother to head to the Stockholm City Hall.

There was a luncheon and she had to schedule when she was going to give her lecture the following week.

That same morning, Ben was also getting ready for the day. He had also flown into Stockholm the day before, but had come very early, catching a red-eye out of New York the night before that. It gave him time to see the city a little before the ceremonies of today.

Mars and Jane had flown with him, leaving the kids at the house with their new nanny. Jane was very uncertain about the woman, but Ben was paying for her services, and they had gone through a rather lengthy interview process with many candidates.

Yesterday, after settling into the five-star hotel in downtown Stockholm, the trio had walked around most of the city center. They had visited the Christmas Fairs and two markets, sampled many of the buffets that seemed to be in every pub and restaurant, and Mars, especially, had fallen in love with the *julbord*.

Both men had eaten their fill of moose and reindeer sausages, and the tiny glasses of Schnapps went well with the many other meat options. Jane couldn't stop eating the local gingerbread and spiced wine. She said she felt like a little girl again. Christmas had always been important in both her and Mar's family history.

They had a late dinner at a very beautiful restaurant and had enjoyed an entire *julskinka,* which was a leg of ham marinated in mustard. As far as the culinary delights of Christmas in Stockholm, all three were over-full as they took an after-dinner walk along streets completely adorned with bright Christmas lights.

It was a small vacation that all three friends had needed badly. They had bought many craft items for the children for Christmas and looked forward to the kids seeing the handmade wooden toys and dolls.

They finally headed to the hotel to sleep when it started snowing heavily. Many people ran to get in out of the wet, heavy snow which quickly started piling up on the streets and buildings around them.

The next morning, as Mars and Jane had joined Ben in his suite of rooms to get ready for the day, the talk was banal, and Mars, in particular, was in a fine humor. There was never any jealousy or negative feelings between the three best friends, and Ben was so happy they had joined him on his trip. He needed their support, especially, he felt, to get through his speech later that evening.

Ben wore a black-on-black tux with a vest instead of a cummerbund. He was happy that in his late forties, he was still in excellent shape, and could still wear the same size pants and jacket as he could when he was in college.

Mars, on the other hand, had grown even larger in girth than he had been in college. He also, wore an expensive tuxedo that Ben had bought for him the month before. Jane constantly argued with Mars to have a healthier diet and to exercise.

Now that their careers were steady and didn't require as much fieldwork, Mars had promised to change his ways in the spring, and to start walking with Ben, if Ben promised to go slow at first.

Ben happily agreed.

As Ben finished up his hair, and put on his jacket, Jane swept into the room, looking quite beautiful in a purple evening gown that showed off her slender frame. Her hair was done up, and Ben watched as Mars looked appreciatively at his wife. Their love made Ben hopeful every single day.

The trio, dressed in their best, walked down to the lobby, and got into the black limo idling at the curb. Ben's lawyer, as well as his assistant, had set up everything beforehand, and Ben was glad that he could relax and enjoy the company of his best friends without any worry.

Once again, he thought that money really made things easier.

As the car drove through the busy streets, covered in the new snow that had fallen in the night, Ben looked down at the two notecards that he had for his speech. Most of it, he had planned, would be ad-libbed. Off the cuff. He had talking points on the cards, but no word for word paragraphs. Until the final one. That one, he needed to have had pre-written.

The three best friends arrived at the Stockholm City Hall, and a young woman, smartly dressed in a business suit, met them at the top of the stairs. She led them to the Blue Hall, where that night's banquet would take place with the Swedish Queen and her royal family.

For the moment, it was set with fewer tables, for an impromptu luncheon. The three friends walked to the round head table, which could hold eight people. At the moment, it only held two. Gwen Murphy and a very attractive older woman sitting beside her.

Ben, Mars, and Jane took their seats, where the paper placards with their names written in gold sat on fine china plates. Ben smiled at Gwen, who returned the smile, and introductions went around the table.

For some reason, Gwen seemed a little nervous, and Ben had never seen her that way. He stuck the information in the back of his mind as he greeted the woman to Gwen's right, who she introduced as her mother.

"Gwen, you met Mars here once before, years ago," Ben said to Gwen. Gwen smiled, acknowledged the memory, and gave pleasantries to Mars and his wife, Jane.

"How ready are you for the speech?" Ben asked Gwen. Gwen smiled again at him and held up a stack of notecards. Ben took his own out of his breast pocket and smiled in return.

Their smiles seemed to be plastered to their faces since they saw each other across the white linen covered table. Mars and Jane both noticed. As did Gwen's mother. Looks went around the table, unbeknownst to the two future laureates.

"It's not so much the speech that I'm concerned about. I was just given word that they have set up a classroom at the Science School for my lecture on Tuesday," Gwen told Ben.

"I received a phone call this morning. I am giving my lecture on Tuesday as well. But in the afternoon," he said.

"I would love to hear you give your lecture, if I may?" Ben asked.

"Of course. Nothing you don't already know, Ben," she answered. Ben smiled at her and knew that she would be coming to his as well.

He suddenly remembered that he had asked her for a drink and wanted to see if she would find time to get that drink with him at the earliest. He would ask her to meet tonight, he knew. He started making plans in his mind.

Ben was looking at Gwen for a little too long when Mars cleared his throat and motioned with his head that the wait staff was coming around with covered dishes for their lunches.

Gwen glanced quickly over at her mother, who had just kicked her ankle under the table. Something flashed in her mother's eyes, and a small smile was on her lips. Gwen squinted her eyes at her mother, knowing what she had been thinking. She chose to ignore the insinuation.

The delicious lunch went by smoothly. They all talked passionately about their various causes and activities, and Gwen and Jane talked mostly about their children. They both stated several times that they should get the children together since their ages lined up so well.

They all enjoyed the lunch and gathered as a group to go to the small meetings that took up the rest of the afternoon. The medal presentation was slated to begin at 5 p.m., local time, and the banquet would start at 7 p.m. It seemed like it would be a long night.

Ben found a quick moment in between a meeting about what was expected of them as laureates and the next about where their guests would be seated for the ceremony to corner Gwen alone and ask her for that drink.

"Gwen, I know today is going to be a very long day, but I would really like to show you a small pub around the corner that I think you'd like. I know your children will probably be sleeping by the time the banquet is finished, so would you mind allowing me to buy you that drink?" he asked hopefully.

He was visibly nervous to ask Gwen out, and he hoped that it didn't show too much on his face. For some reason, he wanted, more than anything, to be strong for this woman.

She looked up at him, impatient to get to the next meeting, as the schedule was tight. But she knew that Ben had probably been thinking of asking her all day, so she gave only a moment's hesitation, and agreed to accompany him that evening for "one drink."

He smiled again and told her he had a plan. That pleased her more than she cared to admit to herself.

The rest of the afternoon went by in a flash, and before they all knew it, Mars and Jane were seated on the right side of the auditorium where the ceremony was to take place, and Gwen's mother sat with members of Gwen's team, the team who had flown in for the presentation of her medal, and to "take a stand when I call out your name," as she had told them she would do.

Ben and Gwen sat in plush red seats on the left side of the stage. There was a person between them. Ben would be presented with his medal and diploma first and was given all the time he needed to give a small speech. But it was pressed on the laureates from the chairman of the prize committee that they should try to be as brief as they could. Gwen would receive her awards third out of the five people receiving the prestigious award that night. She was glad that she could enjoy most of the ceremony before it was her turn to be in the spotlight. Gwen looked over at the large stage, seeing the deep blue of the carpet, the bright gold of the Royal Family's seats, and the stone podium with the face of Albert Nobel on the front.

The auditorium filled quickly, and everyone present stood as the Queen of Sweden entered from the right side of the stage. She took the large, regal chair at the right of the stage, directly to the right of the podium where the awards were to be given and the newly crowned laureates would say a few words. Her husband and three growing children gathered behind her, finding their own seats. Ben knew that Queen Victoria was very lucky to have the crown. Only right after her birth had the country changed the Succession Act, allowing the first born of the reigning monarch to gain the throne, regardless of gender.

Soon after the arrival of the Queen, the chairman of the committee stood and gave opening remarks, which included a short description of the winners of this year's Nobel Prizes, and lists of their accomplishments.

Gwen was surprised when the chairman declared that Benjamin Reeves has sold over 100 million copies of his books through his decades-long career, and that they had been translated in over 150 languages worldwide.

She had known that he was successful, and that he was an amazing writer, but she was unaware at just what an impact he had had on the literary world. She was under the impression that he was receiving his award in conjunction with his additions to her own work, but at that moment, as she looked over at Ben sitting two places down from her, she realized that she had given the man too little credit.

She suddenly saw him in a different light, and she wasn't sure how she felt about that revelation.

When the chairman got to Gwen, she turned back to the podium, and listened as he listed her accomplishments, which mostly surrounded the work she had done in clean energy. She was a little disappointed that while her work had changed the world, and brought about many other technological advancements, her lists of accomplishments were much shorter than most of the other future laureates, especially Benjamin Reeves.

She suddenly felt down on herself. Why was she feeling jealousy, while sitting on the stage to receive the most prestigious award in science?

She tried to clear her mind but was not able to.

Ben looked over at Gwendolyn while the chairman spoke of her work. She was settling and resettling in her seat. He wondered what was bothering her. He could see the confidence she had worn on her face all day slowly drain away. He tried not to think about what she could be thinking about.

He shifted his eyes off of Gwen and back to the chairman, who stood at the podium to the side of the Queen. Ben was nervous that he would be receiving his award first. He always hated being first at things.

He had the notecards in his hand, and he knew that his hands were sweating. He put the cards back into his breast pocket and casually wiped his hands on his pant legs.

As the chairman wound down his introduction, he invited the Queen to the podium to say a few words. The

Queen wore a beautifully adorned ball gown with full skirts and the crown of state on her head.

Ben thought she looked too young to be a Queen, but knew that, just like in Great Britain, the Crown was mostly a figurehead, and the country was run by Parliament. Her position was mostly a public affairs one, without having power to change policy for the small, yet rich, country.

The Queen gave her remarks in Swedish, her native tongue. It was her right, as the Monarch of the host country, to use her native tongue, and the guests who did not speak Swedish would get a transcript of her remarks at a later time, they had all been briefed. Ben knew that the Queen was heavily educated and spoke at least four languages. She wasn't the first Queen in Sweden for more than 200 years for nothing. He knew not to underestimate her when she presented him with his Nobel.

As the young Queen finished her own remarks, she gestured to the student at the side of the stage holding the medal and diploma for Benjamin Reeves to step forward. At the same time, Ben stood up and approached the Queen. She smiled at him and told him in perfectly clipped English that she had read all of his books. He smiled at her, feeling much calmer.

The Queen then switched to English and read Ben's list of accomplishments in literature, ending with his inclusion into the august company of Nobel laureates, and gestured for Ben to step closer as she hung the heavy golden medal around his neck, handed him the custom artwork that was this year's diploma, and shook his hand. He was surprised at the strength of her grip.

She gestured for him to take the podium, and as he stepped up to the microphone, his mind suddenly went to a place he didn't expect at all.

He saw himself, sitting in the back of the dirty white van as a ten-year-old child who had just lost his entire world, bumping along the West Texas road out to the home he didn't want, in a land so alien to him, he didn't even realize what he was seeing.

He remembered the lost feelings, the despair, the loneliness already creeping in, where it would find a home for many years.

Ben was suddenly caught up in the moment and had to take a few minutes to compose himself. He knew that this was expected in this ceremony and knew that the crowd waiting for his words would forgive him.

He cleared his voice, wiped his eyes with the handkerchief from his inside jacket pocket, and gathered himself. His mind came back to the present, and he knew it would be tough to get through the next several minutes. But he needed to tell this short story. His most important one.

And what better place to tell it? He cleared his throat and started speaking as clearly as he could.

From her seat, Gwen watched a man who was comfortable weeping in the presence of so many learned professionals and a royal family. She grew even more impressed with as he took enough time to compose himself before his strong, deep voice resonated across the auditorium.

She sat forward, hanging to every one of Ben's words. As the speech went on, and she looked out into the crowd, she saw all eyes were on the tall, dark, and handsome Ben, and many leaned forward to hear his story.

"Follow laureates, family and friends, and Her Royal Majesty, thank you for being here, supporting those receiving this very prestigious award tonight, and to the Nobel Committee, thank you for your choices for this year.

I would also like to say a brief word of thanks to my best friends and family who join me here tonight, Dr. Markson Gray, and his wife, Dr. Jane Gray. I wouldn't be here tonight if it wasn't for your constant love and devotion, Mars, and Jane. Please stand, and everyone, please give these amazing people a round of applause for their love and support," Ben said.

Mars and Jane sheepishly stood to a thundering round of applause, made louder by Ben's own applause into the microphone. He smiled down on his best friends and nodded to them. Jane waved back and Mars's face was bright red.

"Now, please allow me a few minutes to tell you a story, as I'm known to do," Ben began, quietly nodding at the scattering of laughter coming from the audience.

"Stories have been my way of life since I was ten years old. I tell stories for a living, and those of us who write, who live in the worlds that we design, often find it hard to discuss our own stories. The stories of our very own lives. I would now like to tell a story most in the world have never heard before," Ben paused. He tried to modulate his voice. To keep it steady. He knew it was about to be difficult to keep up such a calm tone.

"Most know that I wrote my first book when I was sixteen years old, publishing it the next year. It has often been reported that I was a bit of a prodigy for literature. Most bestselling authors have lived long lives before they are able to tell a decent story. I was extremely lucky to be published at seventeen, and I have never taken it for granted. But what I want to speak about tonight, here in front of so many fellow believers in the study of life, are those first sixteen years of my life. And then the few after. The years that most don't know about," he continued.

"I never knew my father. I knew his name, since I shared it, but in all of my life, I have never been face-to-face with the man. That fact should have made my life much more difficult than it was, but I had an amazing early childhood thanks to my mother, Lorraine. My gentle, beautiful mother was the center of my entire life, until the day I lost her. I was ten years old, and my life would change drastically, and tragically." Ben paused.

"I was sent from my life on Long Island, New York with my beautiful and strong mother, to West Texas, to a boy's home, where I lived until I graduated. It was there that I learned a little healing, found strength in my God-given gifts, and saw my future clearly for the first time." Ben paused again.

"I lost the only woman who had loved me as a child, and it would be years before I was able to properly process that fact. And it was with another woman, years later, who had reminded me so much of my own mother, who helped me heal. The only love of my adult life, Neeley." Ben had to wipe his eyes again. This was the first time he had publicly spoken of Neeley.

"Neeley and I met in college. I had already written a few books, and I was a bit of a celebrity on campus. She didn't care. She was a much more gifted writer than I was. She saw what life really was. And it wasn't the harsh, dark landscape I had always taken if for. She saw life for the beauty and happiness that it could be. She was amazingly beautiful, inside, and out, caring to a fault, and loved everyone around her. She had this unique ability to make the most downtrodden person around her feel bright pleasure to just be alive. She brought out the best in people, including me. She believed in me in ways I didn't deserve. And in ways I still don't," he said.

"We were meant to marry, start a family, and grow together. We often spoke of our future together, and it wasn't the normal things she would speak about. She didn't care about the wedding. She cared more about our relationship. That we worked every day at it. That we talked about absolutely everything. She made me want to tell her the minute details of my day. We were always completely honest with each other, which was rare for me. I never spoke to others in truth, because I didn't want to let anyone in. But Neeley found herself at the very center of me without trying. She made her own, comfortable, home inside of my mind and spirit. I knew her much better than I ever knew my own mother, and I knew more than anything her proven love for the broken young man that I was because of all of the loss I had suffered," he said to the listening crowd.

"And then one night, as I was researching the book that brought me here tonight, *Eve's Plight*, I got a knock on the door of the home we were supposed to end up one day sharing, and it was a deputy sheriff with the news that I had lost Neeley as well. She was gone in a blink of an eye. A life that should have glowed brighter than any other, was snuffed out in a split-second accident," his voice broke. But he recovered very quickly.

"And for the longest time, I felt like it was completely my fault. I was supposed to have met her that night for our weekly date night. I would have driven her home in my own car rather than her being in a taxi that didn't make it to its destination," Ben broke down once again.

A couple of minutes later, he finished his speech.

"I have known for several years now that our lives are not dictated by the tragedy we all experience, but rather by the joys that we should strive every day to find. As hard as it is to lose those closest to you, and as hard as it is to picture the lives we should have had if nothing tragic ever happened, we must find the little joys. For me, it's in my writing love stories that I myself have never fully experienced. It's in the family and friends that have stuck

262

by my side even when I try with all of my might to push them away," he said, looking at the crowd.

"And it's in the higher purposes that are given to each of us from a higher Being. It's to all this joy, all of this happiness, that I dedicate this medal. I don't deserve to be here with all of you. But Neeley did. My best friends do. The stories that have given me so much in my life, they all deserve to be here, and be recognized."

"So, I thank you for listening to me tell this small, simple story. I believe when the situation is the heaviest, and the company around you is the strongest, and the world is the darkest, that a simple story of hope is what is needed most," he said.

"Thank you all for allowing me to be here, and for keeping the memory of Neeley and my mother Lorraine alive, if even for a brief time. Thank you," Ben finished.

There was a moment of calm and quiet, with the feeling of potential energy strong in the large room, and then the hundreds in attendance leapt to their feet, thunderously applauding for the simple story Ben had given them.

The gravity of the situation was lost on no one. There weren't many dry eyes in the room, and for a normally formal, intellectual conference of learned people, it was suddenly heavy with emotions. Even those on the stage stood and applauded. The Queen wiped her eyes and clapped her glove-covered hands together.

Gwen watched Ben bow his head graciously and walk back to his chair. She noticed he had never taken his cards out of his pocket. She was overcome with emotions and had no way to navigate how Ben's words made her feel. For a woman who was usually in complete control of her mind and emotions, she was awash in feelings.

The applause faded away, and the rest of the evening went by in a blink for Gwen. Her own speech, nowhere near as moving as Ben's, went by while her mind was on other things. She read from her notecards, knowing in her heart the gravity of the situation. She gave each member of her team their due credit. Each were given applause as they stood. But her mind was on Benjamin.

Through the lengthy banquet following the awards ceremony, more speeches were given, but days later, when asked what she had eaten, she couldn't answer. Her eyes never left the face of the tall, dark-haired man sitting down the table from her in the banquet hall. A million questions were on her mind.

As she watched Ben's face, she could see his friends try to talk to him, to open him up and make him enjoy the meal. But he never smiled back. He wore his pain in his eyes. She wondered if they were still going to have that drink that evening.

Unconsciously, she knew her own mother and colleagues were trying to talk to her about the ceremony. She still wore her medal around her neck, as did all the other winners in the banquet hall.

But she didn't hear much, remember much, or eat much.

An hour later, as she bid her mother goodnight at the door of the dark car waiting at the curb in front of the Hall, she felt Ben's presence beside her. They both wore heavy jackets against the chill of the night, and the briskness of the wind.

They both still wore their medals, and Ben had escorted her and her mother to the line of cars. Mars and Jane had bid them all a goodnight and took Ben's limo back to the hotel.

As the dark sedan pulled away with Gwen's mother, Gwen turned to Ben, looked up at him, and remembered how tall he was all over again. He smiled sweetly at her and offered his arm. They started walking the two blocks to the pub he had briefly described to her between the ceremony and the banquet, as they had stood in line to enter where the dinner had been served.

She felt his strong body next to her, his arm hard under her hand. Their long legs kept stride with each other, and he had kept her from slipping at least twice on the short, brisk walk.

They approached a dark, two-story building down a short, narrow alley, and entered the warm, invitingly dim pub. They walked up to the bar, took two stools at the end away from the door, so as not to feel the draft every time someone walked in.

He took her coat, she kicked off her green high heels. She ordered a local stout and saw Ben's look of approval. He had ordered a bourbon from back home, as he explained that he had sampled several different local spirits the day before.

As they settled in with their drinks, the talk between them started slowly, but built up steam. She wanted to ask him about Neeley so much but knew that he would not speak of her again. He had gotten Neeley out of his system tonight, and she knew instinctively that if she mentioned it, the wound would be too raw.

So, she spoke of their work. She spoke of the kids. After three beers, she spoke of her marriage. Stewart was still a sore subject. But he listened, interjecting at the perfect spots, saying the perfect things. She got a real sense from him of his vast intellect and his views of the world and life in general.

The time went by faster than they both realized. This was the first time that they really talked to each other.

She enjoyed it.

As they sat in silence, finally, after having shared stories and ideas back and forth faster than either had done with anyone else, they both felt a combined contentment to just be in the moment.

A while later, she started tapping her fingers, thinking of the late hour. The pub was open all night, as it was close to Christmas, and two days away from the many Processions of Lucia. They had both overheard several people speaking in multiple languages about the special day.

When Ben placed his warm, heavy hand on top of hers, and she felt the overwhelming emotions it caused in her, she looked over at him.

She saw what she had searched for all of her life. He was looking into her. Into her soul. He saw her.

His look. At her. Her breath caught.

She almost passed out.

And as his deep, dark eyes bore into her soul, and she felt light and heavy at the same time, something electric passed between them.

She could see the invitation in his eyes. She could see in herself how this man saw her.

It did not match with how she saw herself.

He saw her as a man should see a woman. Her own mental image of herself was as a scientist first, and a woman second. Ben saw the woman she was, right at that moment. And it scared the living shit out of her.

So, she did the only thing she could think to do.

She ran.

Chapter 28

Ben caught her at the end of the alley, where she was already shivering without her coat. He walked up behind her and put her jacket around her shoulders.

She slipped her arms into the sleeves. He walked around in front of her and zipped up the heavy coat for her. He reached into his own jacket's pocket and placed her Nobel medal around her neck.

She couldn't believe she had left a damn Nobel Prize medal in a bar. She kept her eyes downcast, shame washing over her at running away from this man. It distracted her from thinking why she had run away in the first place.

No words were spoken. She didn't even know how he had paid for the drinks, or how he had caught up to her so quickly. She was even more surprised when his black limo pulled up at the street in front of them.

Ben opened the door for her, before the driver could get out. She got into the warm interior of the car, appreciating that Ben somehow had the car close by, idling to stay warm, and that he had had the presence of mind to have planned all of this out.

He didn't even ask what hotel she was staying at. He nodded to the driver and watched as the divider between them in the back, and the front where the driver sat, slowly slid up, giving them privacy.

Ben didn't say a word. She didn't either.

But her took her hand and rested them both on the seat between them. She jerked and looked over at him, but he didn't let go. She wasn't strong enough, physically, or mentally, at the moment to remove her hand from his. She knew she didn't want to.

She had no idea where he was taking her, or what his intentions were, but at that moment, she didn't care. She didn't give one thought to not trusting him. For once, she wasn't making the plans. She wasn't making the decisions, even for herself.

She sat back against the soft leather seat of the large automobile, feeling Ben's strong fingers gripping her own, and closed her eyes. She didn't even think about his reaction after she had run away from him.

It was like he knew what she was going to do and had planned accordingly. She smiled, but kept her eyes closed. She could feel herself slowly giving up control. It was one of the most alien feelings she had ever had. But it made her glad. On this night, she thought, she did it willingly.

Still no words were spoken between them in the back seat of the roaring vehicle. She kept her eyes closed until she felt the car pull to a stop, and finally opened her eyes to see that they were under the front vestibule and in front of the valet station of the hotel where she and her family were staying.

She looked at Ben in confusion, and he explained that he was staying at the same hotel. She assumed that he either got lucky choosing the same hotel, or he was better at doing his homework than she gave him credit for. Either way, it didn't matter as he got out of the limo, took her by the hand and led her into the warm and bright lobby.

She did not take her eyes off of Ben's back. He gripped her hand tighter as they got on the elevator. The hotel was deserted at so late an hour, but she didn't care. She didn't care about anything at the moment and knew that she was putty in the hands of this tall, hard man.

She didn't know if it was the alcohol, or the late hour, or the fact that she had not made love to a man in well over a year.

She was surprised she didn't feel her usual nervousness before sleeping with a man. Not that she had that much experience in her life, but almost universally, she had felt a very high degree of tension beforehand.

This night, she felt nothing but calm. She was introspective on the ride up in the elevator and wondered why she felt so at home.

But deep inside, she knew the truth. She would let this man that she had actually known for over twenty years to have his way with her simply because of the way he had looked at her in the pub.

The entire ride up to the top floor of the hotel, down the long hallway to the end where double doors led to the largest suite in the hotel, and into the interior of the suite, which was well- lit and smelled of pine and Christmas, she thought of Ben's look.

She stood by the door, finally having let go of Ben's hand as he took a few minutes to light several candles around the living room of the suite. Gwen looked around at the Christmas tree in the corner, the holly strewn about the suite, and the red-and-white Christmas candles scattered in decoration.

But she really couldn't take her eyes off of Ben's practiced, precise movements. She realized suddenly how tall and strong he looked. She had never known a man like Benjamin Reeves, and she wondered just how much she was going to get to know him in the next several minutes.

She felt awkward standing in the entryway of the suite, but she didn't dare move. She wrung her hands together as she watched Ben. He took off his winter coat, and then his tuxedo jacket.

He looked over at her as he took off the bow tie. He took his Nobel medal from around his neck and placed it on a table. He removed the black vest and lay it with the growing pile of garments on one of the chairs of the small dining area.

He then stood at the other end of the suite and looked over at Gwen. Gwen's knees got weak as she wondered what she was to do, and as he again used his penetrating gaze to look deep into her, she swallowed hard and didn't dare move.

She felt a shudder in her belly.

The hotel suite was now in a gradual dimness, broken by the many flickering candles, but without any other artificial light.

Ben walked over to the ornate couch in the center of the living area of the suite. She watched as he took a seat.

She only just realized that a fireplace next to the couch snapped with flame. She wondered when he had lit the wood logs.

The sudden smell of wood smoke and the sound of the crackling logs made her think of long-ago memories of childhood Christmases. Her mind was scattering, she thought. Gwen was getting quite warm in her winter coat.

Finally, he spoke.

"Gwen, please take off your winter coat, your medal, and put them on the floor next to you," he said in a soft, yet firm voice.

She didn't know what came over her, but suddenly she wanted nothing more than to please this man. She was never this way. She was always the one taking charge, doing what she wanted, relishing in controlling the situation.

She was surprised at herself as she dropped both her medal and jacket on the floor with a thunk. She hoped, fleetingly, that she hadn't damaged the medal. She also didn't care. She looked back up into Ben's eyes as he took her in with his own. She realized that they were so dark they looked black in the glow of the candles and the fire snapping next to the couch.

"Step out of your heels, and put them next to your jacket," he told her in the same firm voice.

Again, without even thinking, she obeyed. She would do anything this man told her at this moment.

"Now, close your eyes. Good. I want you to slip out of your dress," he commanded her. She didn't even hesitate. With eyes closed, she reached around behind her and unzipped the dark green ball gown.

As she moved the small zipper head down to the small of her back, the dress fell away of its own accord. It puddled at her feet, and she stepped out of the folds of silk and kicked it over towards her belongings next to her. She kept her eyes closed as she felt his dark eyes on her body.

She was wearing matching black bra and panties. She was distractedly glad that she had decided to wear a matching set and had not embarrassed herself by not being somewhat prepared for what was happening. Where she got that thought, she didn't know.

His voice sounded again, this time from farther away. She opened her eyes, expecting him to be seated on the couch near her, staring at her tall, slender body. But he wasn't on the couch. He had moved towards the bedroom door on the left-hand side of the suite.

She looked down at herself to make sure nothing was out of the ordinary. It wasn't. She was proud of how she looked.

"Come here," he told her firmly.

She walked on stocking-covered feet over to him, standing in the doorway of the bedroom. He was still completely dressed, and she could feel his command of the situation. She respected that he had put her in the more uncomfortable position of being practically naked in front of him when he was still fully dressed. She was deliciously aroused by his actions so far. She anticipated so much more.

He held out his hand, and she walked up to him, never taking her eyes off of his. She took his strong, warm hand in her cold one, and he pulled her into the room. He left the door open and spun her around to stand in front of the foot of the large bed. She still had not uttered a word of protest, completely trusting in Ben to know what he wanted her to do.

She was shivering with a chill, but also with the anticipation of what this man was going to do to her. He had already shown in the last fifteen minutes that he could command her completely, even if it was slightly against her will. But she didn't voice her will.

She realized again the alien-ness of the situation, but it was sending waves of chilly pleasure through her stomach, and she could feel the wetness at her middle, staining her black silk panties. She stood for this man's inspections.

He stood in front of her, not moving, not talking, just eating in her figure with his strong gaze. She stood stock still as he devoured her body with his gaze. She was afraid her knees would buckle if he only touched her once. She shivered at the thought. He smiled lopsidedly at her small shake and approached her slowly.

As he stood in front of her, she could smell his cologne. It was a subtle, manly smell. She wondered if it was more a smell of him, rather than a chemical fragrance. She swallowed hard at the thought. She felt like she was about to find out.

He lifted her chin, her eyes looked up into his. She realized how very tall he was. He was the biggest man she had ever been with in this kind of situation. Her mind was scattered once more. She had stood in front of this man, being commanded to take off her clothes, and she obeyed without thought.

He had commanded her across the suite, and she had complied. She had no will of her own as she looked up into his dark eyes. He suddenly took her by the outsides of both of her arms and pulled her willingly against his hard body. He aggressively moved his face down to hers and their lips touched for the very first time. He parted her lips with his tongue, and she opened her mouth to his without hesitation.

He pulled her scantily clad body harder against his taller and broader frame, and she suddenly felt the bulge where her stomach met up against his crotch. She moaned into his mouth when she felt the size of him against her flat stomach.

Her mind was mixed with the pleasure of his strong mouth eating into her own soft one, and the hardness of him against her. She was overwhelmed with desire for this man. Whatever he demanded of her - she was going to give it all to him. She had never felt this aroused. And she could sense that Ben knew it.

He broke off the kiss suddenly. She groaned in disappointment. She wanted to taste his mouth for hours. She could taste the slight bitterness of the bourbon he had drank. It seemed like hours earlier, but she realized it had been less than a half hour.

She was overcome with lust for this man. He kept his strong hands on the outside of both of her arms, slightly squeezing her.

She was aware of how strong he was. She looked down at his left hand on her pale arm and saw the veins on the back of his hand standing out. His skin was much darker than hers. Everything was darker about this man.

She looked back up into the intensity of his eyes and he pushed her backwards. She tried to use her arms to catch herself, but he held her strongly in his grip. Her back hit the soft bed and she moaned at the sensation of falling and him controlling her fall.

He moved above her, and practically lifted her upper body and moved her head up the pillows at the head of the bed. My God, she thought, he was so strong!

He released her arms and told her in a soft, firm voice to close her eyes. She obeyed instantly. He told her to keep them closed. She affirmed with a nod of her head.

And then his hands were on her body. With her eyes closed tightly, and her arms at her sides, she felt his heavy, warm, oh-so-strong hands start exploring her body. She felt the weight of him settle next to her. She wondered if he was sitting cross-legged next to her. She didn't dare open her eyes to check, however.

Both of his hands were on her body. One of his large hands was on the side of her face. It moved down to her throat, a slight pressure scaring her deliciously as he cupped his hand around her slender throat. At the same time, his other hand was on her flat stomach.

The hand on her throat disappeared for a minute, but she felt it settle on her upper chest, above her breasts, and it lay there, heavy, feeling her heartbeat speed up as his hands explored her body. She still did not dare to open her eyes.

His strong hands roamed all over her body, and she had no idea what he was doing as he resettled his body. She had no idea of time or space. All she felt were his hands. She barely realized when one hand reached under her back and deftly snapped her bra open. He removed it, and she knew that he was looking at her naked breasts.

She hoped in her mind that he liked her pale nipples, hard in the chilly air. She hoped he approved of her lack of color around her nipples. She knew that her breast were considered "ghost breasts," as it looked like she had no areolas. Curse of a redhead, she thought fleetingly.

She soon lost that track of thought as both of his strong, warm hands found her breasts. He kneaded them gently, and then not so gently. She felt her nipples harden almost painfully under his fingers as he suddenly pinched them between two of them.

She arched up her pelvis as the jarring shock of the pain aroused her on even higher level than she thought possible.

She felt his weight shift again as his strong lips moved to her nipples. Even more waves of pleasure enveloped her in the middle of her belly. She felt the muscles of her abdomen flutter. Her breath caught sharply as his tongue found each nipple in turn, and then again when his teeth found them. They felt harder than they had ever been in her life, and she wanted to scream for him to touch the parts of her he had purposely ignored.

She thrust her pelvis upwards again, until one of his hands rested on her stomach, pushing her back into the mattress under her. My God, she thought again, this man was strong. He could do anything he wanted to her. She wondered if she was more afraid or turned on by that fact.

And then his mouth was on her stomach and she could feel the slight scratch of the end-of-day stubble on his chin and cheeks. She loved the way his face felt heavy on her midsection. And then his hand was on her thighs. He didn't even have to move his hand, she purposely spread her legs for him, opening up, and letting him know with her movements that she belonged to him, and he could do anything he wanted.

Without opening her eyes she felt his weight shift once again, only this time he was between her legs. Yes, she thought. Please. She didn't realize until after she heard both words that she had said them out loud.

She heard his small chuckle. He suddenly pulled down her stockings, and grabbing ahold of her panties, she lifted her butt to assist him in making her completely naked.

She felt his weight leave the bed. She still did not dare open her eyes to see what he was doing. She wondered if he was finally removing his own clothing. She hoped so. She wanted to open her eyes with all of her being, to see his body, to see all of him. But he had instructed her to keep her eyes closed.

So, she obeyed against her own desires. She lay in the middle of the large bed, completely exposed for this man. What was he going to do now? She wondered. She shivered in the still-chill air and strained to hear what he was doing.

She felt him back on the bed. She heard his breath start to quicken. She could feel him at the foot of the bed, and then felt as he moved up between her spread legs once again. And then he was deeper inside her than anyone else had ever been. It happened so suddenly. She was completely caught unaware and felt sinfully filled by him. He moved slowly, oh-so-tortuously, slowly. She pushed back into him, and he chuckled and pulled away. She moaned in despair for him.

She arched her back, thinking she had all of him inside of her finally, thinking that it was time to start the age-old pattern of rocking together. But he surprised her one last time. Just when she thought he had penetrated her completely, he slammed an additional inch or more into her, making her scream.

And then there was suddenly no tenderness in their lovemaking. He lay his heavy frame down on her, pushing all the way up inside of her, and almost angrily made love to her. She was instantly overcome in his treatment of her body. He was not gentle. But her body responded in a way that both surprised and excited her. She lay her head back, caught in the passion of his lovemaking, and the wave after wave of completion she was feeling.

As her passion intensified, he moved her body with a precision she had only ever read about in his books. He controlled every aspect of her body. He would make her orgasm, but only when he wanted her to. He whispered commands into her ear, and she obeyed immediately. When he told her to change position, she spun around faster than she thought possible. And when he thrust into her from behind, she screamed into the pillow under her head.

How this man could maintain the level of stamina that he did, she wondered. She knew she would be sore the next day, but it didn't matter at all at this moment. She felt wanton. She felt liberated. Her body was his, and he used it in every way he wanted. And she wanted him to, more than anything she had ever wanted in her life.

Soon, as it seemed the rest of the night flew by while they consummated their new union, it was over in a final, shared explosion.

Her body spasmed in their shared conclusion. She could feel his strong body doing the same. She finally opened her eyes and saw all of him. And tendrils of emotions and feelings that she hadn't allowed herself to feel started creeping into her mind. And into her heart.

After several bliss-filled minutes of the two lovers looking so deeply into each other, she closed her eyes again, and didn't remember anything else after.

She easily fell into the deepest sleep she had ever had, and barely felt him lift her, carry her into the second bedroom of the suite, and cover her still naked body with heavy, warm, and comforting blankets.

She was falling deeper into unconsciousness as she felt him kiss her forehead. She had not a care in the world.

Sweet, sweet darkness enveloped her, and her entire body fell all the way into the darkness with her.

Chapter 29

She woke to the sound of soft music and the smell of coffee. She suddenly remembered the entire night before, and her body certainly let her know it was all so very real. As she came fully awake, she panicked slightly.

Her family would be wondering where she was. The kids would need their mother. She jumped out of the bed, slightly recognizing the music. It was Tom Petty. The *Wildflowers* album.

She had loved this album as a teenager. Why was it playing? She wondered as she looked around for her clothes.

She looked over at the table next to her side of the bed and saw a folded piece of paper leaning against a crystal vase holding a single red rose. She picked up the folded letter and saw strong, neat handwriting.

Gwen,

279

Please take your time and get a shower. You'll find all of your toiletries in the bathroom connected to this room. There is a robe hanging in there as well. Please join us for breakfast when you are ready.

Ben

"Us?" she wondered aloud. Well, she had gotten used to doing what Ben told her to do the night before. She went into the well-appointed bathroom and saw that her own travelling toiletry case was on the sink, and her shampoo and soap with its loofah was in the shower, all ready for her.

She marveled at the man's preparedness and wondered embarrassingly how he had gotten her personal items out of her room, several floors below where she was at the moment. She had a fleeting suspicion of just who the "Us" was before she got into the shower.

Well, she supposed she needed to walk into that situation with her head held high. She wasn't going to be embarrassed. She was in her forties for god's sake.

The hot shower felt wonderful on her sore muscles. She felt like she had run a marathon the night before. As the hot water cascaded over her body, she thought back to the long night. Her body tingled as she thought of Ben and how he had treated her. How he had treated her body. How willingly she had given herself to the man.

She felt a familiar tingle in her belly but decided to ignore it. She felt like people were waiting on her out in the living and dining area of the large suite. She was ready to face whatever she had to face.

She thought she would feel shame and embarrassment. She did not, and she wondered, as she washed her body, why that was. Why being with Ben the night before suddenly felt like some foregone conclusion that she was the last one to know about.

She grudgingly left the shower, and brushed her long, wet hair. She put on the thick white terry cloth robe, with nothing underneath. She squared her shoulders, took a deep breath, and walked out of the bedroom to the living area of the suite.

She was not shocked at what and who she found waiting for her. Ben seemed to have charmed her entire family and they were all here. She walked into laughter from her mother and father, who sat at the dining room table with Benjamin, who had just said something to them to make them laugh.

Gwen then saw her children playing on the living area rug with Tiffany, who was pushing toy cars along with her small son. She caught laughter coming from the kitchenette area, where Mars and Jane soon joined the rest holding plates of breakfast foods.

The table was already spread with more food than Gwen thought they could all eat.

As she walked out of the bedroom, closing the door behind her, the entire group turned to her. There was a comfortable silence until Ellie squealed at Gwen and ran to get a hug. Gwen sheepishly looked at her parents as she hugged her daughter to her legs, but they were both smiling at her.

Ben, sitting across from the most important people in her life, smiled as well. He stood and walked over to her. He kissed her cheek, as she looked up at him with complete trust, but a little shock as well.

"Your family has only been here for about twenty minutes love," he whispered to her. She separated Ellie from around her and looked at her parents.

"Are you guys okay?" she asked. Both looked up at her, and both wore identical smiles.

"More than okay, darling," her mother said quietly.

"Yes, honey, everyone is doing well," her father joined in with her mother.

Gwen let out a deep breath. She hadn't realized that she had been holding it in until she saw the approval in both of their eyes.

They smiled knowingly at her again, and Gwen looked over at Ben, who was getting both kids up to eat breakfast. She marveled that this man had set this all up. Again, she wondered if he had known what would happen, and had set this all up beforehand.

He never failed to amaze or challenge her ideas of what reality was around him. She also wondered just when he had slept, or if he had at all.

She did not like how fuzzy her mind seemed around Ben now. Several thoughts of the future went through her mind. From the company, to where they both lived, what Stewart would think, and if Ben had real feelings for her. She tried very hard to stop thinking of the future.

But she also couldn't quite stop the feelings of hope she felt as well.

As she sat down to the large breakfast with every person she loved on the planet, she looked over at Benjamin, who was telling Ellie a story about Mars's son, who was also named Benjamin. She couldn't help but to start running through lists and plans for the future in her overactive mind.

And as if Ben could tell what she was thinking, he suddenly looked up at her, smiled a secret little smile at her, and winked. For some reason, she suddenly felt better. Almost as if she didn't have to do any of it alone anymore.

That got her onto another track of thought, but the laughter and boisterous conversation around her brought her out of her head, and as breakfast continued deep into the morning, she felt suddenly at ease, like life suddenly made sense.

She still couldn't help glancing at Ben's face over and over though, and it seemed that he could tell, and met her eyes every time. She did not notice all of the smiles and looks around the table aimed at the pair, and the comfortable feeling in the air from all of the really good people gathered together.

All too soon, breakfast was over, and her family had to start packing for the return trip home.

Everyone knew that Gwen and Benjamin had to stay in Stockholm for the following week to give their Nobel lectures. Now, everyone else was also aware that it would be an exciting time for the new couple to have some moments of peace together before getting back to their lives in the States.

As hugs were given around, and promises to see each other soon, the entire company, except for Gwen and Ben, left for the airport together. They all piled into the huge car that Ben's assistant had rented for him, but which others seemed to have used more than he did.

The children would be met in DC by Stewart, who would be taking them for the next two weeks. Tiffany would dutifully return to the home office of Gwen's home, which she had a key to, as well as to several duties to perform before Gwen returned home.

Mars and Jane took their plane back to New York, feeling both longing to see their children, but also a sense of extreme joy for Ben, as well as a little trepidation. The future for Benjamin suddenly wasn't as cut and dried as they assumed. They were happy for their best friend, but worried about the change to his life as well.

They both knew that Ben wasn't the best with change.

And, after seeing Tiffany and the children off in DC, Gwen's parents caught a connecting flight back to

California, feeling for the first time in several years that Gwen was going to be just fine, finally.

They talked quietly together for the entire flight back to their home about what they knew about Benjamin, and how happy they were that Gwen had finally seen in the man what they had known for years. Decades, actually. As if a lifelong goal had finally been met, the Murphy's turned their talk and attention to their son, and how to start getting Daniel McCarthy Murphy II to take over the family business, finally.

Retirement and long moments together were in their immediate future, and both relished the thought of slowing down a little. Several small kisses and hand holding happened on the flight home, and it felt a bit like their own honeymoon again.

Not too bad for a couple who had spent more than sixty years together.

Back at the hotel in Stockholm, after Gwen was dressed and more composed, and Benjamin was cleaned up and had taken time for some reflection, they found themselves in the hotel coffee lounge, looking at each other. After the hustle of the morning and getting all of their loved ones off to the airport, the quiet of being alone together was explosive.

The quiet between them was so loud.

Several minutes went by as they continued to look at each other across the small marble table. They were both lost in their thoughts. And they both were wondering what the other was thinking.

Finally, Ben took a drink of his latte, placed the delicate china cup back onto the saucer in front of him, cleared his throat, and started speaking.

"I want to tell you a story," he said to her.

"Alright," Gwen answered with trepidation.

"The night that Neeley died was the first time I saw you. Earlier that day, Mars had given me your name and what you were working on early in your career. I was looking for someone to help me solidify the research I had done in the clean energy field. It was so very early on, but the bones were there," he told her without looking at her.

He was looking at his coffee cup and fiddling with the handle.

"As you know, I was supposed to meet her in the City for a date night. But I got home and got on the computer. I started reading your research that you had published at that time. At the end of one of the articles, I saw your picture," he said.

He gulped visibly, finally meeting her eyes. She was suddenly very nervous about where this conversation was going.

"I started changing my search right after that. I started searching for your pictures, and anything else you had posted and published. And I found quite a bit. A video of your graduation speech from college, several interviews that you had given when you started with the government, and so many pictures of you from your childhood up through your time at MIT," he admitted.

"As you can imagine, as I looked for your picture, and read about your life, I was becoming a little smitten, and I didn't even think of my date with Neeley. I didn't think of Neeley at all, actually," he said.

Here it comes, she thought. She gripped her coffee cup tighter.

"And then there was the knock at the door. I thought it was her," he said. He looked down at the table again. "I was ready for a little lecture for standing her up, but she always forgave me for stuff like that. She was so very loving," he said.

285

"It wasn't her, thought. It was a Long Island patrol cop, and he gave me the news that Neeley had died in an accident, not even a half hour earlier. And a half hour earlier, I saw your picture for the first time," he said.

And there it was, she thought.

She felt his suffering. She was suddenly overcome with feelings for Benjamin that she could not currently quantify.

And she suddenly felt a sharp feeling of guilt. She looked at Ben as he raised a pain-filled face to her, tears shimmering in both of his dark eyes. She knew that he felt the same guilt.

Their souls, at that moment, more than the night before, were aligned.

"Anyway, it took me a lot of years to get over that night. I felt guilt for so long. I'm glad that I was finally able to move past it, but it hampered several years when I should have been dating or trying to have another relationship, and I just couldn't," he explained.

"I'm the same. Not with the tragedy, but it was the work," she said, in answer to his pain.

"I tried to date. I really did. All of my girlfriends were getting married and having kids, and I was just going to the lab, day in, day out," Gwen said in reply.

She wanted to say so much more, but she didn't have the words. She wondered if she ever would.

"Well, it's a good thing you did. Your work changed the world, Gwen. But, what happened with your husband?" he asked suddenly.

And then she told him Stewart's excuses. How he couldn't keep up in her shadow. How she had outgrown him and had left him behind. She took a lot of the blame for that on herself.

"When Stewart proposed, it was such a shock. I really had never seen him like that. That he would be so bold to propose the way he did. It was against his character, and more in line with what he knew I would want," she said.

"I know now that it had been a mistake to get married. But I got two beautiful children that are more me than him out of it. The hard truth is, though, I know in a lot of ways, I was his unicorn," she answered Ben.

"His unicorn?" he asked, puzzled.

"You know, a mystic creature, that you want to have, to possess, but that you can never keep," she explained.

"Ahh, I like that, actually," he said. She smiled at him. He smiled in return. He had such a terrific smile, she thought.

She was so damn beautiful, he thought.

His heart fluttered a bit in his chest. He reached for his cooling coffee, taking a longer sip.

"So, may I ask you a question?" she looked at him suddenly. She was a little nervous.

"Sure, anything," he answered.

"What happened last night? What was that?" she looked down after she asked. Her hands started to move together as if on their own. She purposely held them together, firm against the table, waiting for his answer.

"Well, Gwen, to be honest, I have never really done anything like that. I really enjoyed it though," he said. "But I can tell you exactly what it was."

Something in his tone made her look up into his dark eyes. When she did, she saw him with the same expression on his face of looking through her, seeing her. She gulped, waiting for his answer.

"What it was, was twenty-five years in the making. I like to think it was fate," he said.

He smiled at her, and she melted on the inside. Thank God, she thought. He felt the same for her that she had for him. She had been afraid that this was something he did all the time, and she was just his next conquest. But she remembered how he had arranged everything, even getting her family to the suite for breakfast so that she could sleep in.

No, she thought with sudden and strong insight. This man was certainly not like that. She suddenly knew, without asking, but based on every single fact she knew about Ben, that he was the man she had always dreamed of.

She reached across the table and took his warm hand. He didn't jerk his hand back like she thought he might. She worried because of his earlier confession about Neeley. She knew he was still feeling negative emotions about that admission. Even with the wonderful words he had said since.

But she needn't have worried. There were still tears in his eyes, however. And it touched her soul to see this tall, strong man being vulnerable. Yes, she thought. She had never met a man like Ben Reeves before.

Instead of jerking his hand back, he opened her hand when she put hers on top of his, interlacing their fingers. He sniffed his grief back, smiled at her through the tears, and she felt tears in her own eyes. At that exact moment, as he lay himself open to her, having admitted his deepest shame and then confessing his feelings for her from the last two decades, she started feeling deep emotions for him.

And as she thought about those emotions, she received the sudden insight that she had felt them ever since that day, twenty-something years in the past, when she had met him for the very first time.

She saw the long years in between suddenly, and the love that had always been there, when she hadn't even realized it. For the first time in a very, very long time, as she sat in a warm café, somewhere in the city of Stockholm, halfway around the world from home, with her fingers intertwined with the fingers of the man across from her, she said a prayer.

She said the strongest prayer she knew how to say, inside her mind, and inside her heart.

And deep in her soul, where she had started feeling the connections between her own, and the soul of the man sitting across from her, she heard an answer to that prayer.

She suddenly knew what was going to happen very soon. Probably that night, she thought. She smiled up at Ben, looking forward to the day they had free, and which he had promised earlier to see the Christmas sights of Stockholm together.

But she felt trepidation for what she knew was coming. The Choice she would have to make again.

At the same time, Ben was thinking the exact same thing.

He wondered if he would be making a Choice himself.

And the answer was already there, in his mind. He knew that this was all a Choice.

And he had not done very well with his Choices, he thought nervously.

Chapter 30

After coffee, and several more minutes of looking into each other's eyes, they decided to hit the city, and have a little bit of fun.

Gwen was very excited to see the bustle and trappings of what was considered the best Christmas destination in the world, and Ben was excited to be able to show Gwen a different side of life than what she was accustomed to.

He thought, as they got back into the black limo which had just returned from the airport, that he rarely himself used his position and prosperity on a day-to-day basis. He had just been brought up differently.

Driving through the snow-laden streets, both watched out of the windows at the crowds of people, heavily wrapped against the cold, walking through several markets and squares where festivities were taking place. Ben instructed the driver to take them to the *Skansen* Christmas market in the center of the busy city.

When they pulled up among the taxis and buses of visitors, looking to do the same kind of shopping and trying different delicacies in the market, Gwen and Benjamin disembarked from the car, door held open by the friendly driver, and walked hand in hand into the crowds.

Ben spent most of the early afternoon watching Gwen's face shining and smiling at all there was to see in the oldest market in the city. Vendors displayed wares from all over Europe, and the market itself was surrounded by tall, centuries-old buildings, looking down majestically at the crowds of happy shoppers and revelers.

Watching Gwen's face light up at the handmade dolls, the fine whale bone pipes, puppets, local artwork, and crafts depicting the waterways around the city, Ben was happier in his heart than he had been for many years. He delighted in her delight. And he was having fun himself.

Every time Gwen commented on an item, he bought it for her. At first, she was chagrined about the purchases, until he had to remind her that he was quite wealthy, and she needed to get used to it.

She knew he didn't flaunt his wealth, and she loved that about him, but she soon became comfortable in his use of money and made sure that what she was purchasing made sense, and wasn't frivolous, which he, in turn, loved about her.

As their arms filled up with packages and bags, Ben took out his cell phone and dialed a number. Very soon, the driver from the limo appeared and took two trips taking their purchases back to the car, releasing their hands to start exploring the foods available only at Christmastime in the city.

Gwen's first adventurous culinary delight was sausage made from reindeer. She felt suddenly guilty, and images from the stop motion *Rudolph the Red-Nosed Reindeer* movie from her childhood flashed in her mind, but she ate the first morsel bravely, and then, finding the meat to her extreme liking, ate more.

Ben enjoyed the gaminess of the sausage as well and promised to have it at every Christmas back in the States. Gwen smiled at him and took another piece of sausage on a white cracker into her mouth.

Ben smiled at her around his own mouthful.

They then moved to the vendors of sweet stuff. The pair sampled candied apples, caramel thick on the fruit. Ben found a confectioner and bought Gwen her very first sample of sugared dates. She loved the mixture of sweet and tartness of the European dessert instantly.

Her favorite though, by far, was when Ben produced two plastic flutes of spiced wine. It was deliciously warm, spiced incredibly fragrantly, and Gwen was instantly in love. It reminded her suddenly of winters in New England. She had a sharp nostalgia for the northeast region of the US suddenly and made a comment to Ben about taking him there next year to visit Portsmouth, which to his literary educated and very phonically sound mind, should not be pronounced as "Port-smith."

She just laughed at his comment, and again told him how much he would love that area.

Soon, both were too full from trying all of the various foodstuff in the market, and as they reached the end of the vendors line with only one or two more purchases of Christmas presents for loved ones back home, she was again surprised to see the car waiting on the curb for them.

Gwen smiled at Ben for his thoughtfulness and jumped into the back of the waiting car. Ben soon got in next to her, and after he informed the driver of their next destination, she couldn't help but to reach over, grabbing Ben by the lapels of his winter pea coat, and kissing him soundly, and for quite a long time, right on his mouth. He reached his arms around her as well, pulled her tightly into him, and kissed her just as soundly right back.

She moaned softly into his mouth, and he pulled back a little, softly putting a finger to her lips and said, "Shhh, later love. Later." She just pulled him back to her, kissing him deeply once again. They came up for air when the car stopped, and she looked out of the window to see water.

"Where are we, Ben?" she asked.

"We are going to an island, dear. I think you'll like it. But bundle up, make sure to wear your gloves, as I'm told the trip is quite chilly," he instructed her.

Gwen grabbed her thick white cotton gloves, slipping them on her hands, and zipped up her winter coat to her neck. She adjusted the crocheted toboggan on her head, and watched Ben do the same.

They embarked from the large car when the driver held the door open for the pair and walked together down a short dock and onto a ferry boat. She wondered why they were the only two on the ferry and made a comment about it.

"No, you're right. There should be more people. But I rented the ferry for this trip for us alone. I wanted you to see the city from the water with just me," Ben answered her. "I hear the sight is quite lovely, especially during a white Christmas."

She again marveled at the man's preparedness and was grateful to him for arranging such a sweet and romantic gesture. They soon stood at the aft end of the ferry, watching the city fade behind them as they travelled out to the archipelago. Ben was telling her about the history of the area that he had researched before coming to Sweden. She was happy to listen to his deep voice behind her, as she leaned back into him, feeling the cold, brisk air on her face.

She closed her eyes, feeling the swaying of the ferry, and the wind against her exposed face, and she was happier than she had ever been. As Ben's voice toned on behind and above her head, she felt a contentment and happy lightness settle over her.

But soon, the ferry came to a stop, and she opened her eyes to see the island they had traveled to.

Ben, who had been holding Gwen up and telling her history of the archipelago, released her, grabbed her glove-covered hand, and walked with her down the gangplank to the dock on the island called *Sandhamn*.

She learned that the island was actually named *Sandön* later on, but was colloquially referred by the same name of the largest settlement on the island.

As they walked down the gangplank to the dock of the small settlement, the ferry master met them at the foot of the heavy board. He smiled, tipped his cap to Gwen, and in a very heavily accented English said, "Thank you for boating with *Cinderellabåtarna* Lines."

Gwen returned his smile and Ben shook his hand. She wondered if the ferry was going to wait for the two of them, but when she looked back to see the ferry master sliding the plank of wood back into the ferry, she knew that they were getting back to the city another way.

"Did he say Cinderella?" she asked Ben. He smiled at her.

"I'm not sure of the translation, but it's one of only two companies that has for generations run all of the ferries through the archipelago and beyond. They do cruise ships as well," he told her as they walked into the heavily snow-covered town.

The streets were somewhat crowded, and Gwen looked forward to seeing the festivities here on the island for Christmas. Ben said something about a procession that evening, and it sounded lovely.

As the afternoon sun sank into the west, and the shadows lengthened on the small island, Gwen was treated with Swedish hospitality from one pub to another, and from one shop to the next. They enjoyed several flutes of the heavily spiced wine, and like Jane a couple of days before, she fell in love with the *pepparkakor,* the famous gingerbread cookies she had heard so much about.

She had never been treated with the respect and dignity that was shown to people with prosperity, and at first, she was uncomfortable, but seeing Ben's easy and affectionate nature with the shop owners, she was soon comfortable and even told Ben to tip the wait staff at the small inn where they had their dinner more than he was accustomed to.

He winked at her and doubled the amount of *kronor* he left on the table. She smiled at him and made a comment about it being Christmas and all. Walking out of the inn, he grabbed her tightly into his side, and kissed the top of her red hair before she could put her toboggan back on.

He mumbled a "thank you" into her lovely smelling and bright hair. She nudged him in the ribs with her elbow and he laughed out loud.

It was very soon quite dark on the island, and they walked together to the brightly lit street where the earliest Procession of Lucia was to take place. Ben maneuvered

Gwen through the light crowd to the front of a row of streetlights. Gwen looked up into the soft white light and saw the smaller twinkling white lights strewn between the streetlights.

The entire settlement was brightly lit with white Christmas lights, and to Gwen's delight, a very soft snow started to fall. The glistening snowflakes, big and bright, shown gaily in the glow of the Christmas lights.

The entire scene was magical, and Gwen was as delighted as a child. She looked up at Ben and saw him watching her. She smiled up at him, and as he smiled back, she heard the first voices taking up a very familiar Christmas carol.

Gwen looked back at the stone street, and saw a woman, blonde as a Nordic goddess, walking at the front of a group of revelers. The woman was dressed all in white and had a crown of electrically lit candles on her head. She held a tall white candle in both of her hands before her, and it was properly lit with a flame.

Behind her walked several other young girls all in white with laurel leaf crowns on their heads. They walked in a wedge-shaped line, and behind the girls in white strode more children, dressed as pixies, nymphs, and several other fictional characters.

The singing was coming from this wild bunch of children, and it was beautiful to Gwen. She could also smell the mixture of the cold snow falling and the saltiness of the sea air, and it gave her a feeling in her chest that she couldn't put words to.

But it felt like home.

And so did the tall man she leaned against, trusting him to hold her up. He didn't so much as move an inch as she leaned further back into him.

As the procession reached where she and Ben stood, the snow falling slowly around them, and the sounds of the caroling in her ears, Gwen felt a magic she had never felt before. In this place, halfway around the world from the home she knew, she felt at peace for the first time in as long as she could remember.

She felt Ben standing close behind her, one heavy hand on her shoulder. She was so happy she could burst. Tears glistened in her eyes, and the procession doubled in her wet vision. But she didn't care. She had never had an experience like this one.

She was so grateful to the Universe, to God, to whatever it was that brought her to this spot, on this night.

She could feel the snowflakes hitting her cap-covered head, and onto her shoulders, but she didn't care. She wanted to burst. She didn't want this night to end.

When the procession of costumed children moved down the street, she turned to Ben, smiled up at him, and he wiped away a tear that had fallen onto her cheek. They grinned at each other in a silly way, both feeling the magic of the moment.

Soon, the crowds started to disperse. Many headed back to the docks and waiting ferries. Ben told her that they had to crowd back in on a ferry to get back to the city, but she didn't care. At the moment, she felt like she didn't care about much. The experience of being on this magical island with Ben, who she felt extreme love for at the moment, was all that mattered.

He grabbed her hand and started walking down the hill towards the dock and the waiting boats. She happily followed, allowing herself to be led by Ben's sure-footed steps. She lifted her head, and stretched out her tongue like a child, catching several snowflakes in her mouth. Ben looked back and her and laughed again. She grinned back to him. They both felt like children.

And as they crossed in front of a dark alley between two rambling inns, she saw a pink light from the darkness and gulped audibly.

She stopped in the middle of the cobbled street, directly in front of the alley, and Ben turned to her to see what the matter was. He followed her gaze into the alley and saw the pink light as well.

They both knew what it was, but neither knew that the other knew what it was. A sudden confusion replaced the giddy feelings of just a few seconds earlier.

Together, silently, they walked into the alley. It was dark at first, and their footing was not sure, but soon, pink light enveloped the pair, and they could see clearly. The alley opened up into a small courtyard, surrounded by tall wooden buildings, making a tidy sheltered area.

As the pair walked into the light pink brightness, they looked at each other, and suddenly they both realized that the other knew what was happening.

But Before either could say a word in surprise, an even brighter light shown from the center of the brick-laid floor of the courtyard.

They both looked up at the floating, seven-foot-tall Archangel hanging several feet above the cobbles.

The pair again looked at each other, and again, both were shocked to their core to see the recognition in each other's eyes.

"CHILDREN OF EARTH, YOU ARE HERE TO EACH MAKE A CHOICE, ONCE AGAIN."

The voice boomed in each of their minds, and they shared a sudden connection, as if each heard what the other heard, and it echoed back to what they themselves heard. A dual voice, booming in each of their minds, and the shock and surprise of the moment held both of their tongues. Neither could process what was happening.

Gwendolyn and Benjamin both looked up at Chamuel, and as their hands squeezed each other harder, Chamuel seemed to change before their very eyes. As the pink fog billowed around the courtyard, a radiating light and warmth spread out from the Archangel, and the falling snow seemed to stop on an unseen force, high above all of their heads.

Soon, Chamuel was in his human form. A short, dark-skinned man stood before the pair where a giant Archangel had hovered seconds before. As the finely dressed man looked at the pair in quiet amusement, their tongues were loosened, their shock gone, and they dropped each other's hand.

Ben spoke first. "Again, Chamuel?" he asked. Chamuel smiled at him as Gwen looked sharply at Ben. She remembered her earlier feelings that she had known that this was going to happen.

"Wait," she said in shock. "You know Chamuel?" she asked Ben. He looked over at her with his own bewildered look on his face.

"You mean, you know him too?" he asked in reply.

"I have met him twice in my life. Once in Colorado when I was seventeen, and again in Massachusetts, right before Stewart proposed," she admitted.

Ben looked over at Chamuel, and then back down at Gwen. "I met him in my mother's room when I was eighteen, and again in San Francisco several years ago," he told her.

They both looked over at Chamuel, who continued to smile at the pair. Ben broke the silence.

"Chamuel, is this what we have been given the choices for? Is the life I chose against...was it supposed to be with Gwen?" he asked the Archangel.

Chamuel spoke again, but out loud this time, walking closer to the pair.

"You two have been given the Choice twice in your life. This is the final time. I cannot tell you where your choices before would have led. I can't even tell you what your choice this time will lead to. All I can tell you is that you have been afforded this chance to finish the work in which you have both been set. Your purpose, both of you, is at hand, and the choices you make today, well, those choices have become your reward," he said in explanation.

Before either could speak again, although both really had something to say, Chamuel spoke for the last time.

"I told you both when you were children that your choice would be the difference of life and love. As your lives have progressed to this night, right now, the choices should have become clear to you both. The destinies of billions lay in your purpose. God has watched you two very closely, and you have both done an incredible job with your purposes. Now, God gives that which no one before you has been given before, a choice of reward," he said.

Chamuel looked at the pair. He saw the invisible red strings which already connected each of them to each other's heart. Only he could see the connections, and it made him smile to see the size of the red strings.

They were thicker than any he had ever seen. Even thicker than those between Cleopatra and Mark Anthony, and between Dante and Beatrice. Much thicker than the strings between Paris and Helen.

The strings he could think of in history that were closest in size to this pairs were between John and Abigail Adams.

Chamuel chuckled at the memory and smiled again at the pair. He waited patiently for each to speak. He knew he only had one last thing to say. It would come after the two made their choices.

Ben, again, spoke first. He cleared his throat, glanced over at Gwen, and knew that the moment of change had come for him. He knew that it was time to put the past in the past and look to the future. He didn't know which way Gwen would choose, but he had a sneaking suspicion that she had already made this choice, and he had ruined years for the both of them.

So, he squared his shoulders visibly, and made the choice he should have made twice already. He also mentally prepared an apology to Gwen.

"Chamuel, I choose love," he said. His voice sounded shaky to him. He didn't have the courage to look at Gwen, but he could feel her shift next to him. He knew she was looking at him.

And then she spoke. Her voice was much calmer and softer than his own, he thought. She didn't hesitate. She didn't waver. He was in awe suddenly of her poise and the direction she saw before her.

"Chamuel, I again choose love" was all she said. And it was all that was needed. As soon as she said the words, combined with the choice that Ben had finally made, a loud, multi-voiced choir of sound hit them with the strength of a gale of wind. They both closed their eyes to the cacophony of sound.

When they finally opened their eyes, the Archangel was again in his seven-foot-tall guise, hovering several feet above the cobbled ground. His wings beat soundlessly behind him, and his loud internal voice boomed in their minds again.

"THE FINAL CHOICE HAS BEEN MADE, AND GOD'S WILL HAS BEEN DONE. LET NO MAN SEPARATE WHAT GOD HAS BROUGHT TOGETHER HERE. FOR HISTORY, AND FOR ALL ETERNITY, LET THIS BOND MARSHAL IN THE CHANGE GOD HAS SET FORTH EONS AGO. AMEN"

301

At that, another loud sound escaped from the heavens, and in a blink, all testament that an Archangel had been in the courtyard was gone. Ben and Gwen stood in darkness, collecting their thoughts, bodies shaking, and minds reeling.

Finally, several moments later, Ben's hand found Gwen's. He knew she would be upset that he had chosen against her in the past. He was ready for her to voice her anger and had a paltry excuse prepared.

But she surprised him again, and as he waited for verbal insinuations to assault him, he just felt her turn, wrap her arms around his neck and pull his face down to hers. Right before their lips touched in what felt like the very first time, she whispered in his ear something that he would never forget.

"You are my soul."

They both knew, in that moment, that their lives had finally started.

Chapter 31

Twenty years later, Ben and Gwen Reeves stood on top of a slightly moving stage set up on top of the floating hub deep in the middle of the Pacific Ocean.

Waves crashed around the large circular legs of the platform, and Ben knew that those legs travelled deep into the waters below, rooting deep into the ocean floor. Ben looked over at his aging wife and shared a now-familiar smile with her.

Before Gwen could start the speech that they had practiced with each other over and over the last two weeks, the crowd standing on the platform in front of the stage took several pictures of the couple with their floating cameras above their heads. Ben just shook his head at all the emerging technology that was lost to him.

His grandchildren seemed to understand it all in a blink, but he was often left far behind when they tried to explain it to him. Gwen understood it all, Ben knew. He was curiously okay with that fact, however.

He nodded to his wife, and she stepped up to the podium to address the crowd of journalists and media representatives who awaited her announcements.

Gwen's strong voice came issuing from the several speakers situated around the platform atop the circular structure below them all. As she spoke, flashes from the floating cameras went off like the pops of fireworks Ben remembered as a child.

He knew that recordings of this historic moment would go on to be watched by billions of people throughout the foreseeable future.

"Ladies and gentlemen of the press, dignitaries around the globe, and all human beings of today, and in the future," Gwen said to the quiet crowd and the dozens of floating cameras around her.

She was recorded from every single possible angle, and most showed her husband and partner, Benjamin, in the background.

"Today marks the conclusion of what my team and I have been working towards for the last fifty years. It started with an idea that many shared, but which my husband, Benjamin Reeves, foresaw in his fiction," she slowly rotated and applauded with the crowd as Ben took a slight bow.

"For the last twenty-five years, the firstly named 'Reeves-Murphy Ovum', and now merely called the 'Reeves' Eggs,' have given everyone on this planet free, clean, and renewable energy. Technological advancements as well as proprietary manufacturing processes accomplished by our company, EnergyOne, have allowed this clean energy source to be available, free of charge, to anyone in the world," she said. The crowd cheered and applauded again.

304

"Today, we have taken that technology, and advanced it to the next level. Sitting a few feet below this very platform, the second-largest 'Reeves' Egg,' ever made, which we have nicknamed 'Eve,' is about to embark on its very long life of supplying power to exactly half of this planet. As you have all read or heard by now, a twin 'Egg' nicknamed 'Adam' has been built in the middle of the Atlantic Ocean, very similar to this one, but slightly larger," she explained.

"Its job, when we start its lifecycle tomorrow afternoon, is to supply free, clean energy to the rest of the planet. These two nodes will power every grid on this planet, new and old, for the next several hundred years, with no disruption of power or degradation of equipment," she said again to thundering applause.

"With these two nodes operational, all old-fashioned power sources that have fallen away in the last couple of decades, like coal, natural gas, and wind and solar power, will finally be put to their eternal rest," she said in conclusion.

The world-famous couple, whose story had been told countless times around the world, cementing their legend in history forever, stepped up to the tall metal box in the middle of the stage. Looking at each other deeply and lovingly, they, together with the entire planet watching, placed their hands on the silver disk in the middle of the short tower, and pushed it down until it clicked and held.

A few moments later, the crowd could feel the humming of the "Egg" begin to create power under them. Ben and Gwen knew exactly what was happening at that moment. A large red laser was shot for the first time into a tritium core the size of Gwen's fist. The resulting catastrophic fissioning of the hydrogen atoms making up

305

the core of tritium released an amazing amount of heat. The resulting shockwave of power ricocheted off of the metallic hydrogen sphere surrounding the fissioning tritium, and its ensuing, much more powerful electromagnetic field then collapsed and pressurized the small sun-like reaction held in the center of the chamber.

The compression of the element resulted in a fusioning of the tritium, reforming it into its original form. That action produced an equal mass of energy and heat from the reaction, caught in the specially made Seebeck Generator and alloyed thermoelectric cable net around the sphere, turning the temperatures equal to those at the center of the Sun into vast amounts of electricity, which was then fed into metallic hydrogen-alloy wires, snaking all over that side of the planet.

The process of both fusion and fission started to take place, in perpetual reaction, over and over. A small amount of the energy created from each reaction was fed into the power unit for the laser. The laser was shot in very specific sequences into the core every second or so.

The whole apparatus was self-sustaining for the amazing amount of time it would be in service.

And so, every grid in place in every land in the hemisphere was overcome in the resulting surge of power. But the entire system held.

And continued to hold for the next several centuries, much longer than the original creators even theorized.

Another surge of applause and loud cheering went up as the screens positioned around the platform, next to the giant speakers, showed power relay stations from every country on the hemisphere of the planet go suddenly full "green."

Gwen made a final statement into the microphone, but it was lost to the sound of the cheers and adulations from the scientists and engineers who had gathered behind the crowd of media members.

But history would fade out the noise of the crowds and the waves breaking below the buzzing sphere so that you could hear the last thing Gwendolyn Reeves said to the planet as a whole:

"We grant this technology, and the abundant power it supplies, to all of mankind, in perpetuity. Let it usher in the Energy Revolution that we all dreamed of half a century ago. Let it be known that in this place, on this node of free, abundant power, that love, and connection made all of this possible. Possible for all of the inhabitants of this planet, and in time, those beyond."

She turned, grabbed her husband's outstretched hand, and climbed into the quietly powered helo-jet standing by at the end of the platform.

As the pair climbed into the sleek flying machine, powered by a much smaller "Reeves' Egg," they looked at the climax of their combined journey, and the legacy they left to the billions of human beings around the planet.

And they smiled at each other, knowing now that they could rest, and many others would take over the work they had started so long ago, and those people, some of whom had the same last name as their legendary parents and grandparents, would make the legacy even grander in the decades ahead.

Over the next several decades, a change, foreseen and pre-ordained from on high, descended onto humanity. The so-called Energy Revolution ushered in an unstoppable and stable era of peace and enlightenment to the human race.

The first benefit of renewable and free energy to the planet, an energy source that you could carry in a knapsack all over the world and into every corner of the planet, was the ability to terra-form lifeless sand and scrub grass-covered clay into fertile, crop-heavy land.

In the regions like central Africa and most of the eastern part of the Middle East, where rain was plentiful, and the ground was mostly desert sand, crops like corn, wheat, and cotton flourished. Third-world countries, which had to beg the rest of the world for sustenance in prior centuries, suddenly became the new breadbaskets of the planet. The economic impact for these countries made them so very essential to the rest of the world for the simple fact that they had the square footage to grow enough crops to feed every single person on the planet.

Communities that had once been poor, struggling, and dying suddenly had resources that they could only dream of. This, in turn, brought about commodities like education, transportation, and global connection to even the most remote regions of the globe.

Areas that saw much less rain were still able to be cultivated and were able to grow heartier crops like cassava, sorghum, and soy. Several types of fruit-bearing trees, like olive, citrus, and banana, were also grown in these areas. Whole new agricultural job markets and careers in the new technology were flourishing around the world. The world economy strengthened overnight, and several new strains of disease-fighting crops were planted and thrived in the new terra-forming technology, which for so long, only needed a portable power source to thrive.

The machinery was in place, it had simply needed power in places where power had not been available.

Once the rest of the human race rose up from the bottom of Maslow's pyramid of needs where they had been stuck for generations just trying to survive, a new

Renaissance emerged around the world that was completely unexpected.

As soon as the vast majority of humanity was given the necessary things to survive, like food, a renewable shelter made from the millions of hectares of hemp planted around the globe, and clothing, all for free, the human mind was released to higher understanding and enlightenment.

The vast amount of new art, literature, music, and other creative ventures that emerged after the onset of poverty, starvation, and early death were eradicated around the globe was staggering. Whole new ideas began to emerge from the billions of enlightened souls everywhere. Concepts that were foreign to so many, like Unity, Love, and Solidarity, started to be basic education for the young.

Those same young, who, within a couple of years, were no longer dying of starvation and disease. Cultural inclusion in the arts also abounded. Young white youth in Canada suddenly had access to a wealth of art and cultural mediums from black tribes from Africa. Chinese youth, who were systemically taught to hate anything from the West, very quickly hungered for stories from the US history of the "Old West." And so on, throughout the entire planet.

Soon, those unknown or forgotten culturally important histories and fables found themselves being devoured by a generation of youth who now had the time and ability to consume knowledge which heightened the achievements of all. Racial tension was eradicated within a generation.

The advancement of free energy to the planet ushered in so many unforeseen advancements in human thinking that the previous world became suddenly unrecognizable, and simply became a hiccup in history lessons given to the healthy youth around the planet.

The next change to the human race came from leadership.

For decades, governments around the world tried to tax the new, free energy. Gwen and Ben Reeves fought against every one of them, with new, vast resources of their own.

Their first victory came from making the energy free for the population, but forcing the governments of the world to pay a tax to EnergyOne, their not-for-profit company, for harnessing the new energy to power their own struggling power grids.

Within a decade, even those government-owned subsidiaries fell under the free-use of the clean energy. The governments were forced to change their tactics to stay viable in an ever-changing economic revolution. So, older politicians, clinging to old-world ideals, were soon ousted, and younger, forward-thinking socialist politicians, raised among emerging culturally-diverse and evolved and enlightened movements in every country, took power.

And then they gave that power back to the people. The vast richness of a world without poverty soon showed itself in the form of lasting peace. There just wasn't anything else to fight over. If countries, which in the last decades of the twenty-first century pervaded their populace with human-rights atrocities, wanted to be included in this new world, then the populations were forced to rise up against their former governments.

Many small skirmishes, and then many more battles, were fought for freedom in every corner of the planet. And the freedom fighters won all over the world, as they had all been secretly funded and helped by the West.

Borders slowly faded as people all over the world saw the future for what it could be, rather than what it always had been before.

For the rest of time, advancements in technology in transportation made moving around the world faster, cleaner, and much cheaper. The use of the most abundant element in the universe as a means of magnetic energy and vacuum travel made traveling from places like New York to London a matter of minutes, rather than hours.

This enabled all of the new crops around the world to be shipped to where they were needed the day they were picked or harvested. Children in rural areas in southern Africa and most of the Middle East now had access to commodities like oranges and lemons, cotton denim clothing, and soy-meat, which they had only ever heard of in stories.

No longer did the economic and military leader of the world, the United States, have power over the management of resources around the planet. The US became the hub for all of the emerging governments around the now collectively minded planet.

At the final meeting of the UN in New York City, the day before that governing body would become the United Global Alliance, or UGA, an old, wise man from an old tribe deep in the Amazon rainforest stepped to the lectern and told, in broken English and a native tongue that was translated in the earpieces of the leaders of the world, of a prophesy of his people.

In the prophesy, the world united around a small, glowing sun, in the middle of a circle of his people, hands held together, and peace was ushered into their region for millennia. As the cheers rose for the old medicine man's story, humanity knew that that prophesy had come true for them all.

From small, thumb-sized Reeves' Eggs, that powered an electric car for thousands of years, to huge manufacturing plants producing everything from hemp paper to green farm equipment, ran by medium sized Eggs, the production of what the citizens of the world needed was done cleanly, cheaply, and in vast amounts never seen before.

The true changes came to the planet itself, though. The Reeves' oldest friends, Mars, and Jane Gray, had left the UN years earlier and ran the group of environmental specialists working with EnergyOne, and watched the impact of the new, emerging technology on the planet itself. And what they saw in the next decade was staggering.

The clean energy replaced the other outdated energy sources almost overnight. Coal was regulated to the past. Natural gas followed closely in its steps. Oil and petroleum followed more grudgingly, but followed, all the same.

The resulting changes to this bright blue marble floating through the expanse of space was, in a word, ridiculous. The polar caps were the first to repair themselves. The ozone layer refreshed, and brackish water and dirty rivers and streams became clear and clean within a decade.

The emerging environment disasters of the previous century were another victim relegated to history. Clean air and water nourished the growing cropland all over the planet, and the inhabitants, likewise, started to heal.

Energy sources available anywhere on the planet ushered in new technology that allowed the cleaning of the plastic islands of trash in all of the planet's oceans.

For the first time in recorded history, the planet was once again completely clean. The global warming epidemic of the previous century was gone, and gone forever.

Advancements in medicines, 3D-printed bio-hybrid body parts, and new, emerging holistic remedies made the human lifespan lengthen to almost biblical-era ages. There were still diseases discovered throughout the world, but the technology to eradicate them as they rose up made morality rates plummet.

New advancements in weather control made life-threatening natural disasters a thing of the past. Using huge, powerful electromagnetic field generators from satellites in space, storms and disasters were soon controlled and dispelled before they could damage coastal cities and settlements.

The vast size of this repaired planet made overpopulation a thing of the past as well. There was just so much livable land available now, that all of humanity took up only a small fraction of the whole.

At the center of all of the global change was an emerging, latent, almost divine understanding of the human condition. Once basic needs were met, and the ensuing Renaissance of creativity emerged, advanced and enlightened thinking rose up all over the world. Religion was soon eradicated, and a basic belief in a Universal Energy started to emerge as a new way of socially accepted worship.

There were no churches or shrines made to this new idealism, rather, a general faith in the goodness of man started to come forth. As natural resources became abundant, and the needs of the previous generational wars and strife became obsolete, a new idea came from deep in the past that we as a human race really were all connected. What happened to one, happened to all.

This, more than any other movement in the emerging peace of the planet, was the catalyst for real acceptance of each other. More borders disappeared. More education in other cultures and languages emerged, and by the time Gwen and Ben settled into a deep retirement, away from the limelight of the planet, children learning the new educational precepts could speak several languages, celebrated many cultural holidays throughout the year, and as that generation grew up to eventually manage the planet, the new ideas took over the entire planet, and peace, finally, was achieved.

Gwen and Ben Reeves settled into obscurity. Their legend flourished, but the world at large didn't know what had become of the famous pair. Their extended family knew where they were, and what they were doing, and were happy to give them their privacy at long last. The famous couple were finally able to mourn the passing of those who came before them.

Gwen's parents' deaths, in particular, hit the pair the hardest. And in the busy day-to-day operation of making their dreams a reality for the planet at the beginning of their marriage, they were not able to properly show their family the impact that Danny and Joy Murphy had really had on them, and in turn, the world itself.

The love that Gwen's parents had shared shown over all of the family gathered together at the Long Island Retreat which they all visited throughout the year. The family gathered together on a warm early-fall day, where the leaves outside the big bay windows in the office in the rear of the large, sprawling home were changing, but slowly.

It was the home that Gwen and Ben had retired to, and from which they dispensed the wisdom and leadership to the rest of the overlarge family. Like they were doing on this beautiful, Long Island evening many years after the power nodes came to life, and Gwen and Ben were able to finally retire, together, alone for all the world knew.

Ben and Gwen sat on a leather loveseat, surrounded by the Murphy-Reeves-Gray clan. Ben looked around at the different generations represented in the room. Mars and Jane's son, Benjamin Gray, had married young and the couple were both engineers with EnergyOne. They had had a prodigious amount of children. Ben chuckled to himself at the seven young Gray's crawling, sitting, or being yelled at by their larger-than-life grandparents. Even a few of those seven had babies in their arms. More would come, Ben thought to himself.

Gwen looked down at her own grown children. Sean and Ellie had grown up happy in two different households. They both regarded their own biological father, as well as the stepfather who had helped them both through most of their childhood and early adulthood, as their two Dads.

When Stewart succumbed to a massive heart attack ten years earlier, Ben had stepped in, as he always had, and fathered the two through the tragedy. He even supported the grief his own wife of over a decade went through when word of Stewart's death came to them as they had begun their retirement after the two nodes that powered the planet were brought to life.

Gwen looked at her daughter Ellie, who resembled Gwen so very much. The media had dubbed her "Gwen-Squared," and she was okay with that.

Ellie was a theoretical physicist like her mother, but unlike her mother, she had taken the technology, and had made the two-node global system live way past its expected life cycle.

Gwen knew that her company, EnergyOne, now the largest not-for-profit on the planet, was in good hands.

Sean Haggerty was so much like his father, but he had been raised by Benjamin as well. So, he was a classic conflagration of two different ideals about being a man.

Now, with Stewart gone for almost a decade, he tended to see the world the same optimistic way that Ben had.

He was married to his high school sweetheart, a raven-haired, outspoken girl named Miracle, whom Gwen adored almost more than her own son, as they often joked. The pair had just welcomed their first daughter into the world.

Gwen had looked down on her first granddaughter, and her breath had caught with how much the little baby had resembled Gwen's own mother, Joy.

Joy was half of the reason for this gathering of the family.

Before Ben could address the growing crowd of family and friends, Daniel McCarthy Murphy II stood up and cleared his throat loudly. He was surrounded by his own overlarge horde of children and grandchildren.

He looked tired, Gwen thought, but he had a right to be. As Ben and Gwen worked to make their life's work feasible for the planet, Gwen had hired her brother to be the face of the movement.

Being a former college and then a professional star in football, he had brought the only celebrity status to the program, besides Gwen and Ben themselves. And he had done an amazing job fundraising and pushing legislature around the world that benefitted the company. And the planet as a whole.

Gwen knew that her brother wanted to retire and hand the reins of the marketing and publicity zones of the company to one of the multitude of next-generation young adults in the family. They were all accomplished in one way or another, so the job was made harder by having to choose a successor, rather than not keeping it in the family at all.

Daniel McCarthy Murphy II cleared his throat again and got everyone in the large room's attention. He looked over at his aging sister and her husband, sitting serenely among the many happy and intelligent scions of their shared lives.

He winked at his sister and told everyone to hush so that the famed couple who were the catalyst of bringing this august company together could speak.

Gwen began.

Chapter 32

"As many of you know, Ben and I retired several years ago, and are planning to spend the rest of our days here at home, surrounded by you all, coming and going. We will stay up-to-date on the happenings around the globe, but we really want to spend what years we have left in writing, telling our story, and watching you all grow," she said to the quiet group.

Only one baby cried out for food but was quickly hushed with a bottle from one grandkid or another.

"I want to tell you all the story of my parents, and what they taught me, and what made me pick this big lug next to me, because of them," she said. She elbowed Benjamin in the ribs, and he grunted in faked pain and surprise. The smallest of the grandkids laughed out loud. Ben winked at the child.

"My mom and dad grew up two houses down from each other in Northern California, many miles from here," she started.

"Danny and Joy fell in love with each other before either really knew what love was. My mom told me, many years later, that she had felt like she didn't even have a

318

choice. That some greater power was at work in their lives, and the connection they both felt for each other as children never wavered in almost seventy-five years together," she said. There was so much appreciation for the family's history in the room that Ben and Gwen both smiled at as many faces as they could.

"When I was a little girl, my father, this great big man who could crush beer cans on his forehead and fix cars and held control of our little family with a firm hand only had one weak spot in him. My mother. 'My Joy,' he called her, when he would come home from the office, and later, from the wine production company he started, and pick her up in a great big bear hug. Every single day he walked through that door, he picked up 'his Joy' the same way, even when he was old, and couldn't quite pick her up as high as he always had before," Gwen said to a rapt audience.

"But it was the look that my father gave my mother that I always saw. And envied. It was a look of recognition, not just for WHAT my mother was, but WHO she was as well. My father saw all the way into my mother, and she could see all the way through him. It was that love, that look, which I waited all of my life to see. As hard as I worked in the labs and in the field, I searched for that look harder," she said.

And then she turned to Ben, who had shared her life and home for over three decades now, and still looked at her the same way every day they had shared as he had during that first date on the other side of the planet.

"I finally found that look. I found it when I stopped searching for it. When I had given up on ever having love in my life again," she said to Ben. Ben smiled at her and reached for her hand. He looked down at their intertwined hands and felt like they still fit the same way they had thirty years prior.

319

"This brilliant man, who all of you have grown up with, who all of you are here because of, this man saw me. He saw WHAT I was, but more importantly, he saw WHO I was," she said with a smile and a tear. Ben reached up and wiped the tear from her wrinkled cheek. He mouthed to her how beautiful she was, and she smiled in return.

"My parents loved Ben from the beginning, because in some ways, Ben had been there the entire time. He just didn't know it, and neither did I," she said, looking back at the large family surrounding them. "But somehow, Danny and Joy had known."

"As you all know, Benjamin grew up an orphan. He went so many years alone, and without the love that we all share here in this room today," she said.

"Your father, and grandfather, and uncle, and best friend is the reason we are all here today, and I want you each to know, if it wasn't for Ben, and for the look that I saw between my parents from my earliest memories, and then saw from his eyes to mine, if it wasn't for Ben's love for this world, this life, and all of you, we may all be poorer for it. He overcame so much, and we all owe him everything," she said with a smile for her husband, and her heart. He smiled back, gave her a kiss (which several younger kids exclaimed over with a "Ewww"), and smiles around the room were shown towards the aging couple.

Ben took over the story from his loving wife. He gripped her hand and readied himself to tell the rest of it.

"What all of you are not aware of, is that your mother, and grandmother, and I were given a choice. Several, actually," he said with a small smile.

"It is the same choice that all of you will be faced with at some point in your lives. It's the choices that we are all faced with that determine the future," he said with wisdom to the room.

"You will all face choices of many kinds, but the biggest one you will all face, is the choice between life and love. And that choice comes from God above," he said.

"God put all of you in this room, to share and hear this story. If any of you have any further questions about how God gives us all a choice, let us know. Gwen and I will be happy to tell you more specifics, but don't all come running at once," he chuckled.

"Finally, Gwen and I want to share with you the family legacy. Everyone in this room has a piece of that legacy. It started with my own mother, Lorraine, and it comes finally home to each of you," he said. The room hung on his every word.

"The family legacy is this: This home, and the love shared here with all of you needs to pass on to the generations that come after you. That come after them, for as long as we have in this world," he told the group.

"You guys are all aware of the monetary and financial legacy, but the real legacy in this room is the love and connection that we all share. That a young boy, alone in the world, with no one to love him, and anger as deep as an ocean, could find a girl, with dreams in her heart to save this world, and a passion and goal to find her own twin flame in this world. And those two could love enough to bring a mass of family together like this," he said finally. He gripped Gwen's hands tightly. "Finally, that legacy of love tells us one solid truth. Just one. That with our choices, absolutely anything is possible," Ben said to the room.

"Dream big everyone, dream big. It's a brand new world for you that we have made. And we made it by choice."

Chapter 33

Several years later, Benjamin sat on a padded Ease-chair held aloft above the sand under him by some kind of technology which he didn't understand. But that didn't bother him like it had at one time. He didn't even give it a second thought.

He did, however, think about how his body had forsaken him, and didn't work like it had in earlier times. All old people must think that upon waking every morning, he thought to himself. He chuckled inwardly, and looked up into the bright blue sky above. He did that a lot lately, as well.

There was a lovely breeze on this early summer day in the first week of June. Ben couldn't guess at the year, but he knew that he approached his centennial birthday. As did his lovely wife, Gwen. He took his eyes off of the bright blue sky and settled them on the woman who he had spent the last fifty years with.

She was still strong, straight, and her beauty took his breath every single day. She was collecting seashells on the beach of their Long Island retreat. His eyes lingered on her still-tall frame as she moved delicately on the sand. A nurse stood nearby, but her presence did not ruin the magic of the moment for Ben.

The magic of the moment, he thought poetically. That line of thought led him back to the day before. He had sat at his desk, dictating his newest, and most important story into the data processor sitting quietly on the desk in front of him. He looked up from the ending of his final book, and looked at the serene ocean waters at the tail end of his piece of land.

His tired eyes were then drawn to the bookcase standing like a sentinel to the left of his desk. On the bookcase were the many first-edition hardbacks of his many published stories.

A lifetime of creativity, all on a six-foot-tall wooden bookshelf that he had built himself, decades earlier. His eyes roamed over the jacket covers of over 150 books. His stories. His contributions to the new world that they had helped create.

And they created it together.

And then he looked back at the screen of the data cube. He saw his final words.

"And we made it by choice."

He said the words that he had waited almost one hundred years to say. He said into the mini-recorder clipped to his cotton shirt the final words he would ever write.

"The End. Benjamin Reeves. June 2079."

And that had been it. His final story was finished, and would be sent to whichever publisher his family legacy was using these days. He no longer worried over trivial things like that.

But the book still needed a title. For this important step, he never used the voice recorder. He always used the barely used keyboard sitting, collecting dust, on top of the green army-issued desk that his mother had purchased secondhand so many decades before.

A lifetime ago, he mused.

He had a perfect title figured out in minutes. He had unclipped the recording mic from his shirt and placed it in its charging dock. Pulling the keyboard closer to him, seeing his gnarled hands he hardly recognized anymore work for him as they had done for almost a century.

He looked at the screen, glowing before him gaily. The story finished. About to be released to the world. And, as he pulled the keyboard closer to him and punched in the letters for the title, finally, he knew that his writing career had come to an easy end.

And it was another thing that he was perfectly happy with.

He finished typing the title, and looked back at the screen to make sure it was perfect.

And it was.

Had I Not Chosen
By Benjamin and Gwendolyn Reeves

Ben heard the sound of the seagulls flying above him on the beach, and was still lost in thought as he looked at his wife who was finding perfectly formed shells, washed up from a now clean ocean. Ben looked off to the west and saw the ever-present encroaching skyscrapers.

The City had for years been moving onto the Island.

The City had for years been moving onto the Island. Buildings which defied the logic he had built up over decades of life pervaded the once serene home of his youth. Progress couldn't be stopped, he knew, but he took the purview of the elderly and acted like he didn't enjoy it. But that was just what was expected by the younger generation.

Secretly, and internally, he was excited about where the human race was headed after he was gone. He relished every new advancement, and couldn't keep up with all of the positive changes himself.

But he knew that he and his beautiful bride had helped marshal in that change, and he knew that he could leave this world with the pride that helping with those most important changes gave. It boosted his spirit on this most important day.

His mind started to wander as he again felt the warm sun on his aging skin. He thought to all those who they had lost. Decades earlier they had lost Gwen's parents, who, in the twilight of their own lives, had adopted Benjamin into their clan, making him as much an equal member as anyone else. He had loved them both fiercely for that.

And then to his lifelong best friends, Mars, and Jane. It had been so many years since he had thought of either of them without the other. They had lost Jane first. She went pleasantly and quietly, surrounded by family and friends, and Gwen had held her hand as she took her last breath. Ben had his arm around Mars, who had stood at the far end of the room and couldn't make himself come closer. In the end, Jane had not even been aware of who was around her, but she went peacefully and happily. Her life was celebrated for what it had been. A life given over to this planet we all called home, and to her family, who she loved above all else.

Ben smiled at memories of Jane, bringing food to his house when he wasn't aware, taking care of him like a brother. They had loved each other fiercely, but they had both loved Mars even more.

Ben took a deep breath and let it out in a long sigh on this beautiful day on the beach, a day that would later ring in history.

They had lost Mars only last year, Ben thought. He had lived without his soulmate for more than five years, but they were years filled with family, friends, and travel. Up until the end Mars had still been so very active.

Decades earlier, he had started walking with Benjamin, and those walks had turned into a surprising love of marathons and global trekking. When he had passed suddenly, Mars was half the size that he had been for most of the years that Ben knew him.

Mars had lost so much weight, that Ben had hardly recognized his oldest friend anymore. But he had become so proud of Mars, and they had shared a bond more than brothers until the very end.

Even in this changing world, where human life was found sacred and the global impact of peace and prosperity had made drastic changes to the human condition, accidents still happened.

Mars had been on a recorded and very popular trek in Nepal, the first centenarian to hike some certain trail that Ben couldn't remember the name of, but which didn't matter, because he had read only last month that they were renaming the pass after Mars.

He had stepped wrong, and had fallen into a crevice where he didn't survive. They were able to extract Mars quickly, but it had been too late.

Ben knew that Mars had died doing what he loved, and that was enjoying this great planet that the human race had been blessed with.

326

Ben missed him terribly, however.

So, as Ben's thoughts drifted back over the story of him and Gwen's lives that they had just finished writing, he knew that the final choice that they had made for this day was the correct one.

He actually looked forward to this evening. A day that would go down in history as a globally celebrated holiday.

He was finally at an age that he felt more tired than anything, and he was ready for his final rest. Gwen and he had spoken about it at great length, and the faith that they had gained over a lifetime of doing the work that God had set before them gave them the strength to look into the next phase of life with hope and delight.

As the world healed, and all of humanity had come together, many antiquated ideas about death and dying had changed. The global society had come to accept many cultural traditions about death.

When elderly members of those tribes wanted to end their lives, they were revered for their choice. Many simply walked off into the jungle, or the prairie, or the desert. Their scions respected their wishes, and celebrated their long and venerable lives.

And the globe had now taken that idea and tradition as a part of its collective consciousness. Elderly people were now afforded the rest they often longed for, and it was simply a matter of a decision and a signature. The process had become streamlined, and families celebrated their elderly for their own choices.

Late last month, Gwen and Ben had once again gathered their ever-growing family and had spoken to them all of their decision. As the pair approached their centennial birthday, they were ready for what came after. They wished to end their lives together, and alone.

The family was unsurprisingly upset and saddened, but were also respectful of the famous couple's last decision.

Their final choice.

And today was that day.

So Ben sat on the beach, gazing lovingly at the bride of half of his life, and thought back to the dark years before they had made the final choice for love. He didn't often think of those years, which to most would seem ideal, and they were, in ways. But without Gwen, they had all been hollow and empty.

Gwen had made his life into the rich fabric of beauty and poetry it had been in the second half. When he finally had the other half of his soul with him every single day.

He thought back to the last fifty years and felt a deep joy and satisfaction. They had not left each other's sides for even a day in that whole time. They had shared so many adventures together, all over the world.

And they had grown their family to the huge clan that it was today. They were leaving behind a legacy of love and prosperity. And at the end, Ben mused, contently, that was all you really could do with this life.

It wasn't much what you did during your life that really mattered to history, he thought. It was what you left behind. It was the lessons and joy that you left with your children and their children.

Ben was very proud that he had left so much of himself and his own ideas about this life behind in his writing. But more than that, it was the final story, the most important story that would go down in history as the final lessons that Ben wanted to leave with his family and the world itself. And he shared every one of them with the love of his life.

Gwen had helped him in the last year tell the story the right way. So that generations to come could read the lessons in that story. And even when Benjamin and Gwendolyn Reeves were forgotten to history, the lessons about love, connection, and the Choices God gave each of us would reverberate throughout human history.

Ben was ready for his rest. He had done his job, and he was proud that he had done his job well.

He looked one last time as his wife, his heart, the other half of his soul stood up, and waved at him. It made a very old memory come crashing into the forefront of his mind.

As his wife stood in her white summer dress, still thin, still strong, and her hair gone almost completely white, Ben's memory superimposed the memory of him as a young boy, on this same beach, watching his mother, Lorraine, stand up and wave at him.

His mother had been wearing a similar summer dress, with a wide-brimmed straw hat. She had smiled at her young son, and Ben's heart had soared with love for the woman.

Nine-and-a-half decades later, Ben looked on at the love of his life, wearing a similar straw hat, white hair cascading down around her shoulders, and a tear escaped Ben's eye. The reality of this day, added on with the age-old memory in his mind, mixed together, made his heart once again soar in love and peace. He no longer had any worries. It was time.

Late that evening, as the famous pair lay in the bed in the dark room that had belonged to his mother, Ben looked up at the large skylight above him. The sky was dark, and the stars were silent because of the light coming from the encroaching city, not far away.

But he could see the bright full moon, hanging majestically in the sky, for him to see and feel its rays on his face.

Ben felt a peace and a sense of accomplishment that he had never felt before. His hand found Gwen's hand, lying next to him, and he turned to look one last time at his love. She was smiling at him, and her face had a look of resignation and peace on it, that he knew was mirrored on his own.

The moonlight above them shone down on the quiet room, and the two finished lives. They had both done the jobs in which they were given, and they were both ready to go home.

Ben's hand tightened around Gwen's and she smiled one last time at him. He nodded slightly to her, and she closed her eyes.

He watched her face as her chest rose and fell. It rose and fell again, and then it stopped for the rest of time. He said a quiet prayer, the last of millions of similar prayers given over the years, and he closed his own eyes.

Very soon, in the quiet of the moonlight shining down on the couple whose love would become legend in history, a deeper quiet arose. The famed couple was gone from this world, but their legacy would remain behind them.

They left this world as they had come into it: quietly, peacefully, and together. Twin flames, jointed in eternity, who were separated, but had found each other again.

Ben's last memory, or the vision he was given as he passed from this world to the next, was of him, as a young man, hands covered in grease and oil, turning in his workshop to see a young Gwen, shining in her own youth and vigor.

She smiled at him, and he smiled his knowing smile back at her. They both climbed into his red convertible, and drove, speeding down a road, wind whipping through their hair.

Ben looked over at his love and saw her head thrown back in laughter, as an old song came from the stereo. "Dreaming" by Blondie. He didn't know if she was laughing at the song, or the thrill of driving fast, reckless, without fear.

Ben looked at the long road unfolding in front of his classic muscle car, and grinned. He punched the gas, the powerful car roaring under him.

The last sound he heard was the beautiful laughter coming from Gwen sitting next to him, red hair long, and streaming behind her in the wind.

The End

Joshua Loyd Fox

Sep 2019 - June 2020

Epilogue

Two figures stood close to each other, looking down on a changed world.

They were in the place where the material cannot see the spiritual, but sometimes, some very special times, the two places could come together, for the greater good.

The pink-robed figure turned to his Father and smiled. He knew that he had done a good job. The pair that he had chosen had done exactly that which his Father had commanded him. The Father looked down from on high and knew that it was good.

"I think an eternal reward for the two is much deserved, wouldn't you say, Father?" The pink robed figure said to the other. The Father looked over at his beloved child and smiled.

A smile that lit up universes.

The pink-robed figure smiled in return, feeling deep satisfaction for a job well done.

But this had been just one job of many, and he knew, knew in his heart of hearts that the next job would tax him considerably. He was ready, however. Gwen and Ben had given him back a strength that he had missed for several centuries.

The Father laid a gentle hand on the shoulder of the pink-clad figure standing beside Him. Chamuel looked up at the smiling visage of the Father of All Things, and the smile on his own face faltered somewhat.

He knew what was coming.

The Father nodded at Chamuel, and Chamuel knew that it was time. It was time for the boy. The boy who would change the course of human history, but not from love, or choices. But rather from a place much more sinister.

This was a thing that Chamuel disliked. Dealing with the opposite forces of Creation was always much more taxing than the job he had just completed. He looked back down on a world that was in balance, finally. And he was glad for it.

The Father then held out his hand, and Chamuel took it, feeling the power radiating from the Creator down to one of His favored children.

Chamuel took a deep breath of celestial energy and prepared to travel back to a time when a different world wasn't quite as liberated, nor as awoken as it was in this current one.

He looked up into the bright face of the Father and nodded in return.

And suddenly the pair were standing up on high, looking down at an earlier time, in the century before the one they had just witnessed.

This land they purveyed was a mixture of dark green and intense summer heat and was intensely enraged in racial tension and hatred.

Chamuel watched with the Father's hand still on his strong shoulder, as a group of five children rode bikes to get ice cream. Chamuel flinched visibly at what was to come.

He continued to watch as events unfolded, which would then become the catalyst for even more change. And it was certainly positive change, but it came from dark means.

He knew that sometimes, for the forest to grow tall and strong, a burning, rage-filled fire would have to destroy everything.

And oh, how he hated this part of the job.

Joshua Loyd Fox is the author of four novels, and one Poetry Collection, to date. "I Won't Be Shaken: A Story of Overcoming the Odds," "Had I Not Chosen: Book I of the ArchAngel Missions," "Amongst You: Book II of the ArchAngel Missions," and the upcoming "To Build a Tower: Book III of the ArchAngel Missions," and "I Don't Write Poetry: A Collection," which will both be available in the summer of 2022.

Please visit the author at www.jlfoxbooks.com.

This work of fiction was formatted using 11-point Georgia Font, on 60lb white stock paper. The page size is 5.06" x 7.81". The margins are industry standard, 0.5" all around, and 0.63" inside, with no bleed, and no gutter.

The cover is full color paperback in a glossy finish. The binding is 'perfect.'